Z

THE INVENTION *of* SOPHIE CARTER

THE INVENTION *of* SOPHIE CARTER

SAMANTHA HASTINGS

A Swoon Reads Book
An imprint of Feiwel and Friends and Macmillan Publishing Group, LLC
120 Broadway, New York, NY 10271

Library of Congress Cataloging-in-Publication Data is available.

ISBN 978-1-250-23627-2 (hardcover) / ISBN 978-1-250-23628-9 (ebook)

Book design by Katie Klimowicz

First edition, 2020

For Stacy and Michelle,
the best sisters a girl could ask for

PROLOGUE

THE WHEELS IN THE POCKET WATCH turned in never-ending circles. Sophie watched the gears move as if hypnotized, until her ten-year-old twin sister, Mariah, nudged her arm.

"Make Edmund smile again. I'm drawing his mouth now."

Sophie dangled Papa's golden pocket watch over her baby brother's bassinet. He cooed and reached for it with his tiny hands. Laughing, Sophie gently touched his dark, downy hair. It was so different from her and Mariah's curly red locks. But then, he wasn't their blood relative; Papa and Mama had taken Sophie and Mariah in when their birth mother died bringing them into this world.

Sophie watched Mariah gently sketch Edmund's upper lip onto the paper in the curve of a smile. Mariah had already drawn Edmund's round head, closely set eyes, and his little button nose. Even without a bottom lip, the picture clearly resembled their little brother.

"What are you two doing to my baby?" Mama snapped as she entered the room, looming over Sophie and Mariah with an accusing look on her face. She had dark circles around her brown eyes, looking as if she hadn't slept since Papa left for the Galapagos Islands two weeks before.

Sophie stepped back, away from the bassinet and her mother. She was always the one Mama accused of wrongdoing.

Mariah held up her sketch. "I was only drawing a picture of Edmund, and Sophie was helping me by making him smile," she explained. "Show her, Sophie. Show her how Edmund laughs."

Sophie reluctantly dangled the pocket watch by its chain over the bassinet again, and Edmund smiled up at them.

Mama lifted her hand—Sophie shrunk away from her, clutching Papa's pocket watch against her chest. She wished he hadn't gone on another voyage, leaving her with a foster mother who didn't love her, or even like her. Mama only cared for Mariah and, now, for baby Edmund.

"I won't hold it over him, if you don't want me to," Sophie said quickly. "I didn't mean to do anything wrong."

"Give me Captain Trenton's watch," Mama said, holding out her hand.

Sophie clutched the golden pocket watch even tighter in her little hands and shook her head. "Papa gave it to me so that I could count the seconds until he returned from his voyage."

"Captain Trenton's pocket watch is not a toy. It's very valuable. Now, give it to me."

"It belongs to Papa."

"It belongs to *me*," Mama said sharply. Edmund began to cry.

"I'll give it back to Papa," Sophie pleaded. But Mama wrenched it out of her hands.

"Go to your room and help Nurse pack your things," Mama said, picking up Edmund, whose cries had become loud wails. "You're leaving."

"Are we going to meet Papa?" Mariah asked.

"You're going to Lyme Regis to stay with Mr. and Mrs. Ellis," Mama said, bouncing her crying baby. "Mr. Ellis was a friend of your dead father's. And since your aunt, Lady Bentley, refuses to have anything to do with you, there is nowhere else to send you."

"How long are we going to stay with them?" Sophie asked.

"Pack all your clothes and ask no more questions."

They'd never visited anyone before without Mama or Papa. Something was not right about this visit; Sophie could feel it. But before she could ask another question, Mariah took her hand and gently led her from the room. They found Nurse in their bedroom already packing their things into one large trunk.

"What can we do to help?" Mariah asked.

A tear slid down Nurse's red cheek, and she placed a soft hand on both of their faces. "Nothing, my dear girls. The carriage will be here soon."

"Are you coming with us?" Sophie asked.

Nurse shook her head, spilling more tears. "I have to stay with Edmund. But you'll be good girls, though, won't you?"

"I'm scared," Mariah said.

Nurse turned and picked up Mariah's doll with the pink ribbons in its hair and handed it to Mariah. "Hug Lydia if you're scared, dear. And you won't be alone; you have Sophie."

Sophie was scared, too, but she didn't dare admit it. Nurse picked up Sophie's identical toy. "I suppose you don't want to bring Dianetha along."

"You know I don't like dolls."

"How about hugs?" Nurse asked, opening her arms. Sophie stepped into them, breathing in the familiar scent of starched linen. Mariah joined the embrace, and for a moment, everything felt right again.

Until they heard carriage wheels on the pavement in front of their house.

Sophie broke away from Nurse to look out the window. The carriage driver jumped down from his perch onto the cobblestone road.

"Grab your bonnets, girls," Nurse said as she closed their trunk—the sound had a finality to it.

Mariah started to cry. Sophie took her hand and helped her sister put on her bonnet and coat. Nurse carried the trunk down the stairs, where Mama stood by the front door, holding it open. The girls followed Nurse out to the street, where the driver took the trunk and secured it to the back of the carriage.

Pulling her hand from Sophie's, Mariah threw her arms around Mama's middle. Mama's face softened for only a moment before she said, "Get into the carriage, Mariah."

Sophie couldn't leave home without Papa's pocket watch. How was she supposed to tell time without it? And how was she to know how long it would be until Papa would return for her?

"I forgot Dianetha," she lied, darting back into the house. Instead of heading for her bedroom, she ran to the drawing room. There was a loose brick on the fireplace where she knew Mama hid her precious pearl necklace. Sophie pulled out the brick and the box behind it. Inside, sitting on top of the pearls, was Papa's pocket watch.

Sophie grabbed it and shoved it in her pocket, then pushed the box back into its secret spot and replaced the brick. Taking the stairs by twos, she dashed to her room and grabbed the doll.

Panting, Sophie ran out of the house. She hugged Nurse one last time before climbing onto the carriage seat beside Mariah, who was clutching her own doll tightly. The driver closed the door and tipped his hat to Mama. She didn't say a word, not to him or her foster daughters.

The carriage started forward, and Sophie glanced one last time out the window. Nurse had tears on her face, but Mama looked grimly satisfied. Sophie reached her hand inside her pocket and felt the watch and its linked golden chain. She rubbed her thumb over and over the scrolled decoration on the front of it.

Papa would come for his pocket watch. He would come for her and Mariah.

After several hours, the carriage stopped in front of a narrow row house with peeling red paint. There was a sign in the front window that read CLOCKS AND REPAIRS. Mariah clutched her doll with one hand and Sophie's hand with the other. She inched closer to her twin, feeling less afraid with her near.

"Why did the driver bring us to a clock shop?" Mariah asked. "Do you think there's been some mistake?"

Before her sister could answer, the driver opened the door and held out his hand to Sophie. He helped Mariah out next and then untied their trunk from the back of the carriage. He placed it in front of the door to the clock shop and knocked three times. Mariah was afraid he would leave them, but he waited until a woman answered the door. She was younger than Mama, but her face was already harshly lined. Her light hair was combed back in a severe bun, and her eyes were a color between gray and blue. The woman's dress was dark and very worn, nothing like the bright silk gowns that their Mama wore.

"Mrs. Ellis," the driver said, and tipped his hat to her, before smiling reassuringly at Mariah and Sophie.

Mariah tentatively returned his smile and looked eagerly up at Mrs. Ellis. "Thank you for inviting us to stay."

Mrs. Ellis laughed; the harsh sound was grating to Mariah's ears. "You weren't invited. The Trentons don't want you no more and my husband is the only person alive foolish enough to take in two strangers."

Mariah looked at Sophie, who was hugging her doll for the first time ever. She looked just as scared as Mariah felt.

"Are you two witless?" Mrs. Ellis asked.

"No, ma'am," Sophie said.

"Then grab your trunk and come in," Mrs. Ellis said. "I don't have all day to stand in my doorway."

Mariah released Sophie's hand and they each took a handle of the trunk to carry it into the house. They walked through the shop that had only five clocks on display, a cluttered table, and a man with a wooden leg sleeping in a chair. He wore a sailor's coat and looked like a rumpled pirate. A door from the shop led to a staircase and a kitchen, which was the only other room on the main floor of the house. She saw a table with dirty dishes on it and four chairs that did not match.

They set their trunk on the floor, unsure what to do with it. Mariah wrinkled her nose; something smelled *very* unpleasant. She looked behind the door and saw two dirty little girls eyeing her doll, Lydia, in wonder. Mariah guessed the oldest girl was three and the younger girl about a year old—her nappy was probably dirty. They reminded Mariah of

Edmund, and she wished she had thought to bring the sketch of him with her.

"Should we take the trunk to our room?" Mariah asked.

"There's a mattress in the attic you can share for now, and no more of your fancy airs," Mrs. Ellis said, spitting on the already dirty floor. "You're a pair of charity cases that ought to be thrown on the parish, and that's exactly what I'll do if you give me any trouble. Now, tell me you're grateful to me for taking you in when no one else wanted you."

"Thank you, Mrs. Ellis, for taking us in," Mariah said, then nudged Sophie with her elbow.

"Thank you," her sister muttered.

Mrs. Ellis smiled, and Mariah noticed that her two front teeth were gray.

"I can tell by your pretty little hands that you've never done a day's work. Well, that'll change right now. You," she barked, pointing at Mariah, "take care of my girls, and you"—she pointed to Sophie—"scrub the kitchen. There's a shared pump with a bucket in the back. I'm going to take your trunk to the pawn shop and see what your things will fetch—not nearly enough to pay for your keep, I reckon. Now, hand over your fancy dolls."

Mariah's arm tightened around Lydia. She didn't want another thing that she loved taken away from her. She glanced at Mrs. Ellis's dirty children, who were holding on to her skirt. "Might we give our dolls to your daughters?"

Sophie immediately handed her unwanted doll to the older girl—it was no sacrifice for her. The little girl's face lit up and Mariah felt a twinge of pity for her.

Mrs. Ellis held out her hand for Mariah's doll. Mariah hugged Lydia one last time and handed it to her. Mrs. Ellis then ripped Sophie's doll out of her daughter's hand. "They need food, not fripperies."

Both little girls began to cry. Mariah's already broken heart cracked further for these unloved little girls, but Mrs. Ellis appeared unmoved.

"The big one is Agnes and the baby is Sarah," Mrs. Ellis said. "I want them both cleaned up by the time I return."

"Yes, ma'am."

Mrs. Ellis set the dolls on top of the trunk and carried them both out the kitchen door. Mariah picked up the crying baby and felt wetness on her hand. The smell up close was unbearable. She'd never changed a nappy before, but she'd watched Nurse change Edmund. It couldn't be that difficult, could it?

"I'd better start cleaning the kitchen," Sophie said, her hand in her pocket. She was clearly hiding something, which was smart if she wanted to keep it. Mariah watched her walk out the back door and pick up a bucket to fetch water. Mariah was going to need water, too, if she was going to clean up the little girls.

The rest of the afternoon and evening passed in a blur for Mariah. Her hands ached from scrubbing out the dirty nappies, and the small bowl of soup she'd eaten for dinner did not even begin to curb her hunger.

When they were finally sent to bed for the night, she took Sophie's hand and together they climbed the stairs, up the ladder, and into the attic. They had no gas lamp or candle, so they had to feel their way along in the dark.

Finally, Mariah touched a lumpy mattress on the floor with a thin blanket on it. Both she and Sophie lay on it, snuggled close together for warmth. She heard the scurrying of little paws and forced herself to hold in her scream.

"Do you think that was a mouse?"

"Or a rat," Sophie said, yawning. "I'm too tired to care."

"Do you think it's true?"

"What?"

"What Mrs. Ellis said," Mariah whispered. "That Mama and Papa don't want us anymore."

Sophie squeezed Mariah's hand. "Our parents are dead and the Trentons aren't our family."

Mariah shook her head. She was sure that Mama and Papa loved her and Sophie. They'd taken care of them for ten years. She pictured their warm, beautiful brick house with five servants, not including Nurse. Mama and Papa sitting at opposite ends of the dinner table, eating beef Wellington, bread, tripe, and then pudding . . . Mariah could almost taste the pudding. Her hungry stomach made a gurgling noise it had never made before.

"We are their daughters. They'll come for us," Mariah said. "There's been some sort of mistake."

She heard Sophie shake her head. "They have a son of their own now. They don't need foster daughters anymore."

Tears began to leak from Mariah's eyes. "Then we're all on our own?"

"You have me and I have you," Sophie whispered. She kissed Mariah's wet cheek. "We don't need anyone else."

ONE

Eight Years Later

MR. ELLIS'S HANDS SHOOK SO much that he could barely hold the curved metal pick, let alone perform the precise movement required to set the snail to the hour wheel inside Mrs. Bidwell's clock. He dropped the pick and it clattered to the floor. Sophie stooped down to retrieve it and accidentally bumped Mr. Ellis's wooden leg. He cursed.

"Sorry," she said, setting the tool next to the clock.

He put his shaking hands on the table and used them to push himself to his feet. Even standing, he was a hunched shell of a man.

"I need a drink to steady my hands. Do you think you could finish up Mrs. Bidwell's clock and deliver it to her?"

"Yes, Mr. Ellis."

"And pick up some more laudanum from the apothecary

on your way back," he said. "My leg is hurting something awful with the change in the weather."

"I will," she said, nodding. "Shall I tell Mr. Fisby to add it to your account?"

"Yes." Mr. Ellis put a shaking hand into his jacket pocket and pulled out a penny, placing the coin in her hand. "You're a good girl, Sophie."

She nodded, knowing the coin was more a bribe for her silence to Mrs. Ellis than payment for the errand. In the eight years that she'd lived with the Ellises, she'd learned that it was best to keep her distance from the missus altogether. Sophie's younger self had found a way to do this by performing small tasks for Mr. Ellis.

At first, she'd fetched hammer pins, click screws, and gathering plates for him. But it wasn't long before Mr. Ellis began showing her how to use the tools and fix the clocks herself. Sophie had steady hands. Mr. Ellis did not—especially when he was sober. And today, since Mrs. Bidwell had paid in advance, he was not going to be sober for much longer.

Sophie watched Mr. Ellis drag his wooden leg out of the shop and into the street before pocketing the penny. She was eighteen years old now, and she needed every cent she could get her hands on to start a new life. Placing the snail over the cannon pinion and hour wheel, she used the metal pick to screw it into place. Next, she put on the minute wheel and secured it with the minute wheel cock. The wheels interlocked and she carefully spun them together so that they turned around in circles.

She cringed when the front door opened, hoping it wasn't Mrs. Bidwell. None of the villagers knew that it was Sophie who fixed the clocks. If they knew a girl and not a master clockmaker was doing the repairs, they would take their business elsewhere and the Ellises would lose the small income that they had.

Thankfully it was only Mariah. "Where is Mr. Ellis?"

Sophie exhaled and shrugged her shoulders. "Mrs. Bidwell paid him in advance."

Mariah stepped closer to the worktable. "So he's gone to the tavern to drink, then?"

Sophie nodded. "I don't expect we'll see him until he's either run out of coins for beer or is blind drunk. Where have you been?"

"Delivering the miniatures I painted of Mrs. Johnson's daughters."

"Did she pay you?"

"She paid Mrs. Ellis."

Sophie huffed in frustration. "Mariah, you should insist that you get at least *some* of the money. You do all the work."

"But Mrs. Ellis pays for the paints and supplies," Mariah said. "And provides us with a home."

"Some home," Sophie scoffed.

Mariah held up a letter. "On the way back, I ran into Postmaster Green, and he thought I was you, so he gave me this letter. At first I thought there must be some mistake, because we've never received a letter before. But then he said that *you* had posted a letter last week."

Sophie released the minute wheel and looked up at her sister. "I was going to tell you about that."

Mariah continued as if her sister hadn't spoken. "He asked me who we knew that lived in London, but I couldn't answer because *I* don't know *anyone* who lives in London."

"Mariah . . . ," Sophie started to explain but found she didn't have the words.

Her sister handed her the letter, and Sophie cradled it in her hands.

"Well, are you going to open it?" Mariah asked.

Sophie looked at her sister, standing so close that their shoulders nearly touched. Mariah had the same bright red hair, blue eyes, dainty nose, and mostly straight teeth. Sophie looked down again at the letter in her thin hands. Both she and her sister were slight of frame—from too much work and too few meals.

She tried to break the seal with her thumbnail, but her hands were as shaky as Mr. Ellis's sober ones. Sophie finally handed the letter to her sister. "The first letter I've ever received and I'm too afraid to read it . . . You do it."

Mariah took the letter. "Why should you be afraid?"

"If Lady Bentley refuses to let us stay with her, I'll never be able to go to London and see the Great Exhibition," Sophie said. She took a deep breath before she continued.

"I've almost saved enough money for a round-trip train ticket to London, but not enough for lodging or food."

"You wrote to *her*?" Mariah asked, her surprise evident.

"I know that she's refused to have anything to do with us," Sophie admitted. "Twice. But I only asked if I could stay at her London house for a short time and see the Great Exhibition. I read about it in Mr. Fisby's newspaper. Queen Victoria and Prince Albert built a special palace all out of glass for it."

"Out of *glass*?"

"They call it the 'Crystal Palace,'" Sophie explained, fiddling with her hands and tapping her foot. "I thought, perhaps . . . perhaps I could find an inventor and become an apprentice and make my fortune."

Mariah's face lit up like a candle in surprise. "I should have known you'd have a plan." She broke the wax seal and unfolded the letter. "All right, stop wiggling and I'll read it."

Sophie began to tap her foot again. Her heart pounded as if she were running from a charging bull. Mariah put one hand on Sophie's shoulder as she read the letter aloud:

To my niece Sophronia,

I received your letter and I am prepared to receive you, my namesake, in my home.

"Oh my goodness, Sophie!" Mariah exclaimed. "I can hardly believe it!"

"Keep reading," Sophie begged, her heart beating even faster.

> *I believe it is my Christian duty to see my poor dead sister's daughters established creditably. I shall pay for your clothing and see that you are introduced to good society—not to exhibitions where anyone may enter who pays the fee.*

"Not go to the exhibition?" Sophie snapped. "Then why go to London at all?"

"Hush and let me finish," Mariah said.

> *You will have one season and one season only to find a suitable husband. I am unable to receive your sister as well at this time.*

Sophie heard Mariah's breath catch, but she continued.

> *I can't possibly be burdened with the care of two young ladies with my health being in decline. Once you are married, it will be your responsibility to see that your sister is well cared for. I expect to see you within a fortnight.*
>
> *Yours sincerely,*
> *Lady Bentley*

Mariah set the letter on the table. "That's settled then," she said in a voice not quite her own. "You'll go and find yourself a husband."

"But I don't *want* a husband," Sophie protested. She wrapped her arms around herself, trying to hide her disappointment. "I want to be an inventor. *You* should go. You'd like a husband, I daresay. Besides, you're prettier than I am."

"We're identical. I can't possibly be prettier than you."

"Your hair is a shade darker and I have half an inch on you."

"She asked for her niece named Sophronia, not Mariah."

"She would never know the difference," Sophie retorted. "Mrs. Ellis still can't tell us apart and we've lived with her for eight years. Lady Bentley's never laid eyes on either of us."

"Sophie, you silly thing. This might be your only chance for a better life, to join good society," Mariah said, her voice thick with emotion.

"I pray that it is, and that you will take it," Sophie said, tapping her foot again. "Can you see me dancing and flirting? I can't. But you would be so happy. You could go to art museums and become a proper artist—"

"What about the Great Exhibition?"

"Lady Bentley clearly wrote that I wouldn't be going," Sophie said glumly. "Society has the most ridiculous notions about a woman's place. I can bake bread or go to local balls, but I'm not to work with mechanisms or create machinery."

"I wish we could both go," Mariah said wistfully. "Mrs. Ellis is with child again, and they don't really have the space for us anymore. Sarah and Agnes are getting big enough now to help with the smaller children. We're only a burden on them."

"Is that why she's so cantankerous? I should've guessed," Sophie said. "Well, then we both should go."

As soon as Sophie spoke those words aloud, her tapping foot stilled, the nervous tension that had caused her fidgeting dissipated. It was the perfect solution, a chance for them both to start afresh. The fragile hope that had sparked within her chest at the prospect of attending the exhibition began to grow into a flame of resolution.

Sophie grabbed her sister by her bony shoulders. "Come with me, Mariah."

"Lady Bentley can only stand the burden of one of us," Mariah reminded her. A tear slipped from her eye and fell down her cheek.

"We won't tell her that there are two of us," Sophie said.

"What?"

"We'll both be 'Sophie' and take turns going on outings and such. We could wear the same clothes and share a bedroom."

"And what exactly will the second Sophie do while the other is with Lady Bentley?" Mariah asked doubtfully, wiping away another tear with the back of her hand.

"Explore London! Perhaps the window to our room will

be accessible by a roof or balcony of some sort," Sophie said loudly, her excitement bursting out into her voice. "Either way, I daresay I could come up with an invention to aid in our exits and entrances."

"The whole idea is ridiculous," Mariah said with a sniff.

"The best ideas always are," Sophie assured her, feeling more and more confident with every passing moment.

"We may be identical, but we are not at all the same."

"Mariah, you know we have nowhere else to go but the workhouse," Sophie said. "And you also know that we can't stay here forever. You can find a husband in London or become a painter, but there is nothing for us here. Unless you'd like to marry the butcher's son. His attentions have been quite marked, and Mrs. Ellis likes the extra meat it gets her."

"I couldn't marry Mr. Adams," Mariah said with a shiver. "He has leering eyes."

"Then stop arguing with me and come to London."

"I suppose we could try . . . ," Mariah said. "But what if we get caught?"

Sophie shrugged. "Lady Bentley would send one or both of us back here, but we wouldn't be any worse off than we are now."

Mariah nodded her head slowly, as if considering the possibilities. "It would be a great adventure to go to London."

"That's the spirit, Mariah!" Sophie said, hugging her sister. "You start packing and I'll finish Mrs. Bidwell's clock."

Sophie and Mariah stood waiting at the train station in Dorchester—a newly built brick building with a steep roofline. Five other people stood on the cement platform: two ladies in fine dresses and three gentlemen wearing tall black top hats. The fashionable travelers gave the sisters a cursory glance before turning away from them as if they were dirt. Sophie looked down at her worn gray dress and scuffed, secondhand boots. Mariah held their shabby carpetbag, and Sophie held a basket of bread and fruit. She had baked the bread herself, and she had been quite touched when Mrs. Ellis had given them some fruit to go with it.

"You'll be hungry on your journey," Mrs. Ellis had said. "Keep your money and belongings close. There are thieves on the train."

"Thank you, Mrs. Ellis," Sophie said, managing a handshake for each of the Ellises.

Mr. Ellis had palmed her a shilling coin as he shook her hand. He then patted her shoulder and said his usual phrase: "You're a good girl, Sophie."

Mariah had wept freely and hugged each Ellis child twice. Then she'd sniffed the entire twenty-five-mile ride to the Dorchester train station. Mr. Fisby had been kind enough to let them sit in the back of his wagon, which saved them a long, dusty walk.

Mariah started to cry again as they stood on the platform. One of the gentlemen raised his quizzing glass and studied Mariah as the tears streamed down her cheeks.

"Would you please stop crying?" Sophie begged. "Your face is redder than your hair."

Mariah sniffed loudly and blew her nose in their shared handkerchief, which was already soaked through. "We may never see them again."

"I sincerely hope so," Sophie said remorselessly. "We were Mrs. Ellis's unpaid servants for eight years, and the only thing Mr. Ellis ever did was spend every penny on drink or laudanum."

"But what about the Ellis children?"

"I hope to never change another nappy," Sophie said. "The world is ours, Mariah. Stop weeping over an attic."

Mariah eventually stopped crying and even accepted a green apple from her sister.

Sophie saw the steam before she saw a train for the very first time. She turned to watch the locomotive arrive into the station; it was *beautiful*. Smoke billowed around them as they made their way to the third-class coach. A porter opened the door for them and took their one-way tickets.

The lower-class coach was quite crowded. Sophie wished she could have ridden in the engine car and learned all about how it worked, but she knew that was not possible. The sisters squeezed onto a bench between a very large matron and a short man who smelled strongly of tobacco. They watched out the window for the first several hours before the green fields started to blend together. Mariah eventually fell asleep on Sophie's shoulder and Sophie allowed her head to rest against her sister's.

Sophie awoke to a bump and the sound of squealing brakes. She looked out the window and saw that the sun had already begun to set. In the dim light of dusk, she could only make out the shadows of tall buildings.

She shook Mariah, who was still asleep on her shoulder. "We're here."

Mariah rubbed the sleep from her eyes. "It's already dark. How late is it?"

"Past eight o'clock," said the large matron. "Is someone meeting you two girls at Waterloo Station?"

"We are to go to our aunt's home, near Hyde Park," Sophie replied.

"That's not too far," the matron said. "Only a couple of miles after you cross Westminster Bridge."

"Oh dear," Mariah said. "Do we dare arrive at our aunt's house so late in the evening? Is it even safe for us to walk after dark?"

"If you're looking for accommodations for the night," the matron said, "my sister runs a respectable boardinghouse not a block from here, and her rates are most reasonable. I could take you there myself. That's where I'm headed."

Sophie looked first at the rapidly fading light outside and then at Mariah, who nodded. "Thank you, ma'am. We'd be most pleased to accept your offer."

The short man who smelled of tobacco helped them out of the train car, and they thanked him. They followed the matron through the various platforms and train tracks to the exit and saw an endless sky of rooflines and air filled with black smoke. The streets went in every direction like a maze. Sophie was glad that they'd decided to wait until the morning to find Lady Bentley's house.

The matron led them to a small house on a dark alley. The boardinghouse was run by Mrs. Mangling, a woman with a red face and large hands, and the establishment looked clean enough. Sophie paid the woman all the coins in her purse, but it still wasn't enough. Mrs. Mangling agreed to let them stay if they shared a bed and left before dawn. For once, Sophie was too tired to argue. She followed Mrs. Mangling up a narrow staircase to a cramped, airless room without any windows.

"It's very nice," Mariah said kindly.

Mrs. Mangling harrumphed and took her candle with her as she ambled back down the narrow staircase.

"I suppose we should go in," Sophie said, stepping into the cramped room.

Mariah followed behind her and closed the door—the room was pitch-black. But they were used to darkness. Mrs. Ellis had never bothered to give them a candle. Trying not to bump into each other, they took off their dresses and lay down on the dusty bed. Sophie pulled at the blanket until it covered them.

"I'm scared," Mariah whispered. "London is so much bigger than I thought it would be."

"You have me," Sophie said, squeezing her sister's hand, "and I have you and we don't need anyone else."

Mrs. Mangling pounded on their door just before sunrise. Sophie and Mariah cracked the door open for some light. Once dressed, they finished eating the meager food left in their basket. Sophie was terribly thirsty, so she traded Mrs. Mangling the basket for two glasses of water. They left the boardinghouse and walked out into the cobbled street, which despite the early hour was already filled with carriages, merchants selling their wares, and street sweepers cleaning up the muck from horses.

"I know it's only a few miles, but I think we'd better hire a hansom cab," Sophie said. "I don't think we'll ever find Lady Bentley's house on our own."

"How would we pay for it?" Mariah asked.

"I forgot," Sophie said, pulling a coin out of her dress pocket. "Mr. Ellis gave me a shilling when we left."

"I just hope it's enough to get us to Hyde Street."

Sophie nodded, then took her sister's arm and walked up to one of the many hansom cabs that waited outside Waterloo

Station. A driver, half-asleep, rubbed his eyes as the sisters approached.

"I'm not seein' double," he said. "There's really two of you."

This comment annoyed Sophie to no end, because it had been said so many times before. Still, she forced herself to smile. "Kind sir, we have only a shilling and must get to number forty-eight Hyde Street. Would you be willing to take us there?"

Mariah smiled sweetly at him and added, "Please, sir?"

The driver accepted their offer with a wink and even jumped off his perch to open the door and assist them into the two-wheeled carriage. The cab smelled of mothballs and horse, but the ride was not too long. They paid the driver their last shilling and stood in front of number forty-eight.

Hyde Street looked like a row of navy officers standing at attention. The white buildings stood erect in an endless line, all sporting black shutters, impeccably clean windows, and tall black doors with brass knockers that sparkled like the buttons of a uniform. Even the trees on the street stood in a perfect row, spaced precisely the same distance apart.

"What do we do now?" Mariah asked.

Sophie gave her sister a small shove toward the front door.

"Knock," Sophie said. "I'll walk down the street a bit and come back. Hang my pocket watch in the window of your room and I'll find a way to get in."

"What if you can't get in?" Mariah asked.

Sophie could hear the worry in her voice.

"I'll find a way in," Sophie assured her. She gave her sister a quick hug, then turned and walked down the street, trying to swallow her own fears as well as Mariah's.

TWO

IT TOOK ALL OF MARIAH'S nerve to walk up to the front door. It was still the early hours of the morning, and she feared no one would be up yet. She looked down the street and watched her sister walking away. There was no turning back now.

Mariah picked up the knocker and tapped loudly three times. Several moments later, a man with white wig askew and black coat unevenly buttoned opened the door.

"The servants' entrance is in the rear," he said condescendingly. "Through the alley."

"I'm not a servant," Mariah said, handing the man her aunt's letter. "I'm Lady Bentley's niece. I've come to stay with her."

The man looked her up and down. Mariah could

practically feel his narrowed eyes take in every wrinkle of her best dress and dowdy straw bonnet. He sneered at her but took the letter and read it before opening the door wider to allow her in.

"I am Mr. Taylor, the butler. The mistress will not be up for several more hours," he said in a monotone voice. "I will place you in the care of the housekeeper, Mrs. Kimball. Wait here. And don't touch anything."

He turned away, walking down the hall and out of sight, leaving Mariah alone in the grand entry. It seemed as large as Mrs. Ellis's entire house—larger even—with gleaming white and gray marble floors. The staircase swept up in an elegant curve of crimson carpet.

Subconsciously, Mariah tried to wipe the dust of her journey off her sleeves, but it was a hopeless cause. She was a dirty speck in this perfectly pristine home.

At least a quarter of an hour later, an older woman with graying brown hair tucked underneath a cap tied at her chin came down the hall.

"Miss Carter, I presume?"

"Yes, ma'am," Mariah said, bobbing a curtsy.

"I am Mrs. Kimball, the housekeeper," the older woman said. "I cannot allow you to see your aunt thus attired. Have you another dress?"

Mariah felt a blush creep up her neck. She was already wearing her best dress of gray cotton. She opened her bag to show her faded blue work dress.

Mrs. Kimball crinkled her nose. "No. Come with me. You will need to bathe before you meet your aunt. And I will see if Miss Golden will lend you some clothes."

"Who?" Mariah asked without thinking.

Mrs. Kimball turned back to look at Mariah. "She is your aunt's lady's maid," she said imperiously. "It is the privilege of a lady's maid to receive her mistress's old clothes. We must find something suitable for you to wear before your aunt takes you shopping."

Mariah followed Mrs. Kimball up a flight of stairs to a spacious room with a large four-poster canopy bed, a wardrobe, a chair, and a table with a mirror. The furnishings were a sumptuous peacock blue, and the floor was carpeted in a lovely floral pattern.

"This will be your room," Mrs. Kimball said, then pointed to a side table. "You may leave your things here."

Mariah set down her bag, surreptitiously taking out Sophie's pocket watch and hanging it on the handle of the window. She watched the light reflect off the golden piece and couldn't believe their luck; it would make a perfect beacon for Sophie to find. Their new room was bright, airy, and large—most unlike their shared attic at the Ellises' or the airless, cramped room at the boardinghouse.

"Follow me," Mrs. Kimball demanded.

Mariah trailed behind her to the end of the hall, where Mrs. Kimball opened the last door. It was a room dedicated to bathing and hygiene. There was a water closet in one corner—

how Sophie would love that! In the other corner, there was a large metal tub with several metal pipes sticking out of the wall and a chain cord. There was also a table with a sink. Mariah had heard of such things, but she had never actually seen them. Back at the Ellises', they had boiled kettle after kettle of water to fill the tin bathtub in the kitchen, and then everyone in the family would use the same water. It was such a laborious process that they only bathed on Sundays.

"You will be expected to bathe regularly," Mrs. Kimball said. "Here is your own soap, a towel, and a robe. I will see what clothes I can find. You do remember where your room is?"

Mariah was nettled by her patronizing tone, but said civilly, "Yes, ma'am. Thank you, ma'am."

She waited until the door was closed behind Mrs. Kimball before she quickly undressed. She pressed the bar of soap to her nose, breathing in the lovely scent of lavender. It smelled nothing like the soap she used to help Mrs. Ellis make from discarded animal fat.

Mariah put one foot into the metal tub and then the other. She wasn't exactly sure what she was supposed to do, but she had been too proud to admit that to the uppity housekeeper. For a moment she stood shivering and rubbing her hands over her arms. Then she saw a metal chain hanging above her and pulled it—and nearly screamed in surprise when water was dumped all over her.

The water was not cold—but not particularly warm either—on her back. Mariah sat down and began using the bar of soap to painstakingly wash every inch of her body and strand of her hair. She pulled the chain again to rinse off.

Mariah stood up to get out of the tub, blindly reaching for the towel to dry her face. When she glanced out the window, she nearly slipped out of the tub: Sophie had a rope around her waist and was climbing up the exterior of the house toward the bedroom window. A window that Mariah, in her hurry, *hadn't unlocked*.

"Good golly! What is she *doing*?"

Mariah didn't bother drying herself further, but instead threw on the robe and ran back to the bedroom.

Her heart fell to her feet when she opened the door. Sophie was holding on to a rope with one hand and was trying to pry the window open with the other. Mariah gasped, running to unlock the window. She took the pocket watch off the latch and opened the window just as Sophie dropped the metal tool with which she'd been attempting to pick the window lock. Mariah leaned forward to see it clink against the house once before landing in a bush.

"Come in quickly," Mariah said, suddenly breathless. "Before you fall."

Sophie pulled herself higher on the rope and stuck one foot through the window, and Mariah grabbed it with both hands. Sophie's other foot kicked out, nearly hitting her sister on the nose. Mariah was pulling her through when she heard a knock at her door.

"One moment please," Mariah called.

"I'm going to swing the rest of me inside now," Sophie said, leaving Mariah only enough time to scoot back before Sophie's whole body slid through the window. Her face was flushed red, but besides that, Sophie looked happier than Mariah had seen her in years.

"Quick," Mariah said, taking her hand. "Hide!"

"I've lost my favorite reaming tool. I'm not going to lose my rope, too," Sophie said, reaching through the open window to yank down the rope of her makeshift pulley.

Mariah heard the doorknob turn and she grabbed her sister by the waist, pulling her from the window and hauling her toward the wardrobe. "Get in!"

Sophie opened the doors to the wardrobe and climbed in, reeling up her rope like a fishing line. Mariah closed the doors behind her as Mrs. Kimball came into the room, her arms full of clothes. She was followed by a young woman with brown hair and the most freckles Mariah had ever seen on one person; she wore a maid's uniform and carried a meal tray. Mrs. Kimball pointed to the side table, and the maid placed the tray there.

Mrs. Kimball then walked toward the wardrobe with the dresses. "Miss Golden no longer has any use for these. You may wear them until you are suitably attired. Adell will help you dress when your hair is dry."

Mariah stepped between Mrs. Kimball and the wardrobe and took the clothes from the woman's hands. "Thank you, but I can dress myself."

Mrs. Kimball gave her another disdainful glance before leaving the room without another word. Adell followed behind the housekeeper and gave Mariah a small smile as she closed the door.

Sophie pushed open the doors of the wardrobe, grinning. She skipped over to where Mariah was standing. "That was close."

They both fell back on the peacock-blue bed in silent laughter and, for Mariah, unmitigated relief.

"Why are you all wet?" Sophie asked, leaning her head on her arm.

"The housekeeper insisted I take a bath before Lady Bentley saw me."

Sophie's eyes lit up. "They have indoor plumbing in this house?"

"Yes!" Mariah said. "You'll love it. There's a water closet and a bathtub with a shower. All you have to do is pull the lever and the water sprinkles all over you."

"Is the water hot?"

"No," Mariah replied, "but you'll love the soap."

Sophie sat up. "Well, I'd better go take a bath then."

"I'm afraid I left the towel and the soap on the floor," Mariah said. She hopped off the bed and took off the damp robe, handing it to her sister. "And I'm sorry everything is already wet."

"I'm more interested in the pipes than anything else."

Mariah slipped on her spare shift, then stepped to the

door and cracked it open, looking both ways before signaling Sophie to follow her. She opened the door to the bathing room for her sister. "Don't dawdle. I would hate for us to be sent home before we get to sleep in that magnificent bed."

Sophie gave Mariah's arm a light squeeze. "I'll be back in our room before you know it."

Mariah returned to the room and couldn't resist lying down on the bed again—she hadn't slept in a proper bed in eight years and it felt *marvelous*.

After a short time, the doorknob turned and Mariah's breath caught, but it was just Sophie wearing the wet robe and holding her old dress crumpled up in her hands. She came and sat on the bed and they shared the breakfast from the tray Adell had brought. There was a pot of hot chocolate, several muffins, and some bread. Even shared, it was more food than either sister had ever eaten for breakfast at the Ellises'.

"We'll get quite fat eating here," Sophie said.

"I think I'd like that very much," Mariah said.

"Although, I'm not sure if I'll be able to fit through the window if I get too much larger."

Mariah grabbed Sophie's hand. "You must promise me that you'll never do that again. I nearly had heart failure watching you hang out the window. What if you'd fallen?"

"I don't think I would have died—it's not high enough," Sophie said, waving her hand. "But you're right. Using a rope pulley is far too noticeable for every day. I was lucky that the bedroom window overlooked the back garden and alleyway . . . Still, finding a way out presents an interesting challenge."

"You'll be careful?" Mariah asked, squeezing Sophie's hand one more time.

"I'll be the very soul of caution," she replied with a smile. "I don't recall ever tasting such delicious food. I'd hate to miss out on it."

Mariah did recall tasting it at the Trentons' home, but Sophie *hated* any mention of their former foster parents.

From the pile of clothes Mrs. Kimball had brought, Mariah selected a lovely frock of the palest blue with puffed sleeves that tightened at the wrists. Sophie helped her put on a large petticoat and buttoned the back of her dress. It was a little too large, but so fine that Mariah didn't mind how it fit. The frock made her feel like a real lady.

Unsurprisingly, Sophie selected the plainest dress—a simple green frock with a high collar. She then twisted her mostly dry hair into a loose bun at the back of her neck.

"Would you like me to style your hair before you meet our aunt?" Sophie asked.

"Please," Mariah said, touching her unruly red curls.

She sat in a chair as Sophie carefully pinned each of her curls in just the right place.

"Now what do we do?" Mariah asked.

"I suppose you ought to go down and meet our aunt," Sophie said as she picked up her plain straw bonnet and tied the ribbon at her neck. "And I need to find a less conspicuous way out of the room, or I'll be a permanent resident of the wardrobe."

"Where will you go?"

"On an adventure," Sophie said, tucking away her pocket watch. "Please don't latch your window, just in case."

"*Our* window," Mariah said.

"Yes, ours," Sophie agreed.

Mariah opened the door and peered down the hallway—no one was in sight. Sophie pointed for Mariah to go toward the grand staircase, and she went in the direction of the servants' staircase. Mariah walked down the hall a few steps and turned around; there was no sign of her sister. With equal parts relief and worry, she continued to walk toward the staircase and then down it. She closed her eyes and pretended she was wearing a fancy ball gown and was making a grand entrance to a party all her own. Her gentle fantasy was broken by a harsh voice.

"Who the devil are you?"

Mariah's eyes popped open, and she saw a tall young gentleman in a long overcoat and beaver hat at the bottom of the stairs. He had dark green eyes and a strong chin, and his face was quite tanned. His hands were gloved, and his clothes were tailored. He most certainly was not a servant and he didn't seem pleased to see her.

"I'm Ma—Miss Sophie Carter. Lady Bentley's niece who has come to stay with her for the season," Mariah said confidently, pretending to be her sister in more ways than just name. Sophie would not have been intimidated by Prince Albert himself.

"I was not aware Sophronia had any living relatives," he said coldly.

"Fortunately for her, she has two nieces," Mariah said.

She saw a reluctant smile play on his lips.

"Are they both staying in my house?"

"*Your* house?" Mariah blurted out in surprise.

"I inherited this house and my title from Sophronia's late husband," the brusque young man explained. "I've been her ward since the age of twelve."

"Then you're Lord Bentley now?"

He gave her an exaggerated bow. She curtsied back, unsure whether he was mocking her. At least she wasn't wearing her old work dress.

"Where's the other one?" he asked.

"Other what?"

"Niece."

"Oh, only one was invited," Mariah said.

"For what?" he demanded.

Mariah blushed and managed to stammer, "I believe m-my aunt thinks that she might help me find a . . . a suitable husband."

"And no doubt that will solve all your problems," he replied sardonically.

"No," Mariah said, nettled. "But if I do, I'll at last have a home for myself and my sister where we'll be treated as equals and not as unwanted dependents or unpaid servants."

He took off his hat and she saw his face more clearly. He

looked younger than she'd originally supposed, not much older than herself. But there were lines around his mouth and eyes, and it looked as if he had recently been unwell. His tanned skin had an unhealthy grayish tinge to it.

"Forgive me, Miss Carter," he said in a kinder tone. "I've been traveling for many weeks and didn't expect a stranger in my home."

"I arrived only this morning," Mariah said. "I haven't even seen my aunt yet. Or maybe I should call her Lady Bentley . . . I'm not sure."

A voice from above them said, "Charles, are you all right? What are you doing here? I thought you were in America for the rest of the year."

Mariah looked up and saw a woman who didn't look at all like she had imagined. Lady Bentley had brown eyes and hair, and a sharp, distinguished face. She was about the same height as Mariah, but she seemed larger, because she wore a voluminous gown of striped purple. Lady Bentley slowly stepped down each stair until she stood in the grand foyer with Mariah and the surly young man she'd called Charles. Her keen eyes scrutinized them, from each strand of hair to the scuffs on Mariah's boots.

Mariah curtsied slowly.

"Sophronia, may I present your niece, Miss Sophie Carter?" Charles said.

"You have the beauty of my sister, though little good it did her." Lady Bentley sniffed. "Sophie, you may go."

Mariah looked right and left. "I'm sorry, but I don't know where I'm supposed to go."

She saw Charles's lips twitch again. "Miss Carter, if you go left, you'll find a comfortable sitting room where you can wait until Sophronia is ready for you."

Mariah bobbed another curtsy and opened the door to a bright room decorated in yellow. She closed the door behind her, but she could still hear their voices. She ought to have sat down on the lovely cream-colored settee, but instead she stood by the door and listened.

"Charles, you look unwell . . . Have you been sick?"

"I contracted yellow fever and even though I recovered after a fortnight, my doctor thought it best that I come back to England for a period of convalescence," he said. "Mr. Merritt will take over the business in New York and I will look after my interests here."

"Don't work yourself too hard, Charles," she said. "I will, of course, send my niece back to her father's friend. It is now most inconvenient to have her staying in the house during your convalescence."

Mariah sunk down on the settee, trying hard not to cry.

"I don't see why she needs to go," Charles said. "There are plenty of rooms in the house, and she seems so thin that I don't think she'll eat us out of house and home."

"I'm not sure it is very wise for her to stay here with an unrelated bachelor in the house."

"Don't worry, Sophronia," he said in his dry voice. "I have no intention of falling in love with her."

"If you are sure that you do not mind, I suppose she can stay," Lady Bentley said heavily. "Although, I only offered out of Christian charity. I'm sorry that it is a great inconvenience to you."

Mariah covered her face with her hands. Maybe Sophie was right: She didn't need to find a husband, she needed to find some sort of employment—some way to take care of herself without the help of anybody. Certainly not *him.*

Footsteps approached. Mariah quickly sat up and placed her hands on her lap, one over the other.

The disapproving butler, Mr. Taylor, opened the door and Lady Bentley walked into the room. Mariah stood up and curtsied to her. Lady Bentley sat down on a chair and motioned for Mariah to sit back down on the settee.

"To be frank, Sophie, I am not pleased that Charles—Lord Bentley—has arrived home at this time," she said. "You must promise me that you will not bother him at all during your stay here while he is recovering. To engage his interest would be a spiteful way to repay both his and my kindness."

"Yes, ma'am," Mariah said.

Lady Bentley smiled coldly. "You may call me Aunt Bentley."

"Thank you, Aunt Bentley."

"I will arrange for us to go shopping in the next day or so, but for now you can make yourself useful by helping me with my correspondence," Aunt Bentley said. "That is, if you are literate? But I suppose you must be since you wrote me a letter."

"Yes, I can write copperplate hand and I would be happy to be of service to you in any way."

She would do anything to be allowed to stay.

THREE

SOPHIE'S FIRST STOP, once she escaped the house through the servants' entrance, was to retrieve her reaming tool from the bush. The prickly bush proved to be a formidable adversary, scratching her arm through her dress and dirtying her new gloves. If she ever encountered it again, it would be with a sharp pair of shears.

As she walked down Hyde Street, Sophie spotted a bit of wire in the gutter—always useful in experiments. She pocketed it, then looked both ways before carefully crossing the cobblestone road, avoiding both horse and dog droppings. She hadn't worn so very fine a dress since the Tren— for a long time, and she didn't want to spoil it.

Hyde Street led her to Hyde Park, and as she approached, she was surprised to see so much space in the middle of a bustling city. Yet there it was, with lakes, lanes, and more trees than she could count. And in the distance, she spied the Crystal Palace gleaming like magic in the early morning light.

Her heart flooded with hope for the first time in years. This beautiful building proved that the impossible could be achieved with hard work and a little ingenuity. Joseph Paxton had built it around the existing trees without felling a single one, and he had shown the skeptics that it could be done both quickly and efficiently. The Crystal Palace drew her toward it like a magnet; her head could barely keep up with her feet.

There were not many people in the park at this early hour. She passed a nursemaid flying a kite with some children. There was an old man walking slowly, using his cane for each laborious step. And then a young man caught her eye. His hat was on the bench beside him and his hair was the color of sunshine. He sat reading his paper.

When Sophie strolled by, he took a pocket watch out of his vest and checked the time. As a connoisseur of all things clockwork and mechanical, she could not help but glance at the highly ornate golden piece. The young man wound it up and held it to his ear, but the pocket watch was clearly not working.

"I can fix that, if you'd like," Sophie offered.

He looked up at her, and his eyes were like a rainbow of color: blue, green, and gray. He smiled and said, "Pardon me?"

For the first time in Sophie's life, she didn't feel quite as confident. In fact, her stomach had flipped in a most pleasantly unpleasant way for no reason in particular.

"I'm sorry to have disturbed you, sir," Sophie said. "I noticed that your pocket watch had stopped, and I'm rather good with clocks. I thought I could repair it for you."

Without hesitation, he unclipped it from his vest and handed it to her. Sophie sat down on the bench beside him and took off her borrowed gloves. She pulled out the bit of wire she had picked up off the street and used it to pry open the back of the watch case.

The problem was immediately clear: The hairspring was detached from the balance wheel. Carefully she reattached it with the help of her reaming tool. As soon as she did, the balance wheel began to oscillate and the wheels in the watch moved.

Sophie snapped the back of the watch closed and handed it to the young man. She sat up a little taller on the bench, feeling awfully pleased with herself.

"That was incredible," he remarked. "May I know your name?"

"Sophie Carter." She pulled on her gloves and stood up. Her stomach behaved abnormally again when she added, "*Miss* Sophie Carter."

He stood up as well and quite towered above her. "What can I do to repay you?"

From the corner of her eye, she saw the glittering light of the Crystal Palace. "Buy me a ticket for the Great Exhibition," she blurted.

"The Great Exhibition?" he repeated.

Sophie put her gloved hand to her hot cheek. "I'm sorry, that came right out. Your thanks is plenty. I'll continue my walk. Good day, sir."

She turned away, hesitating when he touched her glove.

"Wait," he said, "is that where you're going now?"

Sophie shrugged. "I'm going on a walk to see the exterior of the Crystal Palace—what a feat of ingenuity and engineering."

"But not to the exhibition itself?"

"I can't go in. I don't have money for a ticket."

"In return for repairing my pocket watch, I would be most honored to escort you to the Crystal Palace and purchase you a ticket to the Great Exhibition," he said.

"I'm sure you have other plans for your Saturday."

"I wish to go with you."

"But I don't even know your name," Sophie half-heartedly protested.

"Mr. Ethan Miller, at your service," he said, offering his arm.

"This is my first time in London," Sophie confided as she placed her hand on his arm. "I'm staying with my aunt, but she doesn't approve of the different classes mingling like they do at the Great Exhibition."

"Should we leave a message for your aunt?"

"No!" Sophie said, too loudly. "I mean, she doesn't even know I'm out."

"Very sly," he said with a hint of a smile.

"Oh, I was," Sophie said. "I had to escape so that I could experience more of London than my aunt's sitting room."

Ethan turned them back toward the direction Sophie had come from.

"Isn't the Crystal Palace the other way?" she asked.

Ethan smiled. "I don't think you realize how large Hyde Park is. It's over a mile walk to the Crystal Palace from here."

They walked to the street and he hailed a hansom cab. For a moment, Sophie wondered if it was wise to go off with a strange man, even in an open carriage on a public street. She placed her hand in her pocket and touched her reaming tool—she could defend herself if need be. Sophie looked at Ethan Miller's handsome face and he smiled back at her. She felt unaccountably warm and entirely safe in his company.

When the horse and hansom cab came to a stop at their destination, Ethan jumped out of it and then offered his hand to her.

The Crystal Palace was even more beautiful up close than she had imagined it would be. It was an enormous building made entirely out of iron and glass. In the middle there was a semicircular transept facade, and below it were three levels of crystal arches.

"It's unlike anything I've ever seen!" Sophie exclaimed. "It's like a magical palace from a fairy tale."

"Wait until you see what's inside," Ethan said, offering his arm again. Sophie eagerly took it, and they wove through people and carriages.

Ethan purchased them each a ticket for five shillings, and as they entered the Crystal Palace, again Sophie's breath was taken away. In the center, there was a pink crystal fountain that was as tall as four grown men standing on each other's shoulders. Sculptures surrounded the fountain, including one of Queen Victoria in all her majesty, and two more sculptures of Queen Victoria and Prince Albert on horseback. All around there were flowers and planted palm trees. Sophie felt like she'd stepped into a different world. In all directions, there was so much to see. So much to explore.

"They say there are over a hundred thousand objects on display," Ethan whispered in her ear.

"How could you possibly see them all in one afternoon?" Sophie exclaimed.

"I don't think you could," Ethan said, opening his official catalogue from Messrs. Spicer and Clowes. "The exhibits are in four main categories: raw materials, machinery, manufacturers, and fine arts. Which should we visit first?"

"Machinery!" Sophie said eagerly. She tugged on his arm, pulling him toward the biggest exhibit of all, a massive hydraulic press, designed by engineer Robert Stevenson.

There was a man standing by it, and Sophie lost not a moment in asking how it worked. The man explained that the hydraulic press was used to lift the heavy iron tubes for Stephenson's Britannia Tubular Bridge. She was dumbstruck when he told her that each metal tube weighed 1,144 tons and yet the press could be operated by only one person.

Sophie and Ethan also saw Nasmyth's steam hammer, which was so delicate it could lightly crack an eggshell; steam-driven plows; adding machines; astronomical clocks; electric clocks; marine chronometers—clocks for ships; machines that could mass-produce nails and pens; a machine that could print five thousand paper copies an hour; textile machines; and every possible type of steam engine.

Ethan led her to a refreshments area that was separated from the exhibits by an ornately scrolled wrought iron fence. He helped her into a seat at a small round table near the statue of an angel and underneath a sprawling tree. A waiter with a shiny, round face and wearing a blue jacket came to take their order.

"I never dreamed so much of this was already possible in 1851," she said, awestruck. They sipped lemonade and ate Bath buns purchased from Messrs. Schweppes. "It seems like something out of my imagination . . . My old neighbors in Lyme Regis would never believe me if I tried to tell them."

"You're from Lyme Regis?" Ethan asked.

"Yes," Sophie said. "But before then I lived in Sidmouth."

"You must like the sea."

Sophie sipped her lemonade and nodded.

"Is your family still in Lyme Regis?"

"No—I mean, I'm an orphan. My father died before I was born, and my mother died in childbed. My sister and I have been living with Mr. and Mrs. Ellis. He was my father's friend in the navy," Sophie said. "But hopefully, we won't need to impose on them any longer."

"Then you'll be staying with your aunt in London permanently?" Ethan asked.

"Only for the season," Sophie replied. "My aunt is Lady Bentley, and she means to find me a suitable husband. But I have other plans."

"What plans?"

"Promise me that you won't laugh."

"I could never laugh at you," Ethan said.

She took a breath. "I want to be an inventor."

"Of what?"

"I'm not sure," Sophie admitted with a slight shrug. "I just like to see how things work, and I think with the proper training and materials I could create new inventions. I'm hoping to find a master inventor at the exhibition to apprentice myself to."

"I don't know of any inventor who apprentices ladies."

"You're probably right," Sophie said with a sigh. She set her glass down on the table, folded her arms, and scowled. "They only apprentice females for sewing or haberdashery. I doubt if even a clockmaker would take me on, though I know everything there is to know about clocks."

"My grandfather owns several factories," Ethan said with a shy smile. "I could ask him if he knows of anyone looking for an apprentice."

Sophie found herself softening despite her frustration. "Do you work at one of the factories?"

"Yes and no," Ethan said. "I don't work *at* any of the factories, but I handle all the finances associated with them."

"You must be quite clever," Sophie said. "What type of factories?"

"All sorts—cotton, wool, paper, machine tools, rolling mills, foundries, and locomotive works."

"Maybe I could see one of the factories someday," Sophie said wistfully. Then, realizing she'd rudely invited herself, she hurried to add, "I'm afraid today that I keep speaking without thinking. You don't have to take me anywhere else. Who knows, we may never see each other again after today. London is such a large city."

"I hope that is not the case," Ethan said. "In fact, I'm sure it will not be."

"How so?" Sophie asked, and found herself leaning toward him.

"My cousin Charles was your aunt's ward," Ethan said.

"You don't say," Sophie said. "Then I suppose you know where I live, too. I'm glad one of us does. With all the turning around we did, I wasn't sure I could find it again."

"It's getting late," Ethan said, looking at his now perfectly working pocket watch. "I should probably escort you home."

"Can we see the Koh-i-noor diamond first?" Sophie asked. "I don't know if I'll get to come back, and I'm simply agog to see it."

She stood up and Ethan offered his arm. He led her away from the refreshments area to the pavilion where the largest diamond in the world was on display, guarded by a clutch of navy-clad policemen. The diamond lay in a case that looked like a birdcage. It didn't sparkle, even though it was lit by a dozen gas jets.

"How very drab it seems," Sophie remarked. "I've always imagined diamonds and gems to sparkle."

"Have you never seen a diamond before?" Ethan asked.

"I'm afraid not," she said.

"Most gems, if they are cut well, do sparkle when the light shines through them."

"Something to look forward to seeing, then," Sophie said. "I was afraid after today that nothing could astonish me. I'm happy that there's more in store for me."

Upon reluctantly exiting the Crystal Palace, Ethan found them a hansom cab and directed it to Lady Bentley's house, on Hyde Street.

"Do you mind letting me out a few houses away?" Sophie asked as they neared their destination. "I would like to reenter the house without my aunt knowing I've been away. If I were to come through the front door, it would be terribly awkward."

"How are you going to get in?"

"I'll sneak through the servants' entrance in the back."

Ethan directed the driver to go a few more houses down, then got out and assisted Sophie down.

"The next time I see you, don't be alarmed if I pretend not to recognize you," Sophie said. "That way my aunt will never guess of our secret adventure."

"I look forward to being introduced to you properly," he said, taking her hand and bowing over it.

Ethan released her hand and Sophie turned to go. She took one step, then pivoted back to him. Standing on her tiptoes, she gave him a butterfly kiss, her eyelashes gently brushing his cheek.

"Thank you for the best day of my life."

Sophie didn't wait to see his response; she turned and nearly ran to the alley that led to the back of Lady Bentley's house. She cautiously opened the back door and looked for servants—there were none in sight. She took the stairs by twos, turned the corner, and bumped into a tall, gaunt man dressed in his dinner coat. He grabbed her arms to steady her and then let her go so abruptly that she almost toppled over.

"Terribly sorry, sir," Sophie said.

"If you were not aware, Miss Carter," he said, "your aunt will expect you to change your dress for dinner."

"I'm on my way to my room to change this very instant," Sophie said over her shoulder as she hurried to her room. As she closed the door behind her, she thought she heard him mutter to himself, "Wasn't she wearing blue before?"

"Sophie! Where have you been for so long?" Mariah cried. "I've been terribly worried."

Sophie took her sister's hands and twirled her around.

"I had the most unforgettable day of my life," Sophie said. "I saw an enormous hydraulic press at the Great Exhibition, and I met the most handsome young man!"

"In that order, I suppose," Mariah said wryly.

Sophie continued to spin her sister around. "No time to talk. I just bumped into a stern man who told me to dress for dinner, so we'd best get you changed into the fanciest dress in the wardrobe."

"You met Charles—I mean, Lord Bentley?"

"Possibly," Sophie said. "I literally ran into him at the end of the hall. But we can talk more after dinner. Come, let me undo your buttons."

Sophie helped Mariah put on their only evening gown—an ornate dress made of purple satin—then pushed her sister out the door. She took off her own green dress and spread out on the bed in only her shift. The mattress was so soft and large, she felt as if she were lying on clouds in the heavens.

All she could think about was Mr. Ethan Miller. Mariah would be shocked if she knew Sophie had given him a butterfly kiss!

FOUR

One Week Later

MARIAH COULD HARDLY BELIEVE THAT she had lived on Hyde Street for only seven days. It was like a beautiful dream—every morning she was afraid she would wake up and find herself back in that old, cramped attic.

Each day the sisters shared the breakfast tray, and then one of them would eat lunch with their aunt and the other one would eat dinner. Sophie never stayed in the room, instead going around to various shops—a bootmaker's, a cigar store, a drugstore, a dry goods store, a bakery, and even a crinoline shop—asking about a possible position. She was looking for any job to pay their way until she found an apprenticeship. But either they did not hire ladies or they were not hiring at all. Mariah was less daring, usually staying in the room feeling bored. She solved this problem by asking their aunt if she could borrow books from the library.

Sophie turned over in bed, taking most of their peacock-blue coverlet with her. Mariah shivered as she smiled; Sophie had been right—no one had guessed that there were two of them.

Mariah startled when she heard a gentle knock at the door. She nudged Sophie to wake her up, but Sophie didn't budge or open her eyes. Then Mariah heard the doorknob turn.

She scrambled over Sophie to the other side of the bed and rolled off, landing on the carpet with a muffled but still undignified thud. Mariah hauled herself under the bed just as the door cracked open. She watched Adell's feet as she placed the tray on the table next to the bed and then left the room.

She scurried out from underneath the bed and saw that Sophie still hadn't stirred. Mariah pushed her wild curls out of her face and picked up her pillow, swatting her sister with it. Sophie closed her eyes tighter, so Mariah rolled her eyes and started eating breakfast alone. As she took a sip of hot chocolate and began eating a muffin, she could hardly wait to dress and go down to the library to get some new books. She had already read every book by Fanny Burney—*Evelina* was by far her favorite.

She selected a peach gown from the dozen dresses now in the wardrobe; Mariah had gone shopping with their aunt two days after they arrived. Their first purchase had been a crinoline cage—the most extraordinary item. It was a steelwork petticoat that looked like a large birdcage that fitted around the waist, making a skirt look circular without the use—and weight—of countless petticoats. Mariah stepped into it, pulling it up to her waist and tying the strings, and then put on her dress.

She arranged her hair before trying to wake her sister by shaking her shoulder. Sophie still refused to open her eyes, so Mariah stuffed a muffin into her open mouth. Sophie's eyes popped open.

"Sophie, be a love and button me," Mariah said. "I want to get us some new books for the week."

Her sister groaned but sat up and buttoned Mariah's dress. Once finished, she fell back into bed and covered her head with a pillow.

Mariah chuckled as she picked up the stack of books to return and opened the door. She walked slowly toward the stairs. Crinolines were funny, bobbing up and down if she walked too fast; the first time Mariah wore one, she nearly fell over.

She held her breath as she walked slowly down the stairs, a firm grasp on the railing, only exhaling when she was safely at the bottom. Then she walked to the library and opened the door.

"Hello, Miss Carter."

Mariah dropped the books she was holding. Standing before her was Lord Bentley, wearing day clothes and a crimson silk over-robe. She tried to pick up the books, but the bottom of her crinoline was stuck in the doorframe. She gave her skirt a tug, only to trip over the books and into his arms.

"I'm so sorry, Lord Bentley," Mariah said. She awkwardly untangled herself from him, trying not to notice how nice he smelled. "But I'm glad to see you out and about. Aunt Bentley said you needed rest and were confined to your room."

"Lucky I was here to catch you," Charles said with a smile that transformed his stern, gaunt face into something rather handsome.

Mariah knew she was blushing, which meant she was red *everywhere*—hair, face, neck. She tried once more to bend over and collect her books, but she couldn't quite reach them because of the wide hoop of her crinoline cage. Charles knelt down easily and helped her, reading aloud each title as he picked it up.

"I see you have quite exhausted our collection of Mrs. Burney's novels."

"Yes," Mariah managed. "I mean, I suppose I ought to read more serious books, but for the last eight years the only book I've had access to was the Bible—"

"All you've read for eight years is the Bible?"

Mariah nodded.

"You poor girl."

She smiled a little at this. "I love the Bible, of course, but one does long for a change. And to experience books written by other women is such a pleasure."

Charles set down the stack of books on the table and turned to the shelf. He pulled out two books that looked brand new and handed them to Mariah.

"*Mary Barton,* published anonymously," she said, reading the title pages, "and *Jane Eyre: An Autobiography* by Currer Bell."

"*Mary Barton* was written by a Mrs. Gaskell," Charles explained, "and Currer Bell is really Charlotte Brontë."

"Really, Lord Bentley?" Mariah exclaimed, louder than she meant to.

"Yes," he said in a conspiratorial voice, a hair above a whisper. "Such secrets always slip out. And you may call me Charles if you like."

Mariah smiled and walked toward the bookcase. Over her shoulder, she said, "I'm glad you're feeling better . . . Charles."

"Better, just bored," he said, picking up another book and flipping through the pages. "Well enough to move about, but not to go back to work; at least, not according to your most solicitous aunt."

Mariah added another book to her pile and turned to look at him. "She speaks of nothing but you."

"She's the only mother I've ever known, and I her only child, even though we aren't related by blood," he said lightly. "But I don't understand how ladies can sit around all day."

"A week ago, I would have given anything to sit around all day. And now that I can, I find I miss having a purpose," Mariah said.

"What purpose was that?"

"Taking care of the Ellises' small children, cleaning,

cooking, mending, teaching the little ones how to read and do math. Sometimes a bit of shopping," Mariah explained. "There was always something that needed doing."

"Sounds exhausting."

"It was," Mariah admitted. "But I had a purpose, and now I'm idle."

"But you are at least putting your idleness to good use," Charles said, "by expanding your knowledge of the world and the people who have lived in it, by reading."

"I thought that maybe I could become a governess. I like to teach children, and I love to draw and paint. But I don't speak French or play the pianoforte—or rather, I haven't since I was a little girl."

"Why did you stop?"

"I—we, my sister and I—had a governess and a pianoforte when we lived with the Trentons, but there were no such luxuries available in the Ellis home."

"Who are the Trentons?" Charles asked.

"They took us in after my mother died when we were born," Mariah explained. "Captain Trenton was my late father's commanding officer."

"If it isn't too impertinent to ask," he said, "why did you leave?"

She shrugged. "Miraculously, she had a son rather late in life and no longer wanted foster daughters."

"That must have been very hard for you."

"It was harder for So— for my sister," Mariah said. "But

I am determined to be a dependent no more. Do you think I might practice on your pianoforte?"

"You're welcome to anything in the house."

"Then . . . might I have some paper and a pen?"

Charles walked over to the desk and opened a drawer. He took out a stack of hot-pressed paper, an inkpot, and two pens, then handed them to Mariah. "Writing letters?"

She shook her head. "Mrs. Ellis is not literate and would never allow me to teach her . . . I was hoping to use the paper to draw, if that is all right?"

"The paper is yours now," he said. "You can do whatever you wish with it."

"Thank you." Mariah picked up her books and set them on top of the paper. Trying to suppress a smile, she turned away to leave the library.

"The look on your face is terribly intriguing," Charles said. "You must tell me what you're thinking."

Mariah pivoted on her right foot. "You're much nicer in your robe than you are dressed in a full suit of clothes."

He laughed loudly. Mariah carefully ducked sideways through the door—so she wouldn't get stuck again—and ran up the stairs with her crinoline bobbing up and down.

"Sophie, you will accompany me on some calls," Aunt Bentley commanded. "We need to expand your acquaintance with single gentlemen."

"Yes, Aunt Bentley," Mariah said.

Aunt Bentley lent Mariah one of her own very stylish hats, complete with ribbons and artificial flowers. They rode in a fine closed carriage, with the family coat of arms on the panel, to the first house, where they were ushered into a sitting room by a wizened butler.

Aunt Bentley sat down on the sofa and gestured for Mariah to sit beside her. A plump woman of forty with a plain face and very ornate puce dress entered the room, followed by an equally plump older man with a similarly plain face. The two were undoubtedly related.

"Miss Blacking, may I introduce my niece, Miss Sophie Carter?" Aunt Bentley said.

Mariah bobbed an awkward curtsy. The older man was staring at her in a way that made her feel quite unwell.

"Lady Bentley," Miss Blacking said, "may I introduce my brother, Mr. Blacking?"

"A pleasure, sir," Aunt Bentley said in her most polite voice. "I believe you are in the business of canals and boats?"

"Yes, ma'am," he said in a gruff, low voice. "My business has been to dig canals and charge for their use. And right profitable it has been."

"My niece grew up in Lyme Regis and has always been fond of the water," Aunt Bentley stated. "Aren't you, Sophie?"

"Yes," Mariah said. "The sound of water is most calming."

"Do you have any property in Lyme Regis?" Miss Blacking inquired pointedly.

Mariah shook her head.

Aunt Bentley smiled. "Alas, my dear niece is an orphan and has only her great beauty, patient temperament, and noble family connections to secure her a place in this world."

Mariah felt her cheeks flame with heat.

I'm for sale to the highest bidder.

Thankfully, they didn't stay much longer. Mariah accompanied her aunt on two more visits, both equally awkward. Mr. Herring lived with his widowed mother and looked to be close to fifty years of age. Mr. Westerham was by far the youngest, perhaps in his early thirties. His face was heavily pocked, and he blew his nose at such frequent intervals as to stop all conversation.

Mariah could hardly muster the strength to get out of the carriage for the last visit. It was a great white house with commanding Roman pillars and was by far the largest residence they had visited so far.

"The others were expecting our visit," Aunt Bentley explained, "but not Mrs. Miller. She is Charles's aunt and therefore no relation of ours. Still, I don't wish to slight her. Mr. Eustace Miller—Charles's maternal grandfather—is very much alive and in possession of most of his fortune; I wouldn't risk Charles's chance to inherit it for the world."

Mariah nodded and followed her aunt into the house. The interior furnishings were as opulent as the exterior suggested. The rooms were as large as the assembly hall in Lyme Regis, and there was enough furniture to comfortably seat at least thirty people. Her aunt chose to sit on a crimson horsehair sofa by the window, and they waited several minutes before a woman entered the room. She had an abundance of blond hair, streaked with white, and wore a deceptively simple blue dress that set off her eyes to perfection.

"Thomasina, allow me to introduce to you my niece, Miss Carter," Aunt Bentley said.

"Miss *Sophie* Carter?" Mrs. Miller inquired.

Mariah almost said no but caught herself. "Yes, ma'am."

"How very knowing you are," Aunt Bentley said.

"Named after you, Sophronia, I believe?" Mrs. Miller said.

"You are positively prescient today."

"I have heard tell of your niece," Mrs. Miller said with a warm smile. "Come to London to seek her fortune."

Mariah could not help but return her kind smile.

"More like to seek a husband," Aunt Bentley said crisply. "I have already introduced her to several eligible gentlemen of easy means. Let us hope that one may find her suitable."

Mariah's smile faded at this.

"If only my son were here," Mrs. Miller said cheerfully. "He is both eligible and of easy means."

Aunt Bentley colored slightly. "I am sure you have other plans for your son, as I do for Charles; a lady from a noble family, with a dowry, and excellent business connections. I only wished to make my niece known to you."

Mariah could only be thankful that she was sitting through

this ordeal and not her sister. What would Sophie have said or done? Mariah almost laughed as she pictured Sophie barking at Aunt Bentley like a fishwife. Sophie had learned several *choice* words, as she called them, living in the poorest part of a fishing town and was unafraid to use them when vexed.

"That is thoughtful of you, Sophronia," Mrs. Miller said, "but I believe Ethan is very interested in meeting your niece. I shall be inviting you all to dinner soon. It has been an age since I have seen Charles. Ethan said he has been much affected by his illness."

Aunt Bentley spoke in detail of Charles's sickness, the doctors they had consulted, and how long he ought to convalesce before returning to social and work duties. When they later departed, Mrs. Miller surprised Mariah by shaking her hand.

It was nearly dinnertime before they arrived back on Hyde Street. Mariah went to her room to trade places with Sophie, but she was nowhere to be found. She felt guilty that Sophie would miss both lunch and dinner, but someone had to be "Sophie."

Adell helped Mariah into her dark blue evening gown, cut low across her shoulders and trimmed with black ribbons. Mariah waited as long as she could before she walked downstairs to dinner.

Aunt Bentley sat at the end of the table and Mariah was placed on her left. *This table is enormous for only the two of us.* Just then, Charles entered the room in the same crimson silk robe from the morning.

"Mr. Taylor, please add another cover," Charles said. "I shall join the ladies for dinner."

"Charles, I'm delighted that you feel strong enough to join us," Aunt Bentley said. "But really, you shouldn't wear a house robe to the table."

"I must," Charles said solemnly. "I've been informed that I'm much nicer when I wear it."

Mariah choked on her white soup and coughed. Charles raised his eyebrows, giving her a quizzical look.

"I can see you are in a teasing mood," Aunt Bentley said. "It is your house, after all, and I suppose you can wear whatever you wish in it."

"I was thinking of wearing it to my club," Charles said. "I thought I might start a new fashion."

"Insouciant dress is never in fashion," Aunt Bentley said in mock severity. "But I won't try to dissuade you further. It will only add to your determination to do it. I remember when you were thirteen years old, I told you that you couldn't ride Lord Bentley's horse because it was too strong for you. You waited until the groom was busy and rode out of the stables on it. Do you remember?"

Charles sipped his wine. "How could I forget? The horse *was* too strong for me. It threw me and I broke my arm."

"Lesson learned," Mariah said, dabbing her mouth delicately with a napkin.

"Not at all," Charles said. "My arm healed, and I got back on that stallion."

"More successfully the second time?" Mariah asked.

"Much," Charles said, with one of his sudden, transformative smiles.

"Yes," Aunt Bentley said, raising her wineglass. "And my late husband was so proud, too. It seems that obstinacy in boys is something to be praised."

"It's always noble to finish what you start," Mariah said. "If it's a good thing."

"Wise words indeed," Charles said. "That is why I mean to return to New York as soon as I'm recovered."

"I was afraid of that," Aunt Bentley said, taking a sip of her wine. "But I won't throw a rub in the way of your American trip or your silk robe."

"Even if I wear my sartorial splendor to Aunt Miller's dinner party next week?" Charles asked.

"I daresay Miss Penderton-Simpson will find you quite handsome in it."

Mariah raised an eyebrow and Charles shifted in his seat uncomfortably. Aunt Bentley had scored a point in their exchange.

"Who is Miss Penderton-Simpson?" Mariah asked nonchalantly.

Aunt Bentley smiled, showing all her teeth. "A most accomplished and well-connected young lady with a dowry few could boast. She quite fancied Charles before he left for New York."

"Is she beautiful?"

"Very," Charles said, standing. "I believe I'm a little done in for the day. I shall excuse myself." He gave the ladies a small bow and then left the room.

"I don't think Miss Penderton-Simpson will allow him to escape a second time," Aunt Bentley said, and took a large bite of duck. She chewed it slowly with a satisfied look on her face.

Mariah swallowed her own mouthful too soon and began coughing again.

FIVE

SOPHIE QUIETLY TIPTOED DOWN THE hall to see if the grand staircase was clear. Mr. Taylor was touching the railing with a white glove, checking for any speck of dirt or dust; Mariah was already out with Aunt Bentley, making it inadvisable for Sophie to be seen by him or any of the other servants. She dashed down the hall to the servants' staircase and saw Adell at the bottom, washing the steps, one at a time. There was no way to get past her without being seen.

"*Botheration!*" she growled under her breath.

She heard Mr. Taylor's firm steps—he was nearly to the top of the grand staircase and he would see her before she could reach her room. There was nowhere else to go but up. She climbed the staircase by twos, past the servants' attic apartments, and to the roof. She unlocked the door and stepped out into the sunlight and fresh air. She still felt trapped, but at least she was no longer in that stuffy bedroom.

For a short while, Sophie amused herself by watching the people on the street down below go about their business. How she longed to go about her own business and find a position so that she could support herself and Mariah. Aunt Bentley had only promised them one season, and it would be over before they knew it. And that was if she didn't discover their deception first and cast them out of the house.

Then Sophie saw something out of the corner of her eye: The door on the roof adjacent to hers was open. It was like a miracle; a way out of her fix. She could escape without any of her aunt's servants seeing her. The only barrier was a two-foot brick wall that separated the two houses, but as she stepped over it, she began to have doubts. What if she were caught and arrested for trespassing? Or as a burglar? Who knew what or whom she would find in a strange house?

Unsure, she sat on the brick barricade between the two houses. Her shadow cast a long silhouette on the roof—if she didn't leave soon the day would be wasted and any opportunity to find work would be lost. She stood up and tiptoed to the door and listened. When she couldn't hear anything, she quietly stepped inside.

Climbing down the stairs, Sophie saw that the entire level was one large room with several easels and paint cans. A large canvas, nearly as tall as her and four times as wide, stood in the center of the room. It depicted a knoll covered in long, wet grass, and a castle in the distance. But the center was surprisingly blank, as if something was yet to be painted.

She took a step back from the canvas and bumped into a table—a paint can clattered to the floor. She heard an angry voice using words that would have made even Mr. Ellis blush. The open door had not been a miracle, but a mistake.

Of all the pigeon-headed things to do!

Quickly she picked up the paint can and put it back on the table, then ran toward the staircase. But her exit was blocked by a bald, portly, middle-aged man wearing a smock covered with paint splatters.

"What in the name of all that is holy are you doing in my house?" he bellowed in a slight Scottish lilt.

"F-f-forgive me, sir," Sophie said. "I was attempting to leave my aunt's house without detection, and I noticed that your roof door was ajar—"

"And that's how you knocked over my paint can?" he said loudly. "I'm calling the Watch."

"Truly, I wasn't trying to steal from you!" Sophie protested. "I was merely borrowing your roof to exit. Surely that isn't a crime."

"It's breaking and entering."

"I didn't break anything, and I was *exiting*."

He picked up a long wooden paintbrush and brandished it at her like a sword. "Lassie, don't think you can escape that easily!"

"Calm yourself, Sir Thomas," a lady's voice said. A woman of middling years came up the stairs behind him. She was neither young nor slender, but undeniably pretty, with large brown eyes, a small nose, and a generous mouth. She wore an apron over her dress and her brown curls escaped from her lacy cap.

The woman smiled warmly at Sophie and gently took the paintbrush-turned-weapon out of Sir Thomas's hand. "Let's start again, shall we?" she said. "I am Mrs. Spooner, and may I introduce you to Sir Thomas Watergate, the renowned artist."

Sophie executed a stiff bow. "I am Miss Sophie Carter . . . I'm Lady Bentley's niece come to stay."

"Aye," Sir Thomas said, rubbing his chin. "You're the one she's trying to leg-shackle to any man under sixty with enough money to afford a chit of a wife with no expectations."

"And how would you know that?" Sophie asked between clenched teeth.

"She paid me a call, seeing if I was interested in meeting you, lass," Sir Thomas said, "and I'm right grateful I had the good sense to decline."

"Not as grateful as *I* am."

"Now, now, let's not be uncivil," Mrs. Spooner said with a barely suppressed smile. "Miss Carter, would you care for some tea?"

Sophie's stomach grumbled loudly before she could answer.

"I'll take that as a yes, dear girl," Mrs. Spooner said. She took Sophie's arm and led her down the stairs to a blue parlor, where she rang the bell and instructed a servant to bring tea immediately.

"Please sit, Miss Carter," she said, graciously pointing to the chair beside her.

Sophie sat down and thanked her.

"Don't be disturbed by Sir Thomas's outbursts," she said. "Geniuses rarely have even temperaments."

A servant set down a silver tray on the table, and Mrs. Spooner poured tea into delicate white cups and matching saucers with pink and blue flowers.

"Is he really a famous painter?" Sophie asked.

Mrs. Spooner nodded. "His paintings are displayed in all the most famous galleries. And people pay him outrageous sums to paint their portraits."

"The detail is so fine and precise on the grassy knoll," Sophie said. "One can almost imagine oneself in the painting, walking through the wet grass."

Mrs. Spooner set down her teacup with such haste that it spilled. "That's it. Why did it not strike me before? Just the thing!"

And with that incomprehensible speech, she stood up and nearly ran out of the room, calling loudly for Sir Thomas.

Everyone in this house is stark raving mad.

Mrs. Spooner reentered the room with her lacy cap completely askew, dragging Sir Thomas by the arm.

"Look at her face, her hair, her form. She's perfect for Joan of Arc," Mrs. Spooner insisted.

Sophie colored under their mutual scrutiny.

"By George, you're right, Prudie!" Sir Thomas said, squeezing her tightly and giving her a great smack of a kiss on the lips.

"Lady Bentley's niece—" Sir Thomas began.

"My name is Sophie Carter."

"Miss Carter, I've decided not to call the Watch, on the condition that you will pose for my painting as its model."

"I'm afraid that I don't have the time," Sophie said matter-of-factly. "I'm currently looking for employment."

"I'll pay you a salary," Sir Thomas said. "Better money than you'll make at any shop in London for doing nothing at all."

"What are you proposing to pay me?"

"Ten pounds."

Sophie tried to hide her surprise by turning away. She'd never possessed any coin close to that much money before.

"Five pounds now," Mrs. Spooner clarified, "and five pounds when the painting is completed."

Sophie opened her mouth and shut it several times. She didn't desire to sit still for hours and have her features memorialized in a fictional painting. On the other hand, ten pounds would enable her and Mariah to see more of London and maybe find a permanent place here.

"I'll be your model . . . on one condition," Sophie said.

"I hardly think you're in any position to make conditions," he retorted.

"Sir Thomas," Mrs. Spooner said, laying her hand on his arm.

"My condition is that my sister, Mariah, who is an aspiring

artist, will be allowed to come and study your painting technique as frequently as she wishes."

"Bless me," Mrs. Spooner said, touching her chest. "I didn't know Lady Bentley had two nieces staying with her."

Sophie swallowed. "I suppose that is the second condition. You can't tell anyone that Mariah is also staying with Lady Bentley, because she doesn't know."

"Where is the poor girl?" Mrs. Spooner asked.

"We're sharing a room, food, and clothing while taking turns being me."

"How is this charade even possible?" Sir Thomas asked.

"My sister and I are identical twins," Sophie explained. "Only a few people can tell us apart."

"But why?" Mrs. Spooner asked. "It seems outrageous and entirely unnecessary."

"My aunt would receive only one of us, and we didn't wish to be parted."

"Is that why you were using my roof, then?" Sir Thomas demanded.

"Yes," Sophie admitted glumly. "Today Mariah is with my aunt, making more house calls."

"Poor single gentlemen should be allowed their peace," Sir Thomas interjected.

"Hush," Mrs. Spooner said. "You poor dears. It's no wonder your stomach was making such sounds. Well, Miss Sophie Carter, you are welcome to come eat any meal with us and use our house as an exit if you please. As is your sister."

Sophie stood, overcome by Mrs. Spooner's rare kindness. "There are no words—"

Mrs. Spooner waved her hand to stop Sophie's gratitude. "Have a piece of cake, dear girl, and then we'll go measure you for your armor."

"Armor?!"

"You don't suppose Joan of Arc fought in her petticoats, do you?" Mrs. Spooner said. "And we'd probably better get you a sword."

"What I wouldn't give to see you dressed in armor!" Mariah said between peals of laughter. "And with a sword!"

Sophie stuck out her tongue. "You'll see me, but you must promise not to laugh. I've arranged with Sir Thomas for you to observe him painting. Maybe you can learn some new techniques."

"Sophie, you didn't!" Mariah exclaimed.

She shushed her.

Mariah clapped her hands over her mouth and danced about the room.

"Stop dancing and help me with my hair," Sophie said.

Mariah twirled twice more before coming over and carefully brushing Sophie's hair until it shone red and bright like maple leaves on an October day.

"Do tell me if you meet a young lady named Miss Penderton-Simpson."

"What a mouthful of a name," Sophie said. "Who is she?"

"Just some person."

"If you want details, I'll get details."

"Very well," Mariah said, pinning a curl in place. "Aunt Bentley mentioned that Miss Penderton-Simpson has taken an interest in Charles."

"Charles?"

"Lord Bentley told me that I could call him Charles," Mariah explained quietly.

"If Miss Pender-whatsit fancies Charles, she must be as disagreeable as he is! Or she fancies becoming a baroness, I suppose."

"Charles is not disagreeable."

"Of course not, sister," Sophie agreed dryly. "He's merely condescending, insufferable, and sneering."

"He can be kind," Mariah said, stabbing the pin through another curl. "He's the one who recommended those books for me that were written by ladies."

Sophie turned to face her sister, her remaining hair falling in all directions. "Don't tell me you *like* him, Mariah."

Mariah flushed. "I-I-I never said that I liked him," she stammered. "I only said that he can be kind."

"When it's convenient for him."

"Stop teasing me, turn around, and let me finish your hair. Or you'll be late for the dinner party with Mr. Miller, who you *do* like."

Sophie obeyed and Mariah barely slipped in the last hairpin before she was summoned downstairs. She gave her sister a quick hug before joining her aunt and Charles in the grand foyer.

Aunt Bentley told her to stand still while she examined her attire and hair. Charles looked away and Sophie clenched her teeth but managed to remain silent. She was wearing a new white dress with a wide neckline, exposing her shoulders. The bertha, or decoration around the neckline, was made of white tulle, and the large skirt over her crinoline had three flounces. Aunt Bentley moved one curl forward over Sophie's shoulder before declaring her presentable.

Charles signaled for Mr. Taylor to open the door. Sophie wished only that it had been earlier in the day, so that she might have seen the way to Ethan's home. When they arrived, Sophie could tell that the house was tall and stately, but very few details beyond that with only the street gaslights to see by. They were ushered into an even greater entryway, where the ladies' wraps and Charles's hat were taken.

An older woman wearing an elegant silk gown of chartreuse, with six flounces and countless artificial flowers, came to welcome them. She was undeniably Ethan's mother; her hair was the same blond but streaked with white. She smiled, and Sophie felt instantly welcomed and wanted.

To Sophie's surprise, Charles actually smiled and embraced her.

"How we have missed you, Charles," Mrs. Miller said as she lightly touched his arm. "I'm so glad that you are enough recovered to join us for dinner tonight."

"If I were twice as unwell, I would not have missed seeing

you," Charles said, with a warmth Sophie had never heard in his voice.

Mrs. Miller nodded to Aunt Bentley and then took Sophie's hand.

"Miss Carter, how lovely you look tonight," Mrs. Miller said, squeezing her hand. "Come, let me introduce you to the other young lady of our small party."

Sophie blinked; she'd forgotten that Mariah had already met Mrs. Miller. But she recovered quickly and followed her into a sumptuous drawing room. Ethan was talking to a young woman with dark brown eyes, mahogany-colored hair, and cream-white skin. There were more flowers in her hair than in a garden. She was dressed in an elegant pink silk dress with pearl beads embroidered in the bodice and short sleeves and wore dainty matching pink slippers. Sophie felt inferior in every way to this girl, even wearing the most beautiful dress she had ever worn.

"Miss Adaline Penderton-Simpson, may I introduce Miss Sophie Carter?" Mrs. Miller said.

Sophie gave an awkward curtsy, and Miss Penderton-Simpson gracefully dipped.

"Miss Carter, may I introduce my son, Mr. Miller?" Mrs. Miller said with a knowing smile. "And Miss Penderton-Simpson, I know that you are already acquainted with my nephew, Lord Bentley, and the dowager Lady Bentley."

Everyone bowed, and Sophie felt a surge of hope when she saw Ethan coming to her side. He offered his arm and led her to a sofa.

"Miss Carter," Ethan said in a low voice, barely above a whisper. "It seems an age since I last saw you."

Sophie could not help but smile widely at this. The strange fluttering in her stomach began again.

"I confess, I've haunted the park hoping to run into you again," he said.

She felt as if her face would crack if she grinned any wider. "I tried escaping only this afternoon through the neighbor's roof exit," she said in a conspiratorial whisper. "But I was caught. It all turned out for the best, however. I've found my first position."

"Congratulations!"

"Don't tell anyone," Sophie said in a low tone. "I'm to pose as a model for a painting by Sir Thomas Watergate."

"That's corking!" Ethan said. "What an honor."

Sophie blushed. "I'm actually getting paid, so it *is* a position. Not what I hoped for, of course, but I'm being paid, so I can't be too picky."

"Does Lady Bentley know?"

"No!" Sophie said, louder than she meant to. "Please don't tell her."

Sophie heard a rustle of skirts and saw Miss Penderton-Simpson coming toward them.

"You two seem to be having quite the conversation," she said. "I'm afraid that I'm here to play gooseberry and sit between you."

"You are welcome," Ethan said, moving over on the couch to make space for her.

"How long have you been out, Miss Carter?" Miss Penderton-Simpson asked as she sat between them. "We haven't met before, I'm certain. I wouldn't have forgotten you."

"Miss Penderton-Simpson, I don't know whether to be flattered or slighted," Sophie replied lightly. "I have been 'in' and 'out' of all sorts of places, but this is my first visit to London."

"You are droll! Please call me Adaline," she said. "'Miss Penderton-Simpson' is quite the mouthful, isn't it?"

"And you may call me Sophie."

"You're named after Lady Bentley, I believe," Ethan said. "She is your mother's sister?"

Sophie nodded.

"Lady Bentley and your mother must have been very close for your mother to name you after her," Adaline said.

Sophie shook her head. "My mother didn't live long enough to name me or my sister."

"You have a twin sister! How very fascinating," Adaline said. "Do you look much alike?"

"Very much alike. You could say we are each other's mirror," Sophie said. "Have you any brothers or sisters, Miss—Adaline?"

"Alas, I'm an only child," she said. "It's quite uncomfortable because my parents have so many expectations of me. I wish I could spread them out between a sibling or two. Poor Lord Bentley has the same burden."

"Mr. Miller?" Sophie asked.

"Four sisters," Ethan said.

"All married," Adaline interjected. "And all beautiful like Mrs. Miller . . . Oh, I think we're lining up to go in to dinner. Pardon me, but I think I'll try for Lord Bentley's arm."

With a rustle of pink silk skirts, she was off. Ethan stood up and offered his arm to Sophie.

"If only it could be so informal between the sexes," Ethan said. "That within moments of meeting you I could call you 'Sophie.'"

"You may call me 'Sophie' when we are speaking privately," she said. "Half the time when people say 'Miss Carter,' I look to see who the lady is that they're addressing."

"Only if you call me 'Ethan.'"

"Seems only fair," Sophie said, and allowed herself to be escorted to the dining room. Ethan pulled out a chair between himself and Charles, who gave her a dirty look. She swallowed as she sat down and placed her napkin on her lap. *This dinner party is going to be as pleasant as a hangnail.*

"What were you and my cousin conversing privately about, Sophie?" Charles asked, suspicion in every syllable.

She bit her lip. Her first impulse was to tell him to mind his own business, but she and Mariah were staying in *his* house, after all. "Only my sister."

"Ah," Charles said, his tone softening. "You must miss her greatly."

Luckily, the staff began to serve the first course, for all Sophie could do was blink back at him—his mood swings were more violent than the sea. She took a few bites of the jardinière soup, followed by turbot, lobsters, and trout à la Genevoise. The servants continued to bring out more dishes until the table was laden with more food than the Ellises ate in a month. As she swallowed a bite of veal loin in béchamel sauce, she thought that perhaps Mariah was right. Charles wasn't such a bad sort for a stuffy lord. In fact, she almost liked him as she listened to him converse merrily with Adaline, who sat on his other side.

Despite the din of conversation, she could hear a steady ticking sound. Sophie looked around the large dining room and saw a tall pendulum clock with Roman numerals on the face.

"What a beautiful longcase clock."

"I wish I could say something interesting about it," Ethan said with his ready smile. "But I'm sure you know more about timepieces than I do."

"I had no idea you were interested in clocks, *Sophie*," Charles said, his sharp eyes watching her closely. He spoke her name like an accusation.

Ethan pulled his pocket watch out of his waistcoat, showing it to Charles. "Miss Carter fixed my watch faster than you can say *nanty narking*."

"I didn't know you'd met before."

Sophie choked on the red wine she was sipping. "I . . . well, uh . . . I mean, Aunt Bentley brought me over to meet Mrs. Miller and . . . and—"

"I happened to be home," Ethan finished for her.

"Exactly," Sophie agreed, placing her goblet on the table before coughing into her napkin.

"You have a great many interests," Charles said. "Art, literature, music, and now mechanics. Is there nothing you don't know something about?"

Sophie coughed once more. "Apparently, I don't know how to swallow."

Ethan laughed and signaled to the butler to bring Sophie more wine, but she wisely didn't drink it. Even sober, she was having a hard enough time convincing Charles she was the same person as Mariah.

SIX

MARIAH GOT OUT OF BED QUIETLY, trying not to wake Sophie, who had not gotten home until well after midnight. Mariah had felt a pang of jealousy after her sister had told her every detail of the dinner party with Ethan Miller. How ironic that her sister, who had no interest in men or matrimony, had met a perfect potential suitor, while she had met only older, disagreeable gentlemen.

She thought of Charles but quickly dismissed it. He was young, titled, wealthy, and rather handsome—even when he was ill. Besides, Aunt Bentley had explicitly asked her to not encourage his attentions.

Mariah dressed silently and gathered up her books. Tiptoeing down the stairs, she walked to the library and carefully returned the books to their proper places on the shelves. She noticed a small green magazine on the table entitled *David Copperfield*, and when she picked it up, she realized it was a book about an orphan that was being published in serial installments. Flipping it open, she read the first pages.

"I didn't think you would be awake for several hours yet."

Mariah looked up and saw Charles standing in the doorway, dressed in a black suit. He was frowning slightly, looking more somber than she had previously seen him.

"I was all out of reading material," she said. "Might I borrow this one? It looks quite intriguing, and I'm also an orphan."

Charles shrugged indifferently.

"Th-thank you," Mariah said hesitantly. She sensed he was upset with her, but she could not begin to imagine why. "Did you have a nice time at the party last night?"

"Nice enough," he said coolly. "My cousin seemed quite taken with you."

"Did he? I wasn't sure that you noticed, given how engaged you were with Miss Penderton-Simpson," Mariah said, piqued. She had no idea whether it was true or not, having only Sophie's account to go on, but Charles's pale face colored a little.

"If you're looking for a wealthy husband," he said, "you could do no better than to get your claws into my cousin. He's one of the wealthiest men in England."

Mariah blushed at his insinuation. "Is Miss Penderton-Simpson not an heiress?"

"Who said I was interested in her dowry?"

"Then why do you think I'm only interested in your cousin's wealth?" she demanded. "Just because I'm poor that doesn't make me mercenary."

"You told me yourself that you were looking for a husband," Charles said.

"Yes, a husband, not a bank account," Mariah said, snapping the magazine shut and walking to the door. "Good day, Charles. I hope you have a nice time at your club."

Charles put his arm out, blocking her exit. "I don't understand you at all, Sophie. You change faster than the weather."

Oh dear. He is beginning to see through our charade and notice the differences between us.

"Are you attempting to change the subject to the weather?" Mariah said, forcing herself to smile. "It does look quite fine out."

"It does, doesn't it?" Charles said. "If I apologize, would you consider going on a walk with me?"

"I don't go on walks with gentlemen until I know how much they're worth per year," Mariah said, folding her arms across her chest. "It saves time."

Charles snapped his mouth shut like he'd just bitten a lemon. Then he suddenly laughed as if he couldn't hold it in any longer. Mariah found her anger slipping away. He removed his arm from the doorway and offered it to her.

"I'm not precisely sure how much I'm worth," he said. "Perhaps I could show you my bank ledger?"

Mariah let out a dramatic sigh and placed her hand in the crook of his arm.

"I suppose that will have to do," she said, and allowed herself to respond to his smile with one of her own.

They put on their hats, and Mariah blushed as Charles helped her don her shawl. *It's just because I've never been helped by a gentleman before*, Mariah assured herself. She took his arm and they walked slowly toward the park. The London air smelled of smoke with a hint of sewer.

"I miss the sea," she said. "The fresh smell of water in the air."

"My last experience on water was less than pleasant, since I was so unwell," Charles replied, "but I did enjoy the sea air on my journey out to America."

"I love the sea because it has endless possibilities," Mariah said. "If you have but a boat, you could go anywhere . . . such freedom."

"Just like reading."

"Exactly!" she said. "You can be anyone and go anywhere for an afternoon in a book and be yourself again before dinner."

"What did you think of *Jane Eyre*?"

"I couldn't put it down," Mariah replied warmly. "I adored Jane. Her story reminded me of my own childhood, and I hope someday to have her strength of character."

"Was your childhood so terrible?"

Embarrassed, Mariah turned her face away from him, staring at the white buildings on her side of the street. "To know every day that you're unwanted and considered a burden," she said softly. "I identified with Jane's feelings of rejection and anger."

"I'm sorry."

She glanced back at him and managed a small smile. "But I had quite the advantage over Jane: I have a sister who loves me, and there is nothing that she wouldn't do for me, or I for her." And then she tried to lighten the conversation by adding, "I confess it took me entirely by surprise that Mr. Rochester had a mad wife in the attic."

"I as well," Charles said. "And I can assure you that I have no wives, mad or otherwise, in my attic."

"I'll have to see for myself, of course," Mariah said. "One can hardly trust men like Mr. Rochester to be truthful after all of his deceiving and manipulation."

"You didn't like Mr. Rochester, then?"

"No. Nor the sanctimonious Sinjin," she said. "I didn't like that Jane's options seemed so narrow. I would have preferred that she went to a larger city and found a nice *young* man who was honest, kind, and loved her."

"It would have ruined the story! She loved Mr. Rochester."

"I liked the idea that love could overcome anything, and that no matter what happened to a person, your love would not change," Mariah said. "I only wish that Mr. Rochester had been worthier of Jane's regard."

"Then you believe that the most important attributes in a suitor are honesty and kindness?" Charles asked, his eyebrows raised. "Not money and position?"

Mariah blushed at her own duplicity; how could she be advocating honesty when she was masquerading as her sister?

"Money and position can change, as they did for Mr. Rochester," she said. "That reminds me of *Mary Barton*. What are your opinions on Mrs. Gaskell's writing?"

"Where have you been all morning?" Sophie asked as she stretched her arms above her head and yawned.

"On a walk with Charles," Mariah said, in a voice she hoped sounded nonchalant.

"You went on a walk with *him*?" Sophie repeated incredulously. "Did he actually speak to you or simply frown from a few feet away?"

Mariah toyed with the idea of telling Sophie what Charles had said in the library about her and Mr. Miller, but she decided not to. Sophie was not one to forgive or forget easily.

"We simply talked about books," Mariah said. "He enjoys reading novels, too, and we gave our different opinions of them . . . I told him quite pointedly that I was going to take a rest this afternoon after my late night, so I think if we're quiet, we can go next door and see how your armor is coming along."

Sophie gave Mariah's arm a playful push and laughed.

Mariah followed Sophie up to the attic, onto the roof, and over the short brick wall to the roof next door. Sophie knocked on the door before entering, then they climbed down the stairs to the art studio.

"Where have you been?" a man in a splattered paint smock asked loudly. "I can't be waiting all morning!"

"We never said a time," Sophie said calmly. "Allow me to introduce my sister: Miss Mariah Carter, Sir Thomas Watergate."

Sir Thomas gave a jerky bow and then walked to the stairs. "Mrs. Spooner, the wretched girls are here!" he bellowed down.

Mariah examined the canvas and was amazed at the intricacy of the details; she could identify each individual blade of grass.

"What intense colors. What exact detail!" Mariah said. "I can't wait to see your technique."

Sir Thomas harrumphed and silently waited for Mrs. Spooner to arrive. When she reached the top of the stairs, out of breath but smiling, she shook hands with Mariah. "Ah, you must be Sophie's sister, just as lovely. I've taken the liberty of preparing some papers, a canvas, and paints for you over here."

"Thank you, Mrs. Spooner."

Sir Thomas made a guttural sound.

Mrs. Spooner said "Ah" and came over to Sophie.

"I'm still working on your armor, but the face and hair

take a great deal of time to paint," Mrs. Spooner said. "Would you mind if I took down your hair and arranged it for the painting?"

"Of course not, ma'am," Sophie said.

Mrs. Spooner deftly took out the hairpins and carefully placed each section of Sophie's hair. She then positioned Sophie with her chin up and her shoulders slightly turned.

"There!" Mrs. Spooner said. "Try not to speak and stay as still as possible. When you get tired, let me know, and we'll have a break for some tea and cake."

Sir Thomas didn't speak as he began to slowly paint the outline of Sophie's face. Mariah looked to Mrs. Spooner to find out what she was supposed to do. Mrs. Spooner understood the look and came over to Mariah's side.

"Now watch the great care that Sir Thomas puts into every stroke," Mrs. Spooner said quietly. "He's a member of the Pre-Raphaelite Brotherhood, and they reject the mechanistic approach of Mannerists that followed the Italian painter Raphael. They focus on abundant detail, lively colors, and the complex compositions of classical Italian art."

"I'm afraid that I haven't seen any classical Italian art," Mariah confessed.

"Sir Thomas and I visited Italy a few years back," Mrs. Spooner said. "I liked it well enough. I particularly liked the paintings on the ceiling of the Sistine Chapel. I tried to get Sir Thomas to paint a mural on the ceiling of the drawing room, but he refused."

"Michelangelo was just as damaging to the academic teaching of art as Raphael," Sir Thomas growled.

Mariah gave Mrs. Spooner a bewildered look.

"Michelangelo is the man who painted the Sistine Chapel ceiling," Mrs. Spooner explained. "Italy may be out of our grasp at the moment, but perhaps a visit to the English Royal Academy of Arts could be arranged?"

"Sir Slousha," Sir Thomas muttered indignantly.

Again Mariah turned to Mrs. Spooner to translate.

"It is an unkind nickname for Sir Joshua Reynolds, a deceased painter," Mrs. Spooner told her. "He founded the Academy, but Sir Thomas doesn't approve of his sloppy technique. Despite its founder, the Academy has many great pieces of art on display. And perhaps this painting of your sister will debut there as well, if Sir Thomas can hold his tongue and not offend anyone he oughtn't until then."

Mariah thought she heard Sophie whisper, "Impossible."

She moved away from Mrs. Spooner and watched every move of Sir Thomas's paintbrush. Each one was slow and portrayed painstakingly perfect detail. The man might not have any manners, nor could he make civil conversation, but he could *paint*. Mariah lost track of time as she watched her sister's face begin to appear in the tiny strokes.

"Let us have some tea before Sophie faints," Mrs. Spooner said.

Mariah felt as if she had been snapped out of a trance, she had been so absorbed in watching Sir Thomas work.

Sophie flapped her arms and jumped up and down. "It's hard to stand still for so long!" she exclaimed.

They went downstairs for a hearty tea that was more food than either sister typically ate for luncheon. Mrs. Spooner kept offering them more savories and cakes until Mariah's corset felt as if it would snap. Afterward, they all went back upstairs to the studio. Sophie stood in the same stance as before, but her eyes blinked frequently as if she were fighting sleep.

Mariah picked up the canvas that Mrs. Spooner had prepared for her. It was a tenth of the size of Sir Thomas's painting of Sophie—about two-feet by two-feet. But she wasn't quite ready for it yet. So she put the canvas down and instead picked up a sheet of paper and a pencil. She lightly began to sketch what she knew best of all.

Two faces—Sophie's and her own.

SEVEN

ON MONDAY, Mrs. Spooner led Sophie to a private dressing room downstairs and helped her out of her dress and crinoline and into a suit of armor. She tied piece after metal piece together until Sophie felt like she weighed more than a carriage.

Mrs. Spooner connected the couter to the vambrace, the last two pieces on Sophie's right arm, and then she declared, "Your armor is perfect."

Perfectly monstrous.

"You look fearsome," Mariah said with an encouraging smile.

Sophie didn't smile back. She could barely see over the metal gorget on her neck. Thank heavens Sir Thomas didn't want her to wear a helmet with a visor or she wouldn't be able to see anything at all.

"Come, dears," Mrs. Spooner said, flapping her arms at Mariah and Sophie like they were her little ducklings she was trying to shepherd. Mariah followed her out the door and down the hall to the staircase.

Sophie waddled slowly behind them; it was difficult to move at all carrying so much weight. Mrs. Spooner and Mariah walked effortlessly up the stairs, but Sophie was unable to swing her foot high enough for the first step. Holding her breath, she lifted her leg with all her strength, but her toe only bumped against the stair.

"Mariah, come and help me."

Her sister laughed before skipping down the stairs to assist her. Mariah lifted her arm and Sophie tried again to raise her foot high enough, but she couldn't quite reach.

"Perhaps if I assist as well," Mrs. Spooner said.

With Mariah on one side and Mrs. Spooner on the other, they both lifted her arms up. Sophie tried once more to lift her leg high enough and she managed to get one foot on the stair tread, but before she could place her other foot beside it, Mrs. Spooner's hold on her slipped. Sophie fell to the floor in a heap, her armor clattering loudly. Mariah, still holding on to her arm, fell heavily beside her.

"What is taking so long?" Sir Thomas complained from the top of the stairs. "You three are louder than an entire army regiment."

"I've dropped Joan of Arc," Mrs. Spooner called.

Sophie felt bruised all over, but she managed to laugh as she tried to get up—a fruitless task. "It appears that I can't get up."

Mariah scrambled to her feet and pulled at Sophie's arm, but the weight of the armor kept her on the floor. Mrs. Spooner tried to lift Sophie up as well, but all she managed to do was press the metal deeper into Sophie's skin.

Sophie yelped in protest. "This isn't working. We need to take the armor off first."

"I believe you're right, my dear," Mrs. Spooner said, chewing her lip. "Sir Thomas, go away for a quarter of an hour while we get Sophie decent."

Sir Thomas passed by them, grumbling in Gaelic. Sophie did not understand the words, but his meaning was entirely clear: He was not happy at the further delay.

Once Sir Thomas had left the hallway, Mrs. Spooner and Mariah began the onerous task of untying and taking off Sophie's armor. Sophie pulled off the breastplate and got to her feet, able to breathe freely for the first time in a quarter of an hour.

"I'd best get you a robe, dear girl," Mrs. Spooner said. "We can't have you scampering around the house in your underclothes. What would Lady Bentley say?"

Sophie didn't think Aunt Bentley would say anything—she'd simply faint at the unseemly sight and, upon waking, demand Sophie leave her house.

Mrs. Spooner brought a lovely pink silk robe and Sophie gladly put it on. Then they carried the armor up the stairs and to the studio piece by piece.

Mariah dropped the gorget on the floor with a clank. "Remind me never to become a knight."

Sophie could not have agreed more, but they needed the money, and if she had to wear armor to get it, she would.

Mrs. Spooner, the only member of their party that was undaunted by their failure, whistled cheerfully as she started putting the armor back on Sophie—piece by heavy metal piece.

For four days in a row, the sky did nothing but rain, and Sophie posed for Sir Thomas. Her limbs ached from holding still for so long and the armor didn't feel any lighter. Mariah was making social calls with Aunt Bentley, so Sophie had no one to entertain her as she posed. She desperately wished to know the time; It would be nice to have some sort of bell or alarm to notify her when she was done . . .

"That's it!" she exclaimed.

"Don't talk!" Sir Thomas bellowed.

Sophie stuck her tongue out at him and returned to her position, but her mind whirred with excitement. She would invent a timepiece that could be set to notify one at a certain time. It could wake people up in the morning for work, it could be used in cooking . . . the uses for a notification clock were endless! And now she had five pounds with which to buy supplies and begin her experiments. She could hardly wait to shed her armor.

"Time for luncheon," Mrs. Spooner said in her pleasant, cheery voice. "Off you go, Sir Thomas, so Sophie can change."

Sir Thomas answered with a grunt and slowly put away his painting supplies before going downstairs. Mrs. Spooner assisted Sophie in untying the strings and removing the various metal pieces.

"Ain't it a wonder that men actually wore these metal suits?" Mrs. Spooner mused.

"I can understand how they were used for protection," Sophie said. "But how do you fight when you can't even lift your arm above your shoulder?"

"A sticky question to be sure," Mrs. Spooner said, helping Sophie into her dress. "You're looking a little peaky, my dear. Let me get you a good luncheon and we'll call it for the day. We can't have you falling ill on us."

Mrs. Spooner did exactly as she said: She stuffed Sophie with smoked ham, kippers, kidney pie, asparagus, potatoes, and bread, and then sent her on her way. When Sir Thomas's footman opened the servants' back door, Sophie quickly ran down the alley and practically skipped to the park.

Finding herself an unoccupied patch of lawn, she raised her arms above her head and twirled around in circles.

I must look mad, she thought bemusedly, but Sophie decided she didn't care. She spun faster and faster until she fell down in the grass, laughing giddily. Then a great gust of wind nearly blew her crinoline up over her head. A much deeper laugh sounded behind her.

She sat up and quickly held her skirt down with her arms, then turned and saw Ethan walking toward her. When he reached her, he helped Sophie to her feet.

"I can't begin to guess what you could be doing, *Sophie*," Ethan remarked. "Some experiment on the wind power of undergarments?"

"Nothing so scientific, *Ethan*," Sophie said, slightly out of breath. "I was reveling in the freedom to move. You wouldn't believe it, but I've spent the better part of the last four days wearing a full suit of armor."

Ethan laughed. "I wish I could see you in it."

"Fear not, brave knight," she replied. "I daresay half of London will see me in it when the painting is displayed next month."

"I'll make sure that I'm the first in line at the Royal Academy of Arts," Ethan said. "Are you done posing for the day?"

"Yes, thank heavens."

"Fancy a visit to the Great Exhibition?"

"Yes, please!" Sophie said, and then blushed at her eagerness. "I mean, if you'd like to go, I would be happy to accompany you."

He took her hand and intertwined it with his arm. "The happiness is all mine, I can assure you."

Ethan took her to see the foreign displays of the Great

Exhibition. They spent the afternoon in a blur of French silks, Sèvres porcelain, Russian urns, and gold watches from Switzerland. Sophie spent a considerable time examining those watches.

"I had an epiphany about timepieces today," Sophie said, as she closely watched the wheels turn in one Swiss watch. "I'm going to invent a notification clock."

"That sounds very useful," he said. "What does it do, precisely?"

"For example, if you needed to wake up at six o'clock in the morning, it would start to ring a bell or make some sort of noise at that time, to notify you to wake up."

"Positively genius," Ethan said, smiling. "Once you've perfected your design, I'll manufacture it in one of my factories for you and we'll both become rich."

Sophie held out her hand. "Let's shake on it."

Ethan took her smaller hand in his and gave it a shake. His touch felt electrifying, but then Sophie caught herself. *This simply will not do,* she reminded herself. *I'm not in London to find a husband, I'm here to create my own future.*

Sophie dropped his hand as if it had burned her. When he offered his arm to her, she folded her arms resolutely and walked forward, trying to pretend that she hadn't seen the flash of hurt on his face.

They continued to wander through the foreign exhibits as if their electric touch had not happened. While they were examining a lump of gold from Chile, Sophie realized that she needed a room with indoor plumbing and quickly. She leaned forward and whispered into his ear, "I'm embarrassed to say it, but I need to use the necessary immediately. What do I do?"

Ethan chuckled and motioned her forward with his hand. "Come, you can try George Jennings's Monkey Closets."

He led her to the Retiring Rooms and paid a penny. Sophie was given a clean seat, a towel, and a comb. She completed her business quickly and spent several minutes admiring the flushing mechanisms before washing her hands and fixing her hair.

"Now you know what it means to 'spend a penny,'" Ethan said as they walked toward the street.

"Thank you," Sophie said warmly. "I'd wager one day every house, even the poor ones, will have one of those water closets."

Ethan hailed them a hansom cab to take them back to Hyde Street. About two blocks from the park, Sophie spotted a clock shop. "Do you mind if we make a quick stop?"

"Of course not," Ethan said, and tapped the side of the cab to get the driver's attention. "Stop here, sir."

The driver pulled his horse to a sudden halt on the side of the street. Sophie jumped out and walked into the shop. Clocks of all sizes were displayed on shelves and tables; the cacophony of different ticking sounds was like a symphony to her ears. She pulled off her gloves and touched several clocks. Some were made of wood and others of metal. Some were weight driven while others were spring driven. She needed a clock that she could easily take apart and put back together in different ways. In the corner, behind a larger wooden piece, she spied exactly what she was looking for: a completely metal oval clock with a face about the size of her palm.

"Can I help you, miss?" the shop clerk asked. He was a small man with a nose like a squashed tomato and beady blueberry eyes.

"Yes," Sophie said, pointing to the clock she'd spotted. "I would like to buy that clock and some assorted spare parts. A few wheels, chime winds, anchors, set lever screws, a barrel bridge, a pallet, and a regulator."

Ethan entered the shop and came to stand by Sophie. "You don't waste any time, do you?"

"This young lady wants clock parts," the clerk said in an unsure voice, turning his squashed tomato nose to Ethan for permission.

Sophie silently fumed.

"Then you'd better get them for her," Ethan replied with an easy smile.

"And this clock," Sophie said, again pointing to the one she wanted. Ethan reached back with his longer arms to retrieve it for her. He carried it to the register, and the clerk came back a few minutes later with a small box full of parts.

The clerk typed the prices into the register. "That'll be three pounds, two shillings, and sixpence, please."

Ethan put his hand in his pocket as if to pull out money, but Sophie touched his arm. "No, you don't need to pay for them. I have my own money."

"As you wish," he said.

Sophie reached into her pocket and took out her five pound note, the most money she'd ever held at once, and placed it on the register. The clerk took it and gave her back several coins in change with a written receipt, which she pocketed. Sophie picked up the box of parts with one hand and Ethan carried the clock out of the shop, where the hansom cab stood waiting.

Ethan told the driver to stop several houses away from Aunt Bentley's. He assisted Sophie out of the cab. She rested the clock in the crook of her left arm and held the box parts with the same hand.

"Shall I see you tomorrow night at the Penderton-Simpsons' ball?" he asked.

"My aunt plans on it."

"May I have the first dance?"

"Of course," Sophie replied, "but you really don't want it. I'm a dreadful dancer."

"I'll be the judge of that," Ethan said with a smile, taking her hand and bowing over it.

She felt the same electric charge that she'd felt earlier, and for a moment she thought he was going to kiss her hand, but he didn't. When he finally released her hand, Sophie told herself that she was relieved, not disappointed. She didn't want or need his kisses. She was going to be an inventor, not a silly girl who giggled over a handsome man.

Still, she was all electric sparks as she walked toward Aunt Bentley's house, trying to convince herself that her excitement was due to her new clock parts and getting to work on her design.

But deep down, she knew the explosive feeling had little to do with set lever screws and ratchet wheels.

Ethan held Sophie securely in his arms as the musicians began to play. With the slightest pressure of his hand on her back, he led her in the dance. Sophie stepped on his right foot twice as they turned.

"I'm terribly sorry," Sophie said, looking down at their feet. "But I did warn you that I'm a dreadful dancer."

"Dance with me again."

"Are you sure?"

"This time close your eyes," Ethan said.

"That would be even more dangerous for your toes."

Ethan grinned, ignoring her trepidation. "Pretend you're a cog in a clock. You spin and turn with the other wheels in perfect synchronization. Keep your eyes closed and trust my hands to turn you."

Sophie reluctantly closed her eyes and allowed herself

to be led. She felt a sense of oneness with Ethan, the music, and the dance. Trusting someone else to guide her was not something she'd ever done before, yet she found herself disappointed when the music ended and she had to open her eyes. They hadn't made a single misstep during the whole dance.

She spied Charles coming toward them and she gulped. She knew Mariah talked to Charles about books—books she hadn't read. Dread filled her heart.

What if I slip up?

"May I have this next dance, Sophie?"

She looked from Charles to Ethan, who nodded. Sophie took Charles's extended hand and he pulled her into his arms. She was so focused on not making a mistake that she didn't say a word.

"You're not usually so quiet," Charles said, surprising Sophie into a misstep.

"Am I not?" Sophie ventured. "I suppose I'm a bit overwhelmed by the ballroom. I've never seen anything quite like it."

"How are you getting on with *David Copperfield*?"

Sophie blinked, no longer worried about her dancing feet. "Great. Just great. I'm almost done reading the book."

"Do you mean the first installment?"

Blast. "Yes, that's exactly what I meant," Sophie said.

"What are your impressions thus far?"

That you're a snobby aristocrat who asks too many questions, Sophie thought waspishly, but managed a smile.

"That it's the best book—*installment*—that Mr. Dickens has ever written, and . . . um . . . Oh look, the music's ended and I see Miss Penderton-Simpson!"

Sophie pulled away from him and practically ran to her friend. "Adaline! This is the most beautiful ball I've ever attended."

"Thank you, Sophie," Adaline said. She looked resplendent in blue velvet with a string of pearls threaded through her reddish-brown curls. "I'm so glad to see you."

"And I you," Sophie said with complete honesty.

Charles finally caught up, bowing formally to Adaline. He seemed to be trying to catch Sophie's eye, but she wasn't about to talk to him alone again and be quizzed on books—or installments or whatever nonsense. Sophie linked her arm with Adaline's. "Would you mind introducing me to some of your friends?"

"I'd be delighted to," Adaline said, leading her to the other side of the room. Adaline introduced her to at least a dozen young ladies and nearly as many young gentlemen. Sophie danced until her feet were sore, carefully staying away from Charles.

She met Adaline again at the refreshments table, where they each took a glass of punch.

"I could use a rest," Sophie admitted, breathless.

"As could I," Adaline said. "Come, let's sit down on a

nice cushy sofa in the corner and you can tell me all about your conquests. I love a good gossip."

They found an unoccupied green sofa with a good view of the entire ballroom and sipped their punch.

"I'm afraid I don't have any conquests," Sophie said. "After one dance with me, I've successfully scared away any prospects."

"Lord Bentley didn't seem scared," Adaline said pointedly.

"Well, he was my aunt's ward . . . He probably only danced with me out of charity."

"My parents are quite set upon me marrying someone with a title—any title," Adaline confided. "I don't think they'd mind if I married a man of sixty, as long as he was the earl of something or other."

"You're so beautiful, you could marry anyone," Sophie said honestly.

Adaline flipped open her ivory-handled fan and fanned herself. "Such nonsense! But so kind of you to say so," she said. "I hope we'll be the best of friends. Too many young ladies are so bent on the competition of finding a husband that they're not even civil to other young women."

"Well, I don't want a husband," Sophie said. "I want to be an inventor."

"Really!" Adaline exclaimed. "Why do you want to be an inventor?"

Sophie sat back against the sofa and tried to think of the reason. She'd always loved working with her hands. The feel of the clock gears on her fingers. The satisfaction she felt when a clock that had stopped began ticking again. The thrill of being completely in control of something in her life.

"I hate to be boastful—" Sophie began.

"I don't mind at all," Adaline interrupted. "Boast away."

"I'm excellent at fixing clocks," Sophie explained. "Sometimes I like to take clocks apart and put them back together in different ways. So . . . I suppose I want to be an inventor because you get to combine curiosity with ingenuity and create something new. Or make something better than it was before."

"How very peculiar, but interesting."

Sophie felt her face flush a little. Perhaps she'd confided too much to her new friend. She changed the focus of the conversation back to Adaline. "What are you interested in?"

"Men."

"Men?"

"Eligible young men with titles," Adaline clarified with a wink.

Sophie nodded her head slowly as if her brain were a clock, and the wheels began to finally fit together and move. "Like Charles—I mean, Lord Bentley."

"Exactly like Lord Bentley," Adaline said with a smile, gently tapping Sophie's arm with her fan. "Why doesn't he fall at my feet? I have everything: birth, beauty, breeding, fortune."

"He must be mad."

"He seems to have his wits."

"I would ignore him and find other, more fascinating, young men," Sophie suggested.

Adaline gave Sophie a one-armed hug. "That is just the thing! I'll arouse his interest by making him jealous."

Sophie was about to explain that was not what she'd meant, when Ethan came and asked her for another dance.

He led her to the floor to line up across from each other for a country dance. The musicians began to play a lively Scottish tune, and the dancers moved together to create intricate figures and turns. One minute, Sophie was away from Ethan and the next moment their hands were clasped together. Then she'd let go and turn away, only to find him again at the end of her circle. Finally, they held their interlocking hands high above their heads and all the dancers promenaded underneath them. The musicians played their final note and Ethan bowed to her. Sophie stepped back, breathing heavily.

"Sophie, I was wondering if you would accompany my mother and me for a tour of one of our factories?"

There was nothing she'd like more—but then she remembered Adaline's words. Sophie didn't want to appear as if she were husband hunting. She *wasn't*.

"I, uh . . . well, the thing is . . . I'm quite busy modeling for Sir Thomas right now and I . . . well, I still haven't found an apprenticeship yet . . ."

Ethan nodded. "I understand. Our visit would be in a professional capacity, of course."

"Professional?"

"And educational," he added, his mouth prim but his eyes smiling.

"I suppose . . . I could—"

"Wonderful. I'll have my mother make the arrangements."

EIGHT

MARIAH LOVINGLY STROKED THE IVORY keys of the grand piano, then placed her fingers in position and began to play a few scales. It was as if her hands remembered a language that her mind did not.

"Up again early after a party. It would seem that nothing exhausts you."

Mariah smiled, turning to look at Charles. "You're up rather early as well, especially considering your condition."

Charles scowled. "I'm recovering from yellow fever, I'm not an invalid."

"Of course," Maria replied. "Your skin is no longer that odd shade of grayish green and your face doesn't hang off your bones quite as much as it did."

"Are you saying that I'm putting on weight?"

"Indeed," Mariah said. "You're looking less and less like Dr. Frankenstein's monster by the hour."

Charles's lips twitched—his reluctant smile that Mariah found all too charming. "Would you consider joining me for my morning walk?"

Mariah assented, and they left the house arm in arm.

"What business did you have in New York?" she asked.

Mariah thought she saw a little color steal into his cheeks. She liked the strong line of his jaw and the smell of his black-currant soap.

"My maternal grandfather has many business interests, and he wanted me to learn about all aspects of his holdings, including his offices in New York."

"Did you like it there before you became ill?"

Charles smiled slightly. "Well enough. The Americans were very kind to me."

"Tell me about them."

"It was probably because of my title, but all the Americans seemed terribly impressed by it and invited me to the most splendid parties. And some of the more daring ladies advocated women's dress reform and even wore trousers called bloomers under knee-length skirts."

"No crinolines?" Mariah asked with a smile.

"Not that I saw," Charles said. "And if you were to wear bloomers, Sophie, you would be able to walk through doorways without getting stuck."

"And be able to bend over and pick up my own books?"

"Yes."

"Their ladies' trousers sound infinitely more reasonable than our enormous skirts."

Charles bit his lip. "I think you would look very pretty in trousers," he said quietly.

Mariah felt a blush travel up from her neck to the roots of her hair. She couldn't look at him, so she kept her eyes focused on her boots.

Charles must have noticed her embarrassment, because he quickly changed the subject. "And I saw a circus where they rode elephants. I was even able to give it a try."

"You rode an *elephant*?!"

"Yes. I paid a handsome fee for the experience, but it was worth it."

"Was it very difficult?"

"Not really," Charles explained. "There was a seat on the elephant, so it didn't require any great skill on my part."

They walked across the street and into Hyde Park.

"I recall you told Aunt Bentley that you planned on returning to America when you were well," Mariah said. "Is that still your plan?"

"Grandfather Miller doesn't think it necessary, but I want to prove to him that I can accomplish the task he set forth," he said. "I've already booked passage for New York in a month."

He was looking at her with such intensity that Mariah turned her head away. "I'll miss you. Will your business take you away for a long time?"

"Ethan stayed for two years to learn about our trade in New York, and I intend to stay that long as well," Charles said.

Mariah touched his arm. "None of us are the same, and we shouldn't compare ourselves to others. Our comparisons are invariably false when we compare *their* strengths to *our* weaknesses."

"Grandfather Miller has measured me against my cousin my entire life, and I've always been found wanting," Charles said bitterly. "Even you preferred dancing with him over me at the ball."

Sophie had clearly left out several details about last night. "Dance with me now," Mariah said, offering her hand to him.

"In the middle of the park?"

"We're the only ones out at this early hour," Mariah said. "Except the birds and squirrels. Surely you don't care what *they* think?"

"There's no music . . ."

"I'll make some," Mariah replied, and began to hum the tune of a waltz.

Charles took her into his arms and Mariah felt every sense in her body tingle in delight. He led her through the waltz with turns and dips. Unlike her sister, Mariah was a natural dancer with grace and rhythm. She twirled and added extra spins to make their dance more intricate, more intimate. Charles twirled her out and then pulled her back into his arms, holding her against him. Mariah could feel his chest rising rapidly and heard her own heartbeat thundering against his.

"Sophie, I—"

"Release the young lady or I'll write you up on charges of public indecency!"

Charles and Mariah separated instantly. Strolling toward them was a bullish constable with a black mustache.

"I don't want none of that carryin' on in the park no more," the constable barked, waving his wooden truncheon.

"We were only dancing," Charles said.

"Looked like a bit more than dancing to me," the constable insisted, separating them further with his baton. "And don't get no ideas about doing that sort of thing on the sidewalk or street, neither. This is a respectable neighborhood, it is."

"Constable," Charles said with a curt nod and led Mariah by the arm out of the park.

Once they had crossed the street, Mariah couldn't hold in her mirth any longer. She laughed so hard that she cried and had to wipe the tears from her eyes with the backs of her hands. Charles looked at her incredulously before laughing with her.

"I feel ridiculous," Charles said as he opened the door to his house for her.

Mariah turned to him. "I feel disappointed . . . that we didn't finish our dance."

Then before he could speak, she ran up the stairs two at a time.

Sophie was not in their room, so Mariah went to Sir Thomas's house to find her. She walked into the art studio and found a man looking at her sketches. He had dark brown hair and thick sideburns that ran all the way down his face to his jaw, and his black clothes were excellently tailored.

The stranger looked up at the sound of her entrance.

"Forgive me for intruding," Mariah said. "My sister Sophie poses for Sir Thomas, and he allows me to watch. I was looking for her."

"You must be the young lady responsible for these," the man said, holding up the sketches.

Mariah blushed.

"No need to be modest," the man said. "They're quite good. But your technique needs work."

"I'm afraid I've never been formally taught."

"That would explain it," the man mused, more to himself than to her. "The wildness, and yet a natural eye for shadows and contrast in your pencil tip."

Mariah turned to see Sophie, Sir Thomas, and Mrs. Spooner come into the art studio. Mrs. Spooner smiled warmly at Mariah. "I take it that you have lost no time in becoming acquainted with Mr. Ruskin."

"We have not yet been introduced," Mariah said primly.

"Then allow me the honor," Mrs. Spooner said. "Miss Carter, this is the famous Mr. John Ruskin: art critic, author, and lecturer. Sir Thomas wrote to Mr. Ruskin about your sketches and asked him to come take a look at them."

"You were correct to write to me, Sir Thomas," Mr. Ruskin said. "She has a natural skill that should be encouraged and developed."

Mariah flushed with pleasure.

"She can't speak," Sophie said with a saucy smile. "She's too overcome."

Mariah *was* entirely overcome, but managed to find her voice and say, "Thank you, sir."

Mr. Ruskin handed Mariah back her drawings. "I wish I had time to tutor you, but my work, *The Stones of Venice,* is all-consuming. Perhaps I could give you drawing lessons via letter?"

"Before I can consent," Mariah said, "I must ask how much these lessons would cost. My sister and I don't have much money—"

"I won't charge you a penny," Mr. Ruskin replied. "It pleases me to assist artists in their works."

"Oh! Thank you!" Mariah said, clasping her hands together. "Thank you. That would mean so much to me."

Mr. Ruskin picked up his black hat from the table and placed it on his head.

"I must go," he said. "Watergate, this will be the most

triumphant painting of your career. Mrs. Spooner, Miss Carter, Miss Carter."

Mrs. Spooner followed him out and Mariah heard her say, "Please give Sir Thomas's best to Mrs. Ruskin."

Mariah covered her mouth with her hands. She still couldn't quite believe it—a real professional had offered to teach her. For the first time in her life, her dreams were within the grasp of her pencil.

NINE

"I'VE TOLD SIR THOMAS THAT you would pose today," Sophie said as she buttoned up the front of her dress. "I hope you don't mind. He was terribly insistent that he not miss even one day, and I'm promised to the Millers all morning."

"I suppose I can wear your armor for one day," Mariah replied.

"Who knows?" Sophie said. "Perhaps you'll discover that you like posing and you'll become both an artist *and* a model."

"Doubtful," Mariah said, making a face.

Sophie laughed and gave her sister a quick hug before leaving the bedroom. She grasped the banister tightly as she walked down the stairs, barely able to hold in her anticipation. She was going to visit a *real* factory with working machines and skilled workers!

Ethan stood at the bottom of the stairs and smiled up at her. Sophie's stomach turned over in a most pleasant manner.

Aunt Bentley was not smiling, but she was gracious enough to civilly ask Mrs. Miller about her day. Mrs. Miller gave a short answer in return and then led Sophie and Ethan out of the house and into their carriage.

Sophie felt shy in front of Mrs. Miller, despite the older woman's benign smile. Sophie had little experience with mothers, and the feminine role models in her life had been neither kind nor caring. What if Mrs. Miller didn't like her or approve of Ethan's friendship with her? She fidgeted with her hands in her lap and she began tapping her foot nervously.

"My son tells me that you're interested in machinery," Mrs. Miller said.

"I'm fascinated by what makes things work," Sophie replied. "We're living in such an age of innovation and industry."

"And we must keep up with it or be left behind," the older woman said sagely.

"My grandfather says the world of his youth is gone," Ethan said. "Industry has changed the landscape of his small village and made farmers into factory workers."

"That is true enough," Mrs. Miller said. "Father Miller remembers his grandfather grinding the grains with a quernstone. Then his father built a water mill, and Father Miller made a few improvements and a fortune by selling his improved machines."

Ethan and his mother took Sophie to a steamboat factory

in Soho. The building was large and square with chimneys on every wall, fires blazing in each one. Hundreds of workers smelted metal, hammered, cut wooden beams, and shoveled coal. It was a gloriously grimy place, and Sophie could not resist asking the foreman all sorts of questions. She wanted to know what every employee was doing, from the lowest coal boy to the highest engineer.

"Where do you work, Mr. Miller?" Sophie asked, as they reentered the carriage some hours later.

"I'm afraid you'll find it disappointing after the steamboat factory," Ethan said. "Just a brick building in town."

"Why don't we take Miss Carter for a tour of the countinghouse as well?" Mrs. Miller suggested.

Ethan looked at Sophie, unsure. "It's only a countinghouse . . ."

"I would like to see it," Sophie said warmly.

"It's decided then," Mrs. Miller said.

Ethan's countinghouse was indeed a redbrick building, and it was the tallest structure for a mile around. It had porticos and columns and a smart sign that read: MILLER AND SON. A footman opened the door, and the three walked in.

"I'm a bit tired," Mrs. Miller said. "I'll rest in your office while you give Miss Carter the tour."

Ethan dutifully took Sophie to a large room with countless clerks at desks adding up their ledgers, then led her up a flight of stairs to the private offices.

"Does your father work here as well?"

"My father died when I was still a small child."

"I'm so sorry that I didn't ask before."

"Grandfather took his place," Ethan said. "He oversaw my education at Harrow."

"And after Harrow?" Sophie asked.

"My grandfather shipped me off to America to work for a couple of years. Then he brought me back to England and has trained me in all aspects of his business," Ethan said. "He's aged greatly this last year, and I've taken over most of his workload."

"How exciting to experience so many different places and businesses. Your life sounds anything but dull."

"I'm afraid I did find it rather dull," he admitted. "That is, until you came upon me that morning in the park."

"What changed?"

"Your enthusiasm," Ethan said with a grin. "Everything that I found tedious, you found fascinating. And now when I look at the numbers and read the reports, I see innovation. I see how exciting you would find it to be on the cusp of science and change."

Ethan turned toward Sophie, but his eyes were not on her, rather on something behind her. She glanced over her shoulder and saw an old man with a full head of white hair and an even fuller white beard leaning heavily on his walking stick.

"Grandfather. I didn't expect to see you, sir."

"Still my name on the front of the building, ain't it?"

"Grandfather, may I introduce Miss Sophie Carter,"

Ethan said. "Miss Carter, this is my grandfather, Mr. Eustace Miller."

Sophie curtsied deeply.

"Come here, young lady," he said in a gruff voice. "You need not bow as if I were a duke. I'm an old man now, and I was born as common as any child in England."

Sophie stepped closer to the gruff old man and returned his piercing stare with a narrowed-eye gaze of her own. She'd learned early in life never to back down, never to show fear. People never respected those who feared them.

Mr. Miller's stare turned into a slight smile, then he stepped away into his office.

"Young Ethan says that you're mad for mechanisms and quite the clock repairer," he said. "Come sit with me in my office. Ethan, order us some tea."

Sophie followed Mr. Miller into a large office with a view of Regent's Park and sat in the nearest chair. Ethan appeared soon after and took the seat adjacent to Sophie's.

"Grandfather, Miss Carter is anxious to learn more about machinery and is interested in an apprenticeship with an inventor," Ethan said. "I was hoping you might have someone to suggest."

"I will think on it," he said curtly.

Mrs. Miller came into the room and sat next to her father. "I see you have met our new friend, Miss Carter, Father." she said cheerfully. "Quite a bright penny, is she not?"

"Plenty of pluck," Mr. Miller said. "I'll give her that."

A clerk arrived with a tray and Mrs. Miller served. Sophie sipped her tea and listened to Ethan's family talk to each other.

"I'm a bit fatigued," Mrs. Miller said. "Ethan, will you see Miss Carter home? I'll ride home with Father."

"I'm not the least bit tired," Mr. Miller growled, sounding more like a scolded child than a grown man.

"Of course you aren't," Mrs. Miller replied, taking his arm gently.

After a pause, he said reluctantly, "I suppose I could go home now. But it's early in the day, and I could have worked for several hours yet."

Sophie and Ethan followed his mother and grandfather out of the countinghouse but entered a separate carriage. She felt a jolt of anticipation that she and Ethan were going to be *alone* in a closed carriage. It took the entire ride home before her heartbeat slowed to a normal rate.

Ethan assisted Sophie out of the carriage and walked her to the front door. He took her smaller hand in his and raised it to his lips, gently kissing it. His kiss was like an electric current that flowed through her entire body and sent the blood singing in her veins. Her stomach flipped again, and she felt curiously weak in the knees.

"May I ask your aunt's permission to call upon you formally?"

Ethan wanted to court her. Sophie pulled her hand back and shrugged, feeling the heat rush to her face. "I'm afraid that I'm looking for apprenticeships at present. Not courtships."

"I understand," he said quietly, his face falling.

Sophie stepped forward to touch his arm. She instantly felt the familiar spark and released it. "I like you awfully . . . as a friend."

He managed a small smile. "As a friend, I will continue to look for apprenticeships for you."

"Thank you," Sophie said, feeling even hotter. "I had such a lovely time at the factory . . . and at your office."

Mr. Taylor opened the front door and they both jumped.

"Goodbye, then," Sophie said, and then dashed into the house and up the stairs to her bedroom. She didn't want Aunt Bentley asking probing questions about her outing or about Ethan. Aunt Bentley would probably throw her out into the street if she knew that she'd spurned a potential suitor—and a wealthy one at that. Sophie opened the door and found Mariah reading in bed. She must have finished modeling early.

"Why is your face red, Sophie?" she asked, even though her own face was redder. She'd clearly been crying.

Sophie didn't cry. Sometimes she wondered if something inside her was broken and she had no idea how to fix it. Still, she always consoled herself with the thought, *Mariah cries enough for both of us—possibly enough for three girls.*

"You're one to talk," Sophie retorted. "You look as if you've wept all afternoon. Let me guess: A *fictional* character died in a book."

Mariah placed *Mary Barton* on the table. "Well, it was sad, but I won't tell you why."

"To punish me?" Sophie asked, pulling out her hairpins to let her long red curls fly free.

"No, to not ruin the ending," Mariah said with a dignified sniff.

"Then *I* won't tell *you* why my face is red," Sophie quipped.

"I may not share your love of instruction manuals and machines," she said, "but that doesn't make me dim. You spent the entire afternoon in a certain young gentleman's company and I'm sure *he* had something to do with it."

Sophie sat next to her sister on the bed. "He kissed my hand and asked if he could formally court me," she whispered.

Mariah sat up straighter with a squeak. "Tell me all the details!" she exclaimed, squeezing her sister's hand. "And I have no interest in any details about the factory; I only want to hear about Mr. Miller. It seems very forward to have asked you instead of Aunt Bentley. What did you say?"

"No."

"What?!" Mariah's hold on Sophie's hand tightened like a vise. "Why not?"

Sophie pulled her hand away from her sister's before it lost all circulation. "You know I don't want to be married. I want to be an inventor."

"Couldn't you be both?" Mariah asked.

"I don't think so."

"I know you said you didn't wish to marry, but I thought . . . I hoped . . . when you met someone you could like, *love* even, you would change your mind."

"What love have you ever seen in a marriage?" Sophie snapped. She stood up and marched over to the washbasin to dab cool water against her hot face.

Mariah didn't answer.

"Even as a child, I knew the Trentons weren't happy," Sophie continued. "When the day arrived for him to return to sea, both of them seemed relieved to part. Mrs. Trenton was much happier when he was away, and I daresay Captain Trenton was, too. Then there are Mr. and Mrs. Ellis, who made no pretense to affection in public *or* private. All Mrs. Ellis ever did was inhale snuff and complain about us, her husband, and her children. What makes you think that the marriage state is so blissful and happy?"

Mariah opened her mouth and then shut it. Finally she managed to sputter, "B-but do you n-not want love, stability . . . and someday, children?"

"What is love?" Sophie asked coldly, shrugging her shoulders. "Mrs. Trenton only had love enough for one child—first you and then her son. And once he came, we were discarded like yesterday's fish."

She heard Mariah come up from behind and place her hands on her shoulders. "If you don't tell Mr. Miller that you want him to stay, he might go. Will you be happy then?"

Sophie brushed off her sister's hands and walked away

from her. "You're one to talk. Since we arrived, you've done nothing but live in a world of fictional characters. What do you know about love in real life? And what are *your* brilliant plans for the future?"

"I . . . I hadn't thought . . ."

"Perhaps you should worry more about yourself and spend less time telling me what to do with my life."

There was a knock at the door and Mariah jumped in surprise.

"Your turn," Sophie said, and scurried into the wardrobe, pulling the door closed with the loop of wire she'd found in the gutter and repurposed as an interior handle. She tried to ignore the battle wounds she'd received—and the deeper ones she'd inflicted.

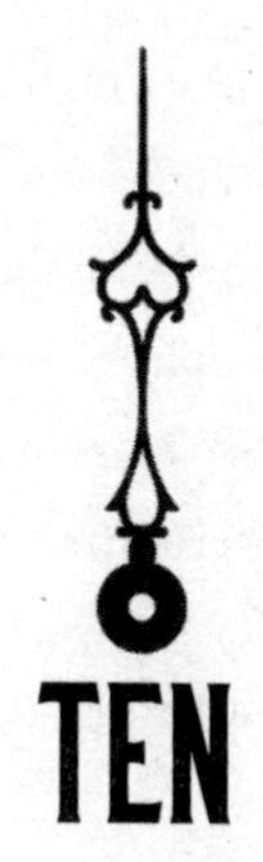

TEN

"MISS CARTER," Adell said with a quick curtsy. "Is somebody else in here? I thought I heard voices."

"I was only reading aloud," Mariah said, glancing at the corner of Sophie's skirt poking out between the wardrobe doors. "I like to use different voices for the characters. It really brings the story to life."

She stepped toward Adell, blocking her view of the wardrobe. "Does my aunt need something?"

"Yes, miss. Lady Bentley would like to talk to you in the parlor."

"Very good," Mariah said. "Thank you, Adell."

She waited for the maid to leave the room before she followed her out. When Mariah opened the door to the parlor, she was filled with anxiety. Her aunt usually left her well enough alone except for morning calls or dinner, and it was much too early in the day for either of those.

Aunt Bentley sat rigidly straight in a wingback chair. Not a dark hair was out of place, and not a wrinkle was to be found on her floral dress. Mariah turned sideways to walk through the door in her crinoline.

"Sophie, thank you for being prompt," Aunt Bentley said in a tight voice. "I would like to speak to you about a most serious offense."

She knows about my walks with Charles?!

Aunt Bentley took a letter out of her skirt pocket and brandished it like a highwayman's pistol.

"This will not be permitted in my home," she said sternly. "Whatever your rearing was, you are now presented to the world as my niece, and I will not have you bringing shame upon me like my sister did."

Mariah stared at the letter, baffled. "I don't understand."

"A man has written to you," Aunt Bentley snapped. "A 'Mr. Ruskin.' For you to receive correspondence from a man in my house reflects badly upon us both. Do you have an understanding with him? If so, you have played Mr. Miller very false, and there is already gossip about the two of you."

Mariah let out a sigh of relief. "Aunt Bentley, there is no need for you to be upset," she explained. "This is all a misunderstanding. Mr. John Ruskin is a famous art critic and he is giving me drawing lessons via letter. Open it and read it. I'm sure its contents will relieve your mind of all concern."

Aunt Bentley cut the letter open with a swift slice of her letter knife and read all four pages intently before setting them down on the coffee table.

"How well are you acquainted with Mr. Ruskin?"

"I've only met him once, and I believe him to be married," Mariah said carefully. "He looked at a few of my sketches and offered some advice."

Aunt Bentley stared at her silently, as if trying to detect a lie.

"I would like to see your artwork," she said stiffly.

"I have a few sketches with me," Mariah replied. "But mostly I painted miniatures for my neighbors, and they kept them. And Mrs. Ellis kept all my paints and brushes, because she had paid for them."

"Perhaps you might consider painting a miniature of me?" Aunt Bentley asked, though her tone made it sound more like a command. "I would like to give it as a gift to Charles before he sets sail for America."

"It would be my honor," Mariah said. "I'll go collect my pencils. May I put the letter in my room?"

Aunt Bentley reluctantly nodded. Mariah scooped the pages off the coffee table and took the stairs by twos. She placed the letter on the bureau and picked up a paper and a pencil, moving quietly so as not to wake Sophie, who was napping on the bed. Mariah brought her supplies to the parlor, where her aunt still sat as straight as a wrought iron gate.

"I will sketch you if I may, Aunt Bentley," she said. "And from the sketch I'll create the miniature. I'm afraid that I don't have the materials—"

"I shall have Mr. Taylor see that they are purchased."

"Thank you."

Mariah carefully began to draw the shape of her aunt's face and was surprised to realize that it was the same shape as her own. She continued to sketch for a quarter of an hour.

The silence between them felt oppressive.

"Aunt Bentley," Mariah asked when she couldn't bear it any longer, "could you tell me about my mother or her family? Mrs. Trenton had only known my mother a few months before she . . . died."

Aunt Bentley breathed in slowly and exhaled. "I don't wish to adversely affect your sketching by movement."

Mariah shook her head. "It won't make a difference at this point."

Aunt Bentley nodded regally but continued to be silent for several more moments. At last she spoke: "My sister Susan and I were very close, although I was nearly six years her senior. She was always a little wild and loved to pick strawberries. She used to pretend to be me and put on my hats and dresses. She wanted so badly to be as big as me, but she never was. Even all grown, I was still several inches taller . . . The smallest things still remind me of her: a skein of blue yarn the color of her eyes, someone singing one of her favorite songs. She was always singing. It was rather irksome while I lived with her, but once she left . . . I missed it."

Mariah soaked up every word and committed them to memory to share with Sophie.

"Are your parents—my grandparents—still alive?" Mariah asked gently.

Aunt Bentley sat up even straighter, if that were possible. "My father died when your mother was four years of age. My mother died two months after Susan's elopement. Mother was always sickly, and the shock and shame of Susan's behavior . . . I believe it killed her. I've never forgiven my sister for her selfishness and stupidity. I never will."

Or us, Mariah thought as she continued to sketch. "May I ask about your home?"

Aunt Bentley sniffed. "Turnberry Manor is a small estate, but a very pretty one. My mother used to say that there was no rose garden in all of England to compare with hers."

"I hope to see it someday."

"I'm afraid that is not possible," Aunt Bentley said stiffly. "I inherited the house when my mother died, but once I married, my property belonged to my late husband. And he left it all to Charles."

"But it was *your* house!" Mariah protested. "That doesn't seem fair."

"Sophie, sometimes I forget how young and naive you

are," Aunt Bentley said with a dignified sniff. "By law, once a woman marries, her property and her dowry belong to her husband. So, besides some dresses and this London season, there is nothing more financially I can do for you or your sister. That is why it is imperative that you find a husband with enough money to keep you both."

Mariah nodded and continued sketching for several minutes. The resumed silence made her feel physically uncomfortable, so she had to break it. "You said my mother liked to sing. Do you remember any of the songs she favored?"

Aunt Bentley again was silent for several moments, before she began to softly sing:

"I've been roaming, I've been roaming
    Where the meadow-dew is sweet,
And like a queen I'm coming
    With its pearls upon my feet.

I've been roaming, I've been roaming
    O'er red rose and lily fair,
And like a sylph I'm coming
    With their blossoms in my hair.

I've been roaming, I've been roaming
    Where the honeysuckle creeps,
And like a bee I'm coming
    With its kisses on my lips.

I've been roaming, I've been roaming
Over hill and over plain,
And like a bird I'm coming
To my bower back again."

Mariah put down her sketch and sat listening, enthralled. Aunt Bentley's singing voice was breathy and quiet, but Mariah sat transfixed. She felt as if she was given a small piece of memory to keep for herself. When Aunt Bentley sang the last word, it was as if she had snapped out of a trance. She colored and coughed.

"Oh, do look at the time," she said, gesturing at the clock on the mantel. "I must go get dressed for dinner, and so must you. I was lucky enough to secure Miss Penderton-Simpson and her parents for our company tonight."

Mariah stood up at the same time as her aunt. Aunt Bentley walked beside her, looking down at the sketch.

"I can already recognize myself," Aunt Bentley said, and attempted something akin to a smile.

Mariah entered their bedroom with trepidation. She saw Sophie lying on the bed, her face turned toward the window. She didn't even glance Mariah's way. Sophie was obviously still angry with her and Mariah's own feelings were wounded, but she didn't want to end up like Aunt Bentley and her mother—estranged. Mariah walked to the bed and sat down on the edge of it. Sophie continued to stare obstinately the other way.

"Aunt Bentley told me about our mother."

Sophie turned over to look at Mariah. "What did she say?"

"That she liked to pick strawberries and that she sang all the time . . . I've never felt more sympathy toward Aunt Bentley," Mariah explained to Sophie. "I think she did genuinely care for our mother."

"Not enough to forgive her," Sophie scoffed, swinging her legs over the side of the bed.

"No," Mariah agreed. "Aunt Bentley still blames our mother for our grandmother's death."

"There is nothing you could do that I would not forgive you for, and I certainly would not abandon your children to strangers. No matter what the circumstances."

Mariah's eyes filled up with tears. "I know."

"I'm sorry for my harsh words."

"They weren't entirely without truth."

"Which makes them even crueler," Sophie said, kicking one foot and then the other.

Mariah leaned her head against her sister's shoulder. "I haven't planned for my future at all. I'd still be at the Ellises' if it weren't for you."

"I understand why you like to read—I prefer books to people, too. But I'm not a heroine in one of your novels. Love is not the answer to all of my problems."

"You'd more likely be the villainess of the book."

"I'd actually prefer that. They're always more interesting than the saintly heroine," Sophie said with a laugh and tugged on one of Mariah's curls. "Come on, you have a dinner party to attend. I'll help you change and dress your hair."

The tension between them seemed to dissolve in the air like steam. Sophie helped Mariah change her gown and then stabbed hairpins into her curls with deadly precision. "Now, don't forget to call Miss Penderton-Simpson 'Adaline.'"

"Is she very elegant?"

"She's beautiful and wealthy and will no doubt be seated next to Charles."

"Will I like her?"

Sophie shrugged one shoulder. "Why wouldn't you? I like everyone when I first meet them. Except Charles."

Mariah blushed and said nothing. *She* liked Charles, and she hoped Sophie's opinion of him would approve. But if he preferred Miss Penderton-Simpson, there was very little purpose in improving Sophie's opinion. With these less-than-happy thoughts, Mariah walked down to dinner.

When Mariah first saw Miss Adaline Penderton-Simpson, she held her breath—Sophie had not exaggerated her perfection.

She stood there without a mahogany curl out of place and wearing the most elegant gown of yellow silk Mariah had ever seen. Her parents stood behind her and were as expensively dressed, but the expressions on their faces were not as welcoming. Coming toward her with a gracious smile, Adaline outstretched her hands to take Mariah's.

"Why, Sophie, how lovely you look tonight!" Adaline said as she squeezed Mariah's hands.

"Thank you, Ad-Adaline," she mumbled.

Adaline took her by the arm and introduced her to her parents, who favored Mariah with a mere nod.

"My parents are pretentious snobs," Adaline whispered in her ear after they stepped away. "Ah, Lord Bentley, you're looking quite recovered and very handsome this evening."

Mariah thought so, too. His smile was dazzling.

"I'm pleased you think so," Charles replied.

The butler announced that it was time for dinner. Mr. Penderton-Simpson held out an arm for his wife and one for Lady Bentley. Charles offered his arms to both young ladies. Adaline eagerly took it.

"I ought to have had a brother and an uncle so our numbers would be the same at dinner," Adaline joked.

"I don't mind walking into the dining room by myself," Mariah said. "You two are so charmingly coupled."

Charles tried to catch her eye, but Mariah would not look at him—not once during dinner, either. She realized as she ate her York ham that she was stupid, silly, and a little heart-broken. Real life was not as pleasant as the imaginary world of books. Sophie was right. Mariah had been foolish and fanciful, waiting for love to solve all her problems.

Mariah was forced to make conversation with Mrs. Penderton-Simpson, who clearly thought it beneath her dignity to speak to a dependent. Meanwhile, watching Adaline and Charles talk and laugh together made it the longest and most miserable dinner of her life.

After the final course was cleared, the ladies returned to the drawing room so the gentlemen could drink port and smoke cigars. Adaline took Mariah's arm again and they sat next to each other on a chaise—it was suffocating for Mariah. She longed to pull her arm away from Adaline, but instead she sat stiffly beside her.

"I'm distressed to learn that Lord Bentley means to return to America so soon," Adaline confided. "I was hoping to be married this year—I'll be twenty in December. But to be engaged to a lord is nothing to sneeze at."

"Has he . . . has he offered?" Mariah managed to ask.

Adaline shook her head. "But I still have more than a fortnight to convince him to throw his name and title at my feet. Dearest Sophie, you were quiet during dinner and you don't seem to be at all yourself. Are you feeling unwell?"

"Oh," Mariah murmured, and then lied, "I have a headache. I'm sorry if I'm poor company for you."

"You must go to bed at once," Adaline insisted. "I shall not keep you. Go on, I'll make your excuses to your aunt."

Mariah thanked her and quietly left the room, her misery complete. Charles was going to marry a beautiful heiress who was so nice that Mariah liked Adaline in spite of herself. She walked slowly up the grand staircase, one foot and then the other.

"Where are you going, Sophie?" Charles asked.

Mariah glanced back and saw that he was standing on the bottom stair. "I am *not* So—" she began to say but stopped herself with a frustrated sigh. "I'm going to bed."

"In the middle of a dinner party?" he asked, climbing the stairs and taking her gloved hand in his. Mariah tried to pull her hand away, but he held on to hers firmly. His closeness made her heart ache.

"Tell me what is wrong?" he asked in a gentle voice that nearly undid her.

"I've been pretending I'm a heroine in a novel and that anything can happen," Mariah said softly. "And now it's time to live in reality. Goodnight, *Lord Bentley*."

Mariah pulled her hand from Charles's and, picking up her skirts, dashed up the stairs to her room, slamming the door behind her.

"Back already?" Sophie said. She sat at their table taking apart the clock she'd purchased.

"Bit of a headache," Mariah lied again. "I'll just go to bed."

Sophie set down the metal piece she was handling and helped her sister undress. Mariah slipped on her nightdress and climbed into bed, turning to face the wall.

For the first time in her life, she didn't want to tell Sophie what was wrong. She couldn't bear her sympathy *or* her scorn.

ELEVEN

"AND WHAT ARE YOUR QUALIFICATIONS for an apprenticeship, *Miss* Carter?" Mr. Packer asked in a nasally, high-pitched voice.

Although he was a prominent London inventor, Sophie thought Mr. Packer looked more like a magician. His long black mustache curled on both sides and was so wide that it nearly reached his thick sideburns. His nose was long and pointy, and his eyes blinked incessantly.

"Well, for the last eight years, I've worked in a clock shop," Sophie replied. "And I can repair almost anything that ticks."

"Clockwork is centuries old. I'm interested in current innovations powered by steam or gas," Mr. Packer said, twisting one side of his mustache around his pointer finger. "What is your educational background, *Miss* Carter?"

Sophie glanced briefly at Ethan, who was sitting beside her. He gave her an encouraging smile. "I had a governess."

Nearly eight years ago, but she didn't have to tell Mr. Packer that.

"Stitching and playing the pianoforte are hardly qualifications for an apprenticeship to a mechanical engineer and one of the foremost inventors in London," he scoffed.

"Self-proclaimed," Ethan whispered under his breath, but loud enough that Sophie heard it.

She cleared her throat to cover her smile. "I'm also proficient in algebra and geometry. I read and write well, and I can sketch very accurately."

Mr. Packer gave her a condescending smile. "Well, should I ever wish for a sketch, I shall send for you, *Miss* Carter," he said. "But I could not in good conscience allow you to work alongside my other apprentices. They are not only much younger than you, but they are also better qualified and have earned their positions through their own merits and not through their . . . *connections*."

He looked directly at Ethan before turning back to Sophie.

"And I suppose all your other apprentices are *men*," she said sharply.

"But of course," Mr. Packer said, twirling his mustache again. "You'd best stick to your sketches and your writing, Miss Carter, and leave the masculine subjects of mechanics and technological innovations to whom they rightfully belong."

Sophie was beyond furious. She wanted to rip that ridiculous mustache off his face, but instead, she stood up. "Thank you for the interview, Mr. Packer."

He nodded benignly at her, seemingly oblivious that his words and manners were insulting. Sophie stuffed her hands into the pockets of her skirt, fighting the urge to pull at his mustache. She looked at Ethan, who leisurely got to his feet and put on his hat.

"Yes, Mr. Packer," he said. "Thank you for your time. It has been a most illuminating discussion."

Mr. Packer smiled and held out his hand. "Then you will invest in our shop, Mr. Miller?"

Ethan didn't take the outstretched hand, instead shaking his head. "I'm afraid not, sir. It seems you're too traditional in your outlook. Your ideas are too steeped in the past for my taste. I'm only interested in investing my capital in movers and shakers—innovators, shapers of the future. Good day to you."

Sophie watched this exchange with her mouth open in surprise. Mr. Packer blinked and blinked as if he didn't trust his eyes or his ears. Ethan then took her elbow and guided her out of the shop and onto the loud, bustling London street. His carriage was only a few steps away and he helped her inside before tossing a penny to the little street sweeper. He hopped in the carriage beside her and sighed. "That could have gone better."

"I thought you were marvelous," Sophie said, attempting

a weak smile. "I only wish I could have ripped the curly mustache off his face."

"I was thinking more of punching his long nose."

"Both would have felt satisfactory, I think."

"Oh, Sophie, I'm so sorry," Ethan said, shaking his head. "He came highly recommended to my grandfather."

Sophie indulged herself in a nice, long sigh. "I'm afraid that most men—and unfortunately even most women—in London, if not all of England, would agree with Mr. Packer."

"He's a narrow-minded fool."

"Most men are."

Ethan looked momentarily affronted and then, to Sophie's relief, laughed loudly. "I hope you don't number me among them."

"Of course not," she said. "I wouldn't be sitting next to you in this carriage if I did."

"I'll keep inquiring after positions for you," he said. "But in the interim, would you consider going to the theater with me . . . as a friend?"

Her first instinct was to say yes—spending more time with Ethan would be delightful. But she didn't want to encourage him because even though she liked him so much, she wasn't ready for a courtship. She might never be. And there was danger in becoming too attached. Ethan would always have a place in the highest society—the kind that Aunt Bentley occupied—but she and Mariah would probably end this season in much different circumstances. Hopefully they would have paying positions and a small place of their own. But certainly not a fancy London mansion like Lord Bentley's home or Ethan's.

He must have sensed her hesitation. "I thought an aspiring inventor like yourself would like to study the stage lights and other engineering and technological advances used in a practical setting."

"So, you're saying that going to the theater is like studying engineering?"

"Precisely," he said with a grin.

Despite her gloomy thoughts, Sophie couldn't repress a smile. "I suppose I could *study* one night next week."

"Excellent," Ethan said. "I'll get some friends to make up a party and I'll ask your aunt for her permission to escort you."

"Oh yes, I suppose you'd better ask her."

Ethan took her hand to help her out of the carriage and Sophie felt the familiar thrill of his touch.

This simply will not do.

She knew better than to get attached to a person who could leave her at any time. He walked her to the front door and lifted the knocker. Mr. Taylor, ever the disapproving butler, let them in and she caught a glimpse of a blue dress darting madly into the library.

Both she and Mariah were "out" at the same time.

"Oh bother," she cursed underneath her breath.

Ethan turned and looked at her solicitously. "Is everything all right, Sophie?"

She touched his arm. A bad idea, because his warmth was a distraction to her already harried mind. She released it. "I, uh, I was just realizing that I needed to talk to my aunt first, before you do. So, um, I'll see you soon."

Sophie opened the door and held it for Ethan, surprising both him and the butler. Ethan walked to the door but before walking through the threshold, asked, "Have I offended you in some way?"

"No, no," Sophie said, starting to close the door, blocking his view of the inside of the house. She leaned through the small gap of the partially opened door and whispered, "My aunt doesn't know about the apprenticeship interview this morning. I'm hoping to avoid a confrontation so that she'll consent for me to go to the theater with you."

Ethan beamed at her, and she wished her body didn't react with the usual butterflies in her belly. He touched his hat. "Then, good day, Sophie. I'll see you on Thursday."

"Thursday," she said, shutting the door.

Mr. Taylor stood behind her, looking at her suspiciously. The butterflies in her stomach fell with a thud—Mariah was still in the library wearing a light blue dress. Sophie's fists clenched the skirt of her most inconveniently dark green dress. Somehow they needed to return to their bedroom without the butler seeing them both.

"Mr. Taylor, would you ask Mrs. Kimball to have tea sent to my room?" Sophie asked in an authoritative voice.

He polished one of the gold buttons on his pristine black

coat with a gloved finger. "I am not an errand boy, girl. And certainly not for the likes of you."

"Did Miss Carter ask you to do something, Mr. Taylor?" Charles asked in a soft voice from the hall. Both she and the butler turned to see Charles coming toward them wearing his familiar frown.

"Lord Bentley," Mr. Taylor said, bowing obsequiously.

Charles raised his eyebrows at the butler, as if unimpressed by his display. For once, Sophie did not mind Charles's sardonic manners.

"I believe that I asked you a question, Mr. Taylor."

The butler fiddled with the same button, but without his previous swagger. "It's not proper for the young lady to ask me to relay messages to the housekeeper."

Charles raised his eyebrows a fraction, but said in the same soft voice, "She is a guest in my house, and if you value your position, you'll do as she asks."

"Very good, my lord," Mr. Taylor said, and bowed so low that she thought his white wig might fall off his head. He then turned on his heel and walked down the hall past the library to the kitchen.

She'd successfully gotten rid of the butler, but now she had to get rid of Charles. "Thank you."

"I hope my other servants are treating you well."

"Yes, they are. Adell in particular has been very helpful."

"I purchased a new book today that I thought you might enjoy. There are several scenes in your hometown, Lyme

Regis. It's called *Persuasion* by Jane Austen. And I know how much you enjoy reading books written by ladies," he said in a pleasant voice. He actually *smiled* at her—Sophie's jaw nearly dropped in surprise. His entire countenance seemed to change when he smiled. He looked almost handsome; it was unsettling. "I left it in the library. Shall we go and get it?"

She blinked. Mariah was already *in* the library. "I would like that very much, but perhaps you can show it to me later? I'm a little tired. And . . . and my aunt wanted to speak to you about something important, she said, something *very* important."

"Oh . . . all right then," he said, shaking his head. His face returned to its usual cold hauteur. "The book is not important. I'll see what Sophronia wants."

Behind him Sophie saw Mariah step out of the library. Instinctively, she grabbed Charles's arm to stop him from turning around and seeing her sister. Mariah put her hands over her mouth.

"Sophie?" Charles asked, seemingly confused by her touch and nearness.

She leaned toward him and brushed her lips against his cold cheek, then mouthed to Mariah over his shoulder, "Run!"

Whether or not Mariah could read Sophie's lips, she dashed to the back of the house toward the servants' staircase. Only once she was out of sight did Sophie release her hold on Charles's arm. "Thank you so much for the book, *Charles*."

Sophie gave him a forced smile and a brief nod, before nearly running to the grand staircase. Her heart was racing by the time she arrived at her bedroom door—Mariah was at the opposite end of the hall, standing at the top of the servants' staircase.

"Quickly!" Sophie hissed and flung open the door.

Mariah lifted her skirts and ran, ducking into the room just as Adell appeared on the stairs. Sophie closed the door to her room and waited in the hall for the young maid.

"I've got the tea you requested, Miss Carter."

Sophie held out her hands and took the tray. "Thank you."

Adell looked at Sophie as if she were behaving oddly. "Is there anything else I can get for you?"

"That will be everything, thank you."

Sophie waited for Adell to walk back down the hall before balancing the tray on one arm and opening the door. Mariah was nowhere to be seen. She set down the tea tray on a table and then opened the doors of the wardrobe, where Mariah was cowering.

"That was close!" Sophie said, taking her sister by the hands and pulling her out of the closet.

"Too close," Mariah said, shaking her head. "And you *kissed* Charles."

"On the cheek," Sophie said with a shudder. "And don't think I enjoyed it. What else was I supposed to do to keep him from turning around and seeing you?"

"I don't know," she said, clenching her teeth.

Sophie smiled at Mariah's ridiculous jealousy. "He bought you a new book—*Persuasion*. Set in Lyme Regis of all places."

"He did?" Mariah said, her expression softening. "How did your interview go?"

"It was all a sham. Mr. Packer had no intention of taking me on as an apprentice. He only wanted the Millers to invest in his shop."

"I'm sorry."

"Don't be," Sophie said, and spun her sister around in a circle. "Ethan is taking me to the theater on Thursday to see the mechanics of a stage play."

She was disappointed to see Mariah's mouth wobble in a pathetic attempt at a smile. "How pleasant," Mariah said in a funerary tone. "Who else will be in the party?"

"Ethan said he would bring some friends." Sophie waved these unknown persons away with her hand. "What's wrong, Mariah? You're acting as if someone died. I barely brushed my lips across his cheek. You have no cause to be angry with me; I don't even like Charles."

Mariah shook her head. "It's not about the kiss."

Sophie took her sister by the shoulders. "We're sisters. I know *something* is wrong."

She wouldn't look Sophie in the eye. "I'm merely thinking about our future. We were almost caught today. What if we *had* been caught? What would we do? Where would we go?"

"Wherever it is, we'll be together," Sophie said, hugging

her sister tightly. "We'll always be together. I have you and you have me. We don't need anyone else."

Mariah's eyes began to water. "I don't want to go back to the Ellises'."

"We won't. I promise." Sophie released her and pulled out a handkerchief, handing it to her sister.

Mariah wiped her eyes and sniffed. "What are we going to do?"

"We're not going to cry," Sophie said softly. "I'm going to find an apprenticeship with someone who is not as narrow-minded as Mr. Packer, and you're going to be a famous painter. Then you can sell your paintings for enormous sums and support us both in the style we have become accustomed to. Everything will be grand. Trust me."

TWELVE

MARIAH CAREFULLY PAINTED AUNT BENTLEY'S face onto the small oval cameo, adding a small stroke to one of her eyes to capture its sharpness.

"Mr. Ruskin is certainly a valuable acquaintance," Aunt Bentley said. "I've inquired about him, and he is quite a respected lecturer and author. In fact, I've purchased one of his books, *Modern Painters*. It's in the library if you wish to borrow it."

Mariah looked up. "I would like to borrow it very much. Thank you."

She paused when she heard the sound of the door to the sitting room opening.

"Charles, how fortunate you're home," Aunt Bentley said. "I'm about to make a call on Mrs. Penderton-Simpson and her daughter. Would you care to accompany me?"

Mariah glanced up at Charles briefly and then stared resolutely back at her painting.

"I'm afraid I will be unable to, Sophronia," he said, holding up a stack of letters. "I have some business correspondence to attend to."

"Very well," Aunt Bentley said. "But before you go, you must look at Sophie's miniature of me. I think it is very like, but you must be the judge."

Charles stood over Mariah's shoulder, and his proximity made her heart beat faster.

"Very like," he said. "You've caught Sophronia's expression as well as her features."

She mumbled a thanks but would not look Charles in the eye. He moved to sit by Aunt Bentley and asked her about their social engagements for the week. Mariah put the miniature down and picked up her letter from Mr. Ruskin. She turned it over and hastily began to sketch Charles's face. The hard line of his jaw, the aquiline angle of his nose, the long sideburns and the definitive cheekbones, and the fathomless depth of his green eyes—more mysterious than any ocean. She longed to trace every curve and line of his face with her fingertips.

Mariah was still staring at Charles when his eyes focused on her. She glanced down at her sketch and didn't look up again until he took his leave. Aunt Bentley left the room shortly after him, and Mariah cleaned up her paints. Carefully placing the sketch of Charles beneath her stack of supplies, she walked upstairs. Sophie was modeling next door, so Mariah had the bedroom all to herself.

She sat down on the heavenly soft bed, relieved to be alone. She was about to pick up Jane Austen's book when she heard a slight knock on the door.

"Yes?"

The door opened and Mariah expected to see Adell, not Charles. She quickly stood up and curtsied.

"I'm sorry," she said. "I thought it was a servant. I didn't realize it was you."

Charles flushed. "I know it is rather untoward to enter your room, but I was hoping that you would accompany me to visit the National Gallery this afternoon."

"I-I would like that v-very much," Mariah stammered.

"Great. Good. Fine," Charles said tightly. He stepped back through the doorframe. "Shall we leave in a quarter of an hour?"

"Yes."

Mariah barely had time to freshen up and put on her shawl and hat before meeting Charles in the grand entry.

"I'm afraid that Sophronia has already taken the carriage," he said. "I hope you don't mind taking a hansom cab?"

"I wouldn't mind if we had to walk."

Charles opened the door. "I would."

They walked down Hyde Street before Charles hailed a hansom cab and directed the driver to take them to the

National Gallery. Mariah watched out the open carriage as they passed by buildings and people. She would never cease to be amazed by the sheer number of inhabitants in the large city. Turning back toward Charles, she gave him a guilty smile.

"I didn't mean to ignore you," she said. "It's still so new and fascinating to be in London."

Charles nodded. "You would like New York, I think. It's much more colorful and varied than London."

"How so?" Mariah asked.

He shrugged his shoulders. "It's so different that it's hard to explain."

"Try."

He gave her a rare smile. "It's such a hodgepodge of architecture and peoples from all over the world. Every day I saw something new or different. Once, there was even a man with a monkey who was preforming tricks in the street."

"I've never even seen a monkey!"

"They're curious creatures, to be sure," Charles said. "Clever, too."

"How I should like to see a monkey," Mariah said. She paused before asking her next question. "What was your favorite part of living in New York?"

"The food. It's like nothing we eat here."

"What's it like?"

"Hot."

"Hot?"

"Spicy," Charles clarified. "They have a Mexican flatbread called a *tortilla* that they place onions and peppers and meat inside and then you eat it with your hands like a pastry. The first time I ate it the spice was so hot that my mouth was on fire and my forehead started to sweat."

Mariah laughed. "That sounds more painful than delicious."

"I got used to the heat, and then I liked it. And they have fruits that are so sweet they taste like a pudding."

"What great adventures you must have had," Mariah said enviously.

"Mostly I worked for my grandfather's business," Charles said, adding in a resentful tone, "and then I got sick and had to come home. But I mean to go back and prove myself."

"I'm sure you shall."

"We're here," Charles announced.

He alighted from the hansom cab and held out his hand to assist Mariah. She blushed as she stepped down and immediately released his hand.

The National Gallery was Romanesque with several columns and a large dome in the center; Mariah was stunned by its size and beauty. Charles offered his arm and escorted her up the stairs to the entrance. She was instantly overwhelmed by the sheer amount of artwork inside; every wall was covered with pictures from floor to ceiling.

"My goodness!" she exclaimed. "There are paintings everywhere but the ceilings!"

"In Rome, even the ceilings are painted."

"Why yes, Mrs. Spooner told me about the ceiling in the Sistine Chapel."

"Is Mrs. Spooner an acquaintance from Lyme Regis?" Charles asked.

Mariah smiled. "She lives next door to you. She's Sir Thomas Watergate's housekeeper and he's a famous artist."

"I'm afraid I've never met either of them."

"Mrs. Spooner is the kindest woman alive. She's even convinced Sir Thomas to teach me some of his painting techniques. Maybe someday one of my paintings will hang on these walls."

She watched him closely to see how he would respond. He looked at her thoughtfully before asking, "Is that what you wish for?"

"Yes," Mariah said. "I've thought quite a bit about it since we first talked of me finding a husband, and I now believe that I would like to pursue painting as a profession. I know that it would be singular to be a lady painter, but I have talent and passion and, luckily, friends who will assist me in this path."

"No more husband hunting because you've already found one, or because of your newfound professional calling?" Charles asked. His voice was light, but his eyes watched her intently.

"If you're thinking of your cousin," Mariah said carefully, "I know for a fact that his intentions are toward another lady."

"It didn't appear so to me."

"Appearances aren't always accurate," Mariah said with the hint of a smirk.

As they stood smiling at each other in the middle of the gallery, it felt like they were the only people in the room. In the world, even. Mariah was not sure how long they stood there before an attendant approached and asked if they needed any assistance.

"No, thank you," Charles said.

Mariah felt hot and turned away before attempting light conversation. "I didn't know you were interested in art."

"I'm not," he admitted.

She looked back at him in surprise.

"I thought you would like to see the National Gallery," he explained quietly.

Mariah blushed and managed a shy, "I did. I do. I . . . thank you."

They began to walk through the other rooms, stopping occasionally to inspect a painting more thoroughly. One painting captured Mariah's attention particularly because it reminded her of Lyme Regis: Joseph M. W. Turner's *Sun Rising through Vapour.* She stood transfixed before it. The lighting was spectacular. The sun shone behind the clouds, its light reflecting on the waves. She drank in the perspective of the ships out to sea and boats near the shore. The delicate brushstrokes of the people on the beach who were cleaning the caught fish. Mariah felt a tear run down her cheek, followed by another.

"This painting has clearly struck your fancy," he said.

Mariah turned toward Charles, and he offered her his handkerchief. She dabbed at the corners of her eyes.

"I didn't mean to cry," she said with a sniff. "My sister is always saying that I cry at everything. This painting just feels so nostalgic to me."

"Does it remind you of your home?"

"I don't have a home," Mariah said slowly, "but the ocean has always been my friend."

"An unpredictable friend, perhaps?"

"Yes, the ocean is always changing," Mariah agreed, "but then the tide always brings her back. Captain Trenton used to take my sister and me out sailing on a small boat. We thought it was the greatest possible adventure."

"Would you like to go on an adventure?"

"Of course," she said. "Doesn't everyone long for an adventure? Something new, something different, to delve into the unknown?"

"You're the only young lady I've ever met who seemed to wish for one."

"You clearly need to meet more young ladies," Mariah said pertly.

Charles laughed. It was a lovely, deep sound. Several heads turned toward them.

"I'll endeavor to meet more adventurous young ladies in

the future . . . However, I'm afraid that I have met my art quota for the day. But I'm not yet ready to go home, and I thought I might take you on an adventure."

"Where are you going to take me?"

Mariah tried to hand his handkerchief back, but he shook his head slightly. Then he placed her hand on his arm and began to guide her out of the large gallery.

"I won't say where we're going, but I think you'll enjoy it."

A footman opened the large double doors for them, and Charles led them out into the bright light of the afternoon. They slowly walked down the stairs, and Charles disengaged his arm and walked toward one of the open hansom cabs. He spoke quietly into the ear of the driver so that Mariah couldn't hear what he was saying. The driver tipped his dirty old hat and smiled with yellow teeth. Charles nodded and took her hand to assist her inside the vehicle, and then climbed in next to her.

"Is looking cheating?" Mariah asked.

"Look as much as you like," Charles said. "I don't think you know London well enough to even guess where we are going."

"True," she conceded.

The cab stopped and Charles got out, offering his hand to Mariah. She looked up and saw a large park, where there were trees as tall as buildings. A loud growl caused her to jump and grab Charles's arm.

"Where are we?"

"Regent's Zoo. It opened a few years ago. I thought you might like to see a real monkey," Charles explained.

Mariah laughed, sliding her hand to the crook of his arm. "And maybe an elephant."

Charles covered her hand with his. "Definitely an elephant."

THIRTEEN

"IT'S NOT EVERY DAY YOU meet a young lady who is not interested in romance," Ethan whispered as they sat next to each other in the dark theater box. "May I be so bold as to ask why?"

"I suppose I haven't been impressed by what I've seen of courtships," Sophie said slowly.

"Not one happy couple?"

She shook her head.

"That's unfortunate. I wish I'd known you when my father was still alive. My parents' marriage is the type that I hope for."

"Tell me about it?" Sophie asked.

"My grandfather wished for both of his children to make 'good matches,'" Ethan replied quietly. "Marriages to families of rank and title. I'm sure you know the type: a fortune in trade for an exchange of old titles. My aunt made that kind of marriage, but my father would not. He married the daughter of one of his clerks, and he always told us that the first time he met our mother, he knew that one day she would be his wife."

Sophie smiled. "How?"

"He just knew," Ethan said, shrugging. "And he always said she brought sunshine into his life."

"They must have passed on the sunshine to you," Sophie said. She was quiet for a minute before adding, "I would like to think my parents were happy for what little time they had together."

"Lady Bentley mentioned it was an unequal marriage."

"Oh, it was very scandalous," Sophie said, raising her eyebrows in feigned shock. "My mother met a sailor in the navy and they eloped. He was considered to be beneath her socially, so her family cast her off. They were married for only three months before he went back to sea. He died on that voyage and later that year, my sister and I were born."

"You're identical twins?"

"Yes, but not at all the same."

"I'm sorry you never knew your parents."

"I am, too," she said. "The lady who took us in after we were born said that we greatly resembled our mother, but there are no portraits of her. All her belongings were sold to pay off her debts. We have nothing of hers."

"I'm so sorry."

"Don't be," Sophie said with a slight smile, subconsciously touching her bare neck. Every woman around her wore jewels. "I have my sister, and she is worth more to me than any foolish trinket."

They sat in silence for a moment, and Sophie noticed several other members of the audience leaving their seats. "Where are they going?"

"People like to walk around the lobby during the intermissions and say hello to their acquaintances," he explained. "Shall we?"

"Please."

Ethan offered his arm to Sophie and they left their box. They were wading through the crowd of fashionable people when someone touched Sophie's arm. She turned to see a familiar face—it was Mrs. Trenton, the woman she had called mother as a child.

How very small she seems!

The last time Sophie had seen her, Mrs. Trenton had towered over her. Sophie was now several inches taller. Mrs. Trenton's dark hair was now more gray than black, and the lines around her mouth and brown eyes were deeper. Her mouth hung agape, and she seemed to be suffering from a great shock.

"Are you all right, ma'am?" Ethan asked.

Mrs. Trenton managed to recover a measure of her composure. "I'm sorry, for a moment I thought I saw a ghost. How fanciful. You're not your mother. You must be Mariah or Sophronia Carter."

"Miss Sophie Carter, *Mrs. Trenton*." Sophie would *never* call that woman "Mama" again.

Mrs. Trenton jerked her head back a little at those words, as if she had been slapped. Sophie and Mrs. Trenton stood across from each other like cats, staring but not speaking a word. Both seeing the other with new eyes.

"Allow me to introduce myself," Ethan said in an obvious attempt to ease the tension. "I am Mr. Miller, a friend of Miss Carter's. I'm afraid we'd best get back to our box before the acting resumes."

"One moment," Mrs. Trenton said, placing her hand on Sophie's arm. Sophie flinched away from her touch. "Captain Trenton is not well. We came to London to consult some physicians. I know he would be delighted if you were to call on him. He's not well enough to go out himself these days."

"Of course," Sophie said numbly.

"We've let a house in Kensington. Seven forty-three Jordan Street."

"I'll escort her there myself," Ethan said, giving Mrs. Trenton a nod before steering Sophie away from her.

Sophie clutched his arm for support and allowed him to lead her through the clusters of people congregating in the lobby.

"Forgive me," she said as he helped her to the chair in their box. "I'm not sure which one of us is more overturned, myself or Mrs. Trenton."

"You were both very pale."

"She's right," Sophie said slowly. "It's like seeing a ghost from the past, and everything comes flooding back like an emotional storm."

"I can take you home now, if you wish."

"No, no," Sophie said, shaking her head. "I want to see the end of the play . . . Mrs. Trenton is the woman who took my sister and me in after our parents died. Then she sent us away when her own son was born. I've wasted eight years being made unhappy by that woman. I shall not give her another moment of my time."

"I'm sorry I was hasty," Ethan said. "I shouldn't have promised to take you to see her husband. Perhaps you could write a letter instead?"

Sophie tried to smile and felt a little of her blood returning to her face.

"I should very much like to see Captain Trenton," she said. "I was his favorite, and he was mine. Mrs. Trenton preferred my sister. She was always much better behaved and infinitely more obedient."

"That doesn't surprise me."

"It shouldn't," Sophie said with a small, humorless laugh. "If there was a tree to climb, I climbed it. If there was a puddle of mud, I found it. If there was something I was forbidden to touch, I touched it."

"And a clock to fix, you fixed it," Ethan continued.

"No, that was later when we lived with the Ellises," Sophie said. "When I lived with the Trentons, my ambition was to be a captain in the navy."

"Naturally."

Sophie heard footsteps and the rustle of skirts behind her. She turned around in her seat.

"I spied you from my box!" Adaline said, holding a pair of golden opera glasses. "I've been looking for you. Why Sophie, you look a little pale."

"It's nothing," Sophie said. "I saw an old acquaintance, is all. I daresay you saw at least a dozen old acquaintances. You seem to be on terms with everyone."

Adaline smiled and whispered conspiratorially, "I do so like to be the center of attention. Do you hate me for it?"

"Of course not."

"Good," Adaline said. "Oh dear, I think the play is about to be resumed. May I call on you so we may have a proper chat?"

"Yes, please."

"Mr. Miller, you may have Sophie back," Adaline said merrily, and Sophie heard her hail yet another friend as she left the theater box.

The other two couples returned to their seats in the box and they exchanged polite pleasantries. But Sophie's mind was not in the conversation. The thought of seeing Captain Trenton filled her with conflict. She had never hated him as she had his wife.

But she had not forgiven him either.

"I can't believe such a small woman scared me as a child," Sophie told Mariah as they lay in bed the next morning. "She was practically a giantess in all my memories."

"Oh, Sophie," Mariah sighed, leaning her head on her hand. "She wasn't always harsh. She was often loving and kind. You should try to think about the happy times, too. Remember the Christmas when she bought us the matching dolls with pink ribbons in their hair?"

"Of course I do," Sophie grumbled. "I wanted a telescope, not a doll."

Mariah laughed. "And we all knew it. I think she was trying to change your nature—and failing miserably."

"I was sorry to hear about Captain Trenton being unwell."

"It's hard to imagine," Mariah said. "He was such a hale and hearty man . . . He could carry both of us around on his shoulders."

Sophie slipped out of bed, taking her pocket watch out of the drawer and showing it to Mariah. "The last time I saw Captain Trenton, he gave me his pocket watch so that I could count the seconds until he returned," Sophie said. "Mrs. Trenton sent us away not a fortnight later. She made me give her the pocket watch, but I stole it back when I went inside the house for the doll. I thought if I had it, he would come back for us and the pocket watch. But he never did."

"I thought we were just visiting Mr. and Mrs. Ellis," Mariah admitted. "I had no idea we were being sent away for good until Mrs. Ellis admonished us to be grateful for her charity in taking us in."

"Charity rarely makes one feel grateful," Sophie said. "Miserable, more like."

"Let's vow not to take charity ever again," Mariah said, holding her hand up for an oath. "I, Mariah Carter, will work very hard and share all my earnings with my sister, Sophie."

"I, Sophie Carter, will work very hard and share all my earnings with my sister, Mariah. Even if I have to wear a suit of armor to obtain them."

"I forgot about the painting with all this talk of the Trentons!" Mariah said. "We ought to be over with Sir Thomas already."

Sophie slipped into a dress and messily buttoned up the front of it; she would only be taking it back off when they arrived anyway. Then she stuffed the rest of her muffin into her mouth and followed Mariah out of the room. Mrs. Spooner and Sir Thomas were waiting when they arrived next door.

"About bloody time," Sir Thomas growled.

"Yes, now off you go for a few minutes so we can get Joan of Arc ready for the war," Mrs. Spooner said, shooing him away with her hands.

Sir Thomas put down his paintbrush and stomped out of the room. Sophie stepped out of her dress, and Mrs. Spooner and Mariah assisted her into the armor. Mrs. Spooner then called for Sir Thomas to return.

"The armor is getting lighter," Sophie remarked, swinging her arms back and forth. "I can almost imagine fighting in it now."

"Quiet, don't move!" Sir Thomas barked.

Sophie returned to her position and held as still as she

could. She watched with amusement as Mariah hovered over Sir Thomas, watching his every movement with the paintbrush.

"Make this lass move!" Sir Thomas complained to Mrs. Spooner. "She's hanging about me like a vulture, waiting to pluck out my eyes."

"Now, now, Sir Thomas, we did agree to let Mariah observe your painting technique," Mrs. Spooner said soothingly. "Mariah, I do believe that you have done enough preliminary sketching on paper and you ought to start on the canvas now. Come."

"I can't thank you enough," Mariah said as Mrs. Spooner set her up with an easel, canvas, and tray of paints on the other side of the studio.

"Oh, don't thank me," Mrs. Spooner replied with a wink. "I've made it my life's work to assist struggling artists. That's why I married Sir Thomas."

"You're married?!"

"Yes," Mrs. Spooner said, grinning. "For more than a decade now. The poor man inherited a title, but not two ha'pennies to rub together. I was left pretty well off by the late Mr. Spooner—he was the one who bought this house and purchased all the furnishings."

"Then why didn't you introduce yourself as Lady Watergate?"

Mrs. Spooner waved her hand. "Who would ever believe I was a lady? Me, a milliner from Cranbourne Alley, putting on airs and pretending to be like her betters."

"Do your friends know that you're married?"

"We don't have many friends," Mrs. Spooner admitted. "Not surprising with Sir Thomas's temperament, is it? But Sir Thomas has many colleagues and acquaintances."

"What about *your* friends?" Sophie asked from across the room.

Mrs. Spooner flushed. "None, I'm afraid. I lost track of my friends from the milliner apprenticeship when I married the late Mr. Spooner. He was much older than myself and not particularly sociable."

"How did you meet Sir Thomas?" Mariah asked.

"Now that story is rather funny," Mrs. Spooner admitted with a smile. "My late husband commissioned him to paint a portrait of me."

Mariah looked surprised, but Sophie laughed so hard that her armor shook.

"Stop moving!" Sir Thomas grumbled.

Sophie laughed even harder and Mariah finally laughed, too.

FOURTEEN

I'M NOT AFRAID OF ANYTHING *or anyone*, Sophie reminded herself. *And certainly not of the Trentons*.

She placed the pocket watch into her reticule; it was time to return it, even if she would miss the timepiece. It had been her secret treasure and her only tie to her past life with the closest thing to a real father she'd ever known.

She took a long breath in and out.

Adell knocked on her bedroom door. "Mr. Miller is here to pick you up for your call, Miss Sophie."

"I'm coming," she said, and wondered where Mariah was, hoping that they were not both "out" in the house.

Something was bothering Mariah. She was becoming secretive and quiet—even more so than usual—slipping off without telling Sophie where she was going. But there was no helping it now. Ethan was waiting.

Sophie put on her new stylish hat with its profusion of feathers. (She thought it looked like a dead bird on her head, but Aunt Bentley insisted it was the latest of fashions.) She tied the ribbon underneath her chin and winked at herself in the mirror.

Ethan stood at the bottom of the stairs, smiling up at her. Sophie offered him a gloved hand, and he bent his head over it.

"Ethan Miller, is that you?" Aunt Bentley demanded from the hall as she entered the foyer.

"Yes, it is, Lady Bentley," Ethan said. "I'm taking Miss Carter to see the Trentons, who were so kind to her and her sister when they were children."

"Curious that they did not keep them," Aunt Bentley replied coldly.

"Mrs. Trenton told us that Captain Trenton was in poor health and wished to see Miss Carter," Ethan explained. "Surely it is Sophie's Christian duty to visit the sick."

Aunt Bentley contemplated this for a moment, her mouth pursed to one side. "One does not wish to be derelict in our charitable duties. Besides, if he really is doing poorly, perhaps he will leave you and your sister something in his will."

Sophie felt the heat rush to her face but managed to contain her fury. "Money is so *very* important, is it not, Aunt Bentley?" she said bitingly.

Ethan took her hand, giving it a reassuring squeeze before placing it on his arm. "We should not keep the Trentons waiting, Lady Bentley."

Mr. Taylor opened the door and Ethan steered her out of the house and into the carriage, directing his coachman to 743 Jordan Street before climbing in beside her. Sophie sat quietly for several minutes.

"It is very kind of my aunt to let me stay for a few months," Sophie said at last. "And she purchased all of my clothes."

"She has certainly been an exemplary guardian and treated Charles more like a son than a ward," Ethan added.

"I wish I could like her better."

"So do I."

Sophie laughed. "Oh dear, I was so close to saying all sorts of things that I shouldn't. It was a good thing you were there, my friend. You saved me from myself!"

"I would save you from anything, including yourself," Ethan said, looking at her with a light in his eyes that filled Sophie up with hope and despair. She avoided his gaze by patting down the wrinkles on her skirt.

"Well, you've had fair warning, friend," she said. "You might need to save me from myself again very soon. Mrs. Trenton and I didn't get on very well when I was a child, and something tells me that she hasn't changed."

"Perhaps not," Ethan said. "But I think we should always give people a chance to change for the better and hope that they give us the same chance."

"Well, I haven't jumped in any mud puddles today and my hair is tidy, so she might not find fault with me."

"I don't know how anyone could find fault with you."

The carriage came to an abrupt stop, and Sophie grabbed his hand tightly. "Please don't leave me alone with her."

"I will be at your side the entire time," he reassured her, gently squeezing her hand back.

Jordan Street was not quite as fashionable as the white buildings of Hyde Street, but it was still a respectable road. Brown brick buildings lined it with countless long, rectangular windows.

Ethan tapped the knocker of number 743 twice. A male servant wearing black livery answered the door, and Ethan gave him his card.

"Mr. Miller and Miss Carter to see Captain Trenton and Mrs. Trenton."

The servant bowed. "This way, if you please, sir."

For once, Sophie actually did need the physical support from Ethan's arm. They walked up a flight of stairs and were taken to a green sitting room with a large fire blazing in the brick fireplace. Mrs. Trenton stood up at once and welcomed them. She was dressed in a somber gown of black bombazine with a black lace mantilla over her shoulders. An old man with white hair sat in a large chair by the fire wearing a nightcap, and his shoulders were covered in four or five shawls. Sophie gasped when she recognized Captain Trenton. He looked so different, as if he had shrunk to half the size of his previous self.

"Forgive me if I don't stand," Captain Trenton said in a weak voice. "I'm afraid that I cannot without assistance."

"Of course, sir . . . Captain," Ethan said, with a bow. "Allow me to introduce myself: I am Mr. Ethan Miller, a friend of Miss Sophie Carter."

"Won't you both sit down?" Mrs. Trenton said, and motioned toward an emerald-colored sofa. "I hope you will not find the room too hot, but the captain gets chilled very easily."

"We're perfectly comfortable, thank you, Mrs. Trenton," Ethan said.

He looked at Sophie, who had yet to speak. He opened his eyes expressively and tilted his head a fraction toward the Trentons.

"Captain Trenton, I have something to return to you," Sophie said, pulling the golden pocket watch from her reticule. She caressed the front engraving softly before standing and walking toward him with her hand outstretched. "I promised to return it to you when you came home from sea."

He looked up at her intently and then placed his gnarled hand over hers. "Some voyages you don't return from the same. I would be honored if you were to keep it, Sophie. I mean, Miss Carter. Although, I'll always think of you as my little Sophie."

Sophie pressed her hand to her cheek and felt something damp through her glove. She was *crying*.

After all these years without so much as a misty eye, here she was crying, and freely.

Captain Trenton tightened his hold on her hand.

"Mr. Miller, would you be so kind as to bring a chair closer? I should like Sophie to tell her papa everything he's missed."

"That might take some time," she said with a sniff.

"Time is our greatest gift, and our greatest curse," Captain Trenton said, his own eyes full of unshed tears.

Ethan appeared at Sophie's side with a chair and a handkerchief. She accepted both from him gratefully.

"Tell me about Mr. Ellis," Captain Trenton said. "He was once in the navy as well, was he not?"

"Yes, he was in charge of the ship's chronometer." Sophie glanced at Ethan and explained, "The ship's clock. He was wounded in an engagement in South America and never recovered his health. He returned to Lyme Regis and opened a clock shop."

"Was he kind to you?"

"He was not unkind," Sophie replied hesitantly. "He cared only for his next dose of laudanum or a visit to the tavern. We were primarily in the care of his wife."

"Was she kind?"

"No," Sophie said. "But she did her duty by us. She taught us how to work and how to take care of ourselves. Perhaps . . . that is better than being kind."

Mrs. Trenton stood up abruptly. "I will see about refreshments." She left the room with a swish of black skirts.

"I didn't know," Captain Trenton said in an imploring voice. His dark blue eyes stared at Sophie intensely.

"About what?"

"That she was going to send you away," he said quietly. "I returned eighteen months later from a voyage around the world to discover my daughters were gone."

"Didn't Mrs. Trenton write to you?"

Captain Trenton shook his head. "I received only two letters during that time, and there was no mention of you or your sister. I thought it was strange, but I didn't think much about it at the time."

"Why did you not come to get us then?"

He heaved a sigh. "I wanted to, Sophie, but it's hard for a man to interfere with the domestic choices of his wife. I had just been promoted to a larger vessel, and I was about to leave again on another voyage. I was afraid if I brought you home, she would just send you away again as soon as I left. She threatened to."

"Perhaps you realized that with a son, you no longer needed foster daughters," she said bitterly.

Captain Trenton reached out his hand for Sophie's, but she pulled hers away.

"I love my son, Sophie. I love you, and I love Mariah. I only wish I could see her one last time. I have always thought of you and Mariah as my daughters, not my foster daughters. The greatest regret I'll be taking to my grave is that I didn't come for you. That I didn't at the very least make sure that you were with people who were kind. I hope someday that you can forgive me."

Sophie dabbed her eyes with the handkerchief and blew her nose. She looked into the tired eyes of the man who was the only father she had ever known. She shook her head slightly. "I don't forgive you . . . but I still love you. That's the best I can say for now."

Captain Trenton began to cough harshly. His face turned red and he covered his mouth with a handkerchief. When he took it away it was covered in bright red blood.

"How long have you been ill?" Sophie asked.

"I returned from the Indies six months ago, and I knew that my next voyage would be the one that no sailor returns from."

"What have your doctors said?" she demanded. "Is there no treatment?"

He gave her a small smile. "I have drunk the waters of Bath and the draughts of a half dozen country doctors and been physicked by three prominent London physicians. My time will soon be up. But I know all about me. I would like to hear about you. My wife surprised me when she told me that you were staying with your aunt, Lady Bentley."

"She'll only allow me to stay for one season. She means to find me a husband," Sophie scoffed.

Captain Trenton lifted his gnarled hand and pointed to Ethan. "I don't think that will be very difficult. It seems like Mr. Miller here is more than ready to fill the position, are you not, Mr. Miller?"

"Papa!" Sophie exclaimed, blushing.

"I am content to be her friend," Ethan said, giving her a reassuring look.

Mrs. Trenton reentered the room, followed by the same servant who had escorted them into the house. He was carrying a large silver platter with a teapot, cups, and a three-tiered stand filled with cakes and biscuits. He set the platter on a table in the middle of the room. Mrs. Trenton sat down stiffly and mechanically poured the tea, looking like a woman about to be judged by a navy tribunal rather than a wife entertaining her guests in the sitting room. As Mrs. Trenton rose and handed out the teacups—first to the captain, then to Ethan, and then her own—Sophie felt a strange sort of satisfaction seeing her discomfort.

Captain Trenton took a small sip of the hot liquid. "Now, please tell me about Mariah."

"Same as ever. Very good, obedient, and tenderhearted. She's taken up novel reading, and whenever one of the fictional characters dies, she weeps as if they were a real person. And there's no persuading her that she's wasting her tears, that it's all pretend. She's also been practicing her drawing and has been corresponding with the art critic, Mr. John Ruskin. He's been giving her lessons via letters."

"So our Mariah is a painter. And what about you, Sophie? Are you still going to be captain of a ship?"

Sophie shook her head. "I would like to be an inventor. I learned a lot about clocks and mechanisms while living with Mr. Ellis."

"Pity," Captain Trenton said, as he shook his head. "You'd have made a fine captain. Still, I hope you'll allow me to give you my old telescope. Parsons, please hand Miss Carter the box from the mantel."

The servant bowed to the captain and did as he was asked. She opened the box, and there lay the golden telescope that she had wanted so badly for Christmas so many years previously.

"Thank you," she said warmly. "I will treasure it."

"May it allow you to see a new perspective in the world around you," he said. "And help you on all future journeys."

Captain Trenton began to cough again. When it abated, he leaned his head back against the chair, clearly tired. Their visit had taken much of his energy.

Sophie stood up. "We must go. Thank you so much for the tea, Mrs. Trenton."

She returned the teacup and held out her hand to Mrs. Trenton, who shook it tentatively. *I don't have to forgive her, but I do have to be civil to her.* Then she walked back to Captain Trenton, placed a soft kiss on his cheek, and then saluted him. Without looking at Ethan, she walked to the door, afraid if she turned around, she might begin crying again.

Parsons opened the door for her, and Ethan followed her down the stairs and out of the house. Ethan didn't speak as he helped her into the carriage and handed her the box that held the telescope. Sophie cradled the telescope's box more gently than she'd ever cradled the doll with the pink ribbons.

"Mariah would've forgiven him," Sophie said quietly. "She would've forgiven them both."

Ethan lifted his hand as if to touch her, but he seemed to think better of it and let his hand fall back to his knee.

"I hope you don't think less of me for being honest," she said wetly.

He shook his head. "No, I don't . . . I think more of you for your strength in visiting people who so greatly wronged you."

Sophie leaned toward him and softly pressed her lips to his cheek. "Thank you for coming with me."

FIFTEEN

MARIAH CAREFULLY BEGAN TO SKETCH the lines of her sister's face onto the canvas, painting Sophie looking forward—fiercely meeting whatever was in front of her. Then Mariah dipped the brush into the paint and began stroking the lines of her own face. She'd drawn herself left of Sophie, her eyes facing away from her sister and off the canvas. They were opposites, and she had drawn them as such, from their facial expressions to their clothing: Her own dress was a soft white, the neckline reaching up to her chin, and Sophie's dress was a contrasting black that left her neck and shoulders exposed.

Mariah looked at her sister, standing in front of Sir Thomas dressed in her Joan of Arc armor. Sir Thomas's painting was nearly complete. On the canvas before him, as large as life, stood Sophie in full armor: solemn, stern, and strong.

Yesterday, Sophie had visited the Trentons. She'd told Mariah all about it and Mariah felt so jealous of her sister.

Why did Sophie get the opportunity to visit their foster parents?

Sophie, who hated them, while Mariah still loved them. Sophie, who had sat with them, talked with them, and touched them. Sophie, who could tell Mariah anything, and Mariah, who could tell Sophie nothing—certainly not of Charles and seeing a real monkey and an elephant. She hated that Sophie made things happen, and she only *let* things happen.

If not for Sophie, Mariah would still be in Lyme Regis changing nappies or married off to the butcher's son with the leering eyes. Mariah knew she should feel grateful, but today she didn't feel any gratitude. She continued to paint, her anger seething within the repetition of the brushstrokes.

One stroke for anger.

One stroke for jealousy.

One stroke for hate.

Mariah embraced these darker emotions that she had never before allowed herself to feel, and they flowed through her fingers and onto the canvas in front of her.

"Shall we break for tea?" Mrs. Spooner asked.

"Please," Sophie said, and placed her wooden sword on the table.

"Another break?" Sir Thomas complained.

"I know, dear," Mrs. Spooner said, taking his paintbrush and palette.

"Aren't you coming, Mariah?" Sophie asked over her shoulder.

"I will when I'm ready," Mariah snapped. "Don't tell me what to do. You always tell me what to do!"

Everyone turned to look at Mariah. She felt the heat rise from her neck and seep into her cheeks.

"Mrs. Spooner and Sir Thomas, why don't you start down to tea?" Sophie suggested lightly. "Mariah and I will follow in a few minutes."

"Of course, girls," Mrs. Spooner said, before descending the stairs with her husband.

Sophie trudged toward Mariah in her ridiculous, clanking armor. She held out her hand to touch Mariah's arm, but Mariah shrugged her off.

"Don't touch me," Mariah snapped.

"What is wrong with you?" Sophie demanded.

"I need a little time to myself. To *be* myself."

Mariah could feel her sister's intense stare but could not meet it. She instead looked down at the paintbrush in her hand.

"I know it's been difficult . . . taking turns being me, never having a moment of privacy," Sophie finally said. "But it won't be for much longer—a month at most."

Mariah slammed down her brush and paint tray with a clatter. "Then what? What are we going to *do*, Sophie?"

"Find a place of our own."

"With what money?" Mariah cried. "You've spent nearly all of the five pounds that Sir Thomas gave you on clock parts, and another five pounds could hardly keep us both for long in any decent situation. Or do you wish to go back to a life of poverty?"

"You know that I don't!"

"Then why do you not encourage Mr. Miller to propose?" Mariah asked, near tears. "He's young and handsome, he's rich, and he loves you! What better offer do you think you'll ever receive? Most of us would be content with far less."

"Are you *jealous*, Mariah?"

"Shouldn't I be?" she asked. "You've always had the better of me."

"The better of what?!" Sophie exclaimed. "Our situations have always been the same! What's mine is yours, and what's yours is mine."

"You always do what you want and say what you want, no matter what the consequences. You must always be in charge. You don't even care that the only father we've ever known is dying, and you refuse to give him your forgiveness."

"I gave him love instead of lies."

"You never consider what *I* want."

"All right, Mariah," Sophie said quietly. "What do you want?"

"I've always wanted to be more like you!"

Sophie gave her a small half smile. "That's funny—"

"It's not funny," Mariah snapped.

"It is a little," Sophie said. "You see . . . I've always wished to be more like you."

"Like me?" Mariah whispered, tears streaming down her cheeks.

Sophie put her arm around her sister's shoulders. "Maybe not your propensity for tears, but I've always been envious of your ability to love those around you, especially the most disagreeable people. Mrs. Trenton, Mrs. Ellis, Aunt Bentley, Charles—even Sir Thomas is more pleasant when you're around. He didn't even curse once when Mrs. Spooner mentioned tea. Think of the improvement. Everybody wants to be near you."

"Not everybody."

"All right, not everybody. But think of the queue that would create," Sophie said. "You wouldn't be able to walk, let alone use the monkey closet."

Mariah let out a reluctant chuckle. "I don't think you're supposed to mention the water closet in polite conversation."

"And when has my conversation ever been marked by its politeness?" Sophie asked. "Yet another area in which you're by far my superior."

"But you're witty and interesting and men like you."

"One man does at least," Sophie admitted, shaking her head. "And I like him awfully. But I don't have your faith in people, Mariah. Your hope. How do I know that this feeling will not die over time, or shrivel into indifference?"

Mariah wiped at her nose with the back of her hand. "You've never failed at anything you've tried, Sophie. Why should love be any different?"

The sisters hugged each other tightly, both ignoring the awkward pieces of armor digging into their ribs.

"You may not yell as loudly as I do, but you're just as strong in your own way," Sophie whispered into her ear. "Stop waiting for what you want and start fighting for it."

Mariah nodded and released her sister, just as Sophie's stomach made a noise.

"Shall we go down to tea?" Sophie asked. "I'm positively famished."

Mariah shook her head. "I want to . . . I'm going to see the Trentons. I want to see Papa before . . . before he dies."

Sophie pulled Mariah into one last painful hug, whispering, "I'm proud to call you my sister."

Mariah felt less bold as she stood outside 743 Jordan Street and her aunt's footman lifted the knocker. A servant opened the door, his eyes widening at the sight of her.

He probably thinks I'm my sister.

"I am Miss Carter," she told him. "Are the Trentons at home?"

The servant gestured for her to come in, and Mariah followed him up a flight of stairs and through a door to a sitting room decorated in shades of green. The large furniture was more comfortable than fashionable, and the room felt more homelike than any room at Aunt Bentley's house on Hyde Street.

"If miss will stay here," the servant said, "I will see if Mrs. Trenton is able to receive you."

Mariah nodded and walked toward an end table. On it sat a wooden toy ship painted bright red. She picked it up.

"That's mine!"

Mariah nearly dropped the toy, turning to see a boy at the door. He wore a navy sailor suit and his eyes were dark blue. He had a smattering of freckles over his pert nose and a determined little mouth. Mariah could see Captain Trenton in the boy's eyes, but his black hair he had inherited from his mother.

She held out the boat to him. "I believe this is yours, Master Edmund."

He snatched it from her hands. "How do you know my name?" he asked suspiciously.

"I knew you when you were a baby," Mariah said. "You were all red, wrinkly, and beautiful."

"Boys aren't beautiful," he said as his mother entered the room. "Mama, this lady says she knew me when I was a baby."

Mrs. Trenton looked older and grayer, and weariness hung over her like a cloud. Mariah's first instinct was to step toward her. But Mrs. Trenton blanched, and Mariah stepped back.

"Miss Carter," Mrs. Trenton said with tolerable command over her voice. She gave a slight bow to Mariah.

"Mariah. Mariah Carter."

Mrs. Trenton stared at her intently. Was she looking for

the little girl she had loved, or seeing the young woman she did not know?

"I thought you were not in London."

"I hope you don't mind my coming," Mariah said quickly. "I wanted to see Captain—Captain Trenton before he d—to see him, a-and you, of course."

"I'm afraid that he was not able to leave his bed this morning," Mrs. Trenton said. "The doctor thinks it may only be a matter of days, possibly hours."

"I see," Mariah said, nodding and trying not to cry. "I'll leave you to take care of him. Please forgive the intrusion."

Mariah walked toward the door. Mrs. Trenton put out her hand to stop her but dropped it immediately upon contact.

"No, please stay," Mrs. Trenton said. "I know that he would be pleased to see you. If you would come with me?"

"Of course."

Mariah followed Mrs. Trenton up a flight of stairs to the first door. When it was opened, Mariah was instantly met by heat—she saw a large fire dancing in the fireplace. In a four-poster bed with scarlet drapes, covered in blankets, lay an old man. Mariah would not have recognized him as her foster father, he seemed so shriveled. She walked toward him and then stopped, unsure of what she was supposed to do.

The old man lifted his head off his pillow. "Please come closer, Mariah."

"How did you know?" she asked softly, sitting on the chair next to his bed. "How did you always know?"

Captain Trenton lifted his gnarled hand and gently brushed her cheek. "You and Sophie might look identical, but your facial expressions were never the same. Sophie always held her head higher, defiantly. And you, Mariah, you always held your head lowered and a smile half hidden—a sort of secret happiness."

He began to cough, and his whole body shook from the convulsions. Looking behind her, Mariah saw Mrs. Trenton standing against the wall as if she wished to disappear into it. Mariah took the captain's hand in her own.

"I won't stay long," she said. "I only wanted you to know how much you meant to me—mean to me. You're the only father I've ever truly had, and I love you. I understand that you did your best, and you can't ask someone for more than that."

Mariah could see tears forming in the old man's eyes before they spilled out onto his weatherworn cheeks.

"I didn't do my best, Mariah," he said, squeezing her hand tighter. "I did what was simplest."

Mariah felt her own tears rise and begin to flow. "I still forgive you."

"Thank you, my child," Captain Trenton said. "You have no idea how much that means to me. Especially now, at the end of my time."

He began to cough violently again.

"Parsons," Mrs. Trenton called from the door of the room. "Send for the doctor at once."

Captain Trenton leaned his head back against his pillows, closing his eyes. Mariah released his hand with a pat from her own. Kissing his forehead, she whispered what he had always said to her and Sophie before bed: "Sail toward your dreams, my darling. I love you."

Mariah turned and walked toward Mrs. Trenton who stepped back until she hit the wall with a slight thump, but Mariah persevered and took the older woman's hands in her own.

"I will always think of you as my mother," Mariah said. "I'm grateful for all that you did for me as a child, and I hope someday that we may be friends again."

Mrs. Trenton sniffed and pulled her hands free from Mariah's. Then she threw her arms around Mariah's neck and began to weep on her shoulder. Mariah returned her embrace and gently patted the back of the woman who had read books to her and listened to her play the piano. The woman who had sung to her at night and held her when she was afraid. Their roles were now reversed, for it was Mrs. Trenton who was afraid. Mariah could feel Mrs. Trenton's body shake with sobs and fear.

Parsons entered the room with a draught on a silver tray. Mrs. Trenton released Mariah.

"Ferguson has gone to fetch the doctor, ma'am," Parsons said. "Shall I administer the captain's medicine?"

"Yes, please," Mrs. Trenton said, attempting to regain her composure and dabbing at her face with a small, lacy handkerchief. "I will show Miss Carter out."

"Very good, ma'am," he said and bowed to her.

Mrs. Trenton walked out of the room without a glance at Mariah or her husband. Mariah followed her silently down the two flights of stairs. Mrs. Trenton stood in front of the large black door and finally turned back to acknowledge Mariah.

"I know that your sister blames me for sending you away," Mrs. Trenton said levelly. "When you have children of your own, you will realize that your first priority must always be for their welfare and security. I believed that all of our money should go to our son, and that someday he would resent what funds had been squandered on strangers."

"We wouldn't have been strangers," Mariah said. "We would have been his sisters."

Mrs. Trenton bristled. "I would prefer that neither you nor your sister ever contact us again."

She opened the door and Mariah stepped out onto the street, the door closing loudly behind her.

Once seated in Aunt Bentley's carriage, Mariah released a long, pent-up breath. She didn't feel better, but she felt finished.

SIXTEEN

SOPHIE DRESSED WITH CARE THAT evening for the Millers' dinner party. She wore a light blue gown of silk with several rosettes clustered on the V-shaped bodice. The neckline of the dress fell just below her shoulders and emphasized her graceful neck; she touched the bare skin and wished she had a necklace to wear. Then Sophie laughed out loud at the absurdity of the thought: Not two months ago, she had only two work dresses, and now she was pining over jewels!

I am completely ridiculous, she thought, tugging on long white gloves that reached her elbows. Then she pulled on her dancing slippers, which had been dyed a matching shade of blue—the color of the sky at the lightest part of the day.

Hearing a knock at the door, Sophie looked around the room before remembering that Mariah had not yet returned.

"Come in," Sophie called.

Adell entered with a quick bob. "Excuse me, miss. This has come for you."

The maid handed her a posy of little forget-me-nots. Sophie inhaled their sweet scent before placing them on the table beside her and opened the card:

Sophie,

My dear friend and future business partner, I would be honored if you wore my flowers tonight. They are but a small token of my great admiration and esteem.

Yours,
Ethan

Forget-me-nots.

She tried to not be too pleased or to smile, but she couldn't help herself.

Adell smiled, too. "I could arrange them in your hair, if you'd like," she offered.

"Please, I would like that very much."

Sophie sat back in her chair and enjoyed the light movements of Adell's fingers as she deftly wove the small five-petaled flowers into her hair. When Adell finished, Sophie looked at her reflection in the mirror and thanked her. She had never felt beautiful before, but in this moment, she defied even Adaline in all her dimpled perfection to eclipse her.

The carriage ride to the Millers' felt constrained. Charles didn't speak once, nor did he give Sophie even a glance. He hadn't looked at her since she came down the stairs with Ethan's flowers in her hair. While Sophie didn't like him particularly, she couldn't help but be offended by his inability to behave civilly. She would never understand what Mariah saw in him. During the carriage ride, Aunt Bentley muttered only a few sentences, which required no response:

"I hope that the rest of the party is genteel. Mrs. Miller can be so democratic in her invitations, with no regard to rank." And: "I wonder if Mrs. Miller's talked to her butler yet about hurrying the courses along at dinner. Last time we dined there, it took nearly two hours."

When they arrived, Mrs. Miller welcomed them warmly. She wore a deep blue dress with the most exquisite lace overlay that Sophie had ever seen. Ethan looked decidedly handsome in a black suit as he bent over Sophie's hand to greet her.

"I'm honored that you wore my flowers, Miss Carter," he said formally, though there was a twinkle in his eye.

"Will I know anyone else at the party?" Sophie asked.

"The Penderton-Simpsons you already know," Ethan said. "But I believe the rest of the party is entirely unknown to you. Come, I'll introduce you."

Ethan led her from the front entry to the sitting room, where she saw Adaline and her parents talking with the Penroses. Four couples were already seated, along with Mr. Eustace Miller. Sophie had not met any of them before, but she knew instantly who they were.

"Your sisters?" she whispered, only loud enough for Ethan to hear.

"They've been eager to meet you. Please don't believe everything that they might say. In fact . . . please don't believe anything they say."

Ethan's sisters and their husbands stood. The family resemblance was marked. Each of the ladies had their mother's blond hair and blue eyes.

"Miss Carter," Ethan said formally, "may I introduce my sister Louisa and her husband, Lord and Lady de Clifford."

Sophie bowed to a very tall, angular man with grayish hair and his much shorter and plumper wife. Lord de Clifford gave a sharp bow, and Lady de Clifford reached out to Sophie. She allowed Lady de Clifford to take her hands and give them a quick squeeze. Her blue eyes were lighter and larger than her brother's, and she smiled broadly.

"I have been very eager to meet you, Miss Carter," Lady de Clifford said in a cultivated, pleasant voice. "There's so much I wish to tell you about my brother."

"Later, Louisa, later," Ethan said, and steered Sophie to the next couple. "Miss Carter, may I present my sister Anne and her husband, Mr. and Mrs. Cartwright."

Anne was as thin as her sister Louisa was plump. Her thinness was exaggerated by a plain black dress, worn off the shoulders with long black gloves. Her blond hair was simply styled in single braids on each side of her head, which became a bun at the back of her neck. She gave a small smile and an even smaller curtsy. Her husband was also wearing only black and merely nodded his head.

"A pleasure," Sophie said, bobbing a curtsy and trying not to feel overwhelmed.

Ethan led her to the next couple.

"And next, my sister Mary and her husband, Mr. and Mrs. Lennox, may I present Miss Carter."

Mary was slight in frame like Anne, but quite a bit taller. She was also well-endowed, which her dress of peach muslin with blue ribbons amply displayed. Mr. Lennox was a good half a head shorter than his wife and twice as broad, with a large belly that his tailoring could not hide. He had a round, red face and an easy smile of good humor. Mary's smile was equally jolly, causing wrinkles around her dark blue eyes.

"And finally, my sister Rebecca and her husband, Lord and Lady Gordon."

Rebecca was shorter than Sophie and looked to be younger than Ethan. She was clearly the beauty of the family, with a perfectly oval face; smooth, porcelain-like skin; and a beautiful smile of straight, pearly teeth. Her hair was dressed in a profusion of ringlets, braids, and gardenia flowers. Her violet silk dress caught the light, and the antique lace at her throat and sleeves probably cost more than all the clothes Aunt Bentley had purchased for Sophie. Rebecca wore long white gloves that reached her elbows and hung on her husband's arm in such a way that made Sophie think that they must be recently married.

"At last," Rebecca said. "I've been begging to meet you for a fortnight at least."

Sophie unconsciously stepped closer to Ethan and managed to say, "I'm delighted to make your acquaintance."

Rebecca released her hold on her husband's arm and took Sophie's. "Ethan, why don't you entertain Charles, and Miss Carter can sit with me?"

Ethan bowed slightly to Sophie before walking across the room to Charles, whose expression was particularly dour. Aunt Bentley sat near Mrs. Miller and Mr. Eustace Miller. Rebecca led her to a settee, and they sat next to each other.

"Now, let me get a good look at you," Rebecca said. "Very beautiful. I can see why Ethan is smitten. Are those his flowers in your hair?"

Sophie felt her color rise, but she was saved from answering by Adaline sitting down on her other side.

"What has Rebecca said to embarrass you?" Adaline teased.

"Nothing," Sophie said, but she felt as if the world had somehow tilted. Ethan's family seemed to assume too much about her and him—about *them*.

"The night is young," Adaline said. "I daresay she'll manage to embarrass you and Mr. Miller before the dinner is over."

"I'll do no such thing!" Rebecca protested.

"It seems very brave of him to have you meet all of his family before an engagement is announced to the papers and you cannot change your mind," Adaline said, winking at Rebecca.

If Sophie were the fainting type, which she thankfully wasn't, she would have fallen to the floor at Adaline's bold announcement. *Engagement?!* It was much too soon to be using that sort of word.

"He made us all promise to behave ourselves," Rebecca said.

Adaline laughed. "Sophie, I know that it's quite without manners to ask, but is everything settled between the two of you?"

"Adaline, such an indelicate question!" Rebecca said, but she still leaned forward eagerly to hear Sophie's answer.

"Like you're not dying to know yourself," Adaline said, shrugging her perfect shoulders. "I've had several people ask me, and I would hate to be the last person in London society to know."

Sophie didn't know what to say. Had her behavior given cause for such talk? *Marriage.* She literally felt sick to her stomach. At last, she found her voice. "Nothing is . . . We are . . . Lady Gordon, do you care for Pre-Raphaelite paintings, by chance?"

Rebecca raised her perfectly shaped eyebrows at her friend. "I'm very fond of art. Are you, Adaline?"

Adaline gave a resigned sigh. "I suppose I'm not un-fond of it."

The butler announced dinner and Sophie was relieved to find Ethan at her side. Adaline took her usual place by Charles, who steadily refused to look at Sophie. Ethan escorted Sophie into an enormous dining room with two large crystal chandeliers hanging from the ceiling. He assisted her to a seat on his left and Lord Gordon sat on her other side. The footmen began to deliver the dishes, which superseded all conversation for a few moments.

Sophie was glad to have a chance to catch her breath and tidy the thoughts in her mind. Adaline seemed to think that all of London society was expecting a wedding announcement any day now. Clearly Ethan's sisters thought they were already engaged, or at least soon to be.

Horrified and embarrassed, Sophie wished that Mariah had come to dinner instead. She stole a glance at Charles, who gave her a withering look in return and then focused his attention on his plate. She wondered what Mariah had said or done to make him feel hostile toward her just when he was starting to behave almost human.

She turned her head to Ethan, who met her gaze with a smile. Her stomach began to turn in the pleasantly unpleasant way that it always did when he was near. But that feeling was overshadowed by the nausea brought on by his family's expectations.

"My sisters weren't invited tonight," Ethan said quietly.

"And yet they're all here."

Ethan shook his head bemusedly. "Yes. My mother told Mary, who told Louisa, who told Anne, who told Rebecca. They were all most eager to meet you."

"Rebecca seems very . . . loquacious."

"A busybody," Ethan said.

Sophie tried to smile but she felt the eyes of the entire party on her—on *them*.

Mrs. Miller diverted the attention. "Charles, how soon will you be departing back to New York?"

"Nine days," he said, with a slight questioning glance at Sophie.

"So soon," Mrs. Miller said. "Are you quite recovered?"

"It's good for a man to be at his business," Mr. Eustace Miller said gruffly.

Charles flushed. "I'm much better, Aunt Miller, and eager to prove myself equal to the task."

"And so you will," Ethan said. "Charles has a great head for business, doesn't he, grandfather?"

"Sound," Mr. Eustace Miller said. "Very sound head."

"I hope you've all received your invitations to my ball next week," Aunt Bentley said. "It will be in honor of my dear Charles's departure."

"We'll certainly be there," Rebecca said with a knowing look at Sophie and Ethan. "It's going to be quite the *family* affair, after all."

Sophie stood up suddenly. Her napkin fell to the floor,

but she didn't bother to pick it up. She walked quickly out of the dining room, covering her mouth with her hands; she felt as if she were about to be sick.

In the hall, she spotted a Grecian urn on the side table. She grabbed it with both hands and brought it to her mouth in time to catch the contents of her stomach.

"Sophie, are you all right?"

Reluctantly she turned to see Ethan standing behind her in the hall. He looked so handsome in the candlelight, even with an expression of concern shadowing his face. She glanced down at the priceless historical artifact she'd just befouled.

"I need some air."

"Let's walk outside to the garden," Ethan suggested. He gently took the urn from her fingers and set it back on the table.

As he began to lead her away, she glanced over her shoulder at the urn. "I was . . . I was sick in that."

"I noticed," he said, a smile tugging at the corners of his lips.

"I'm so sorry."

"Isn't that what bowls are for?" Ethan said. "You don't need to worry about it. It's not an heirloom."

He opened a door that led out to a dark garden. The light from the house's windows wasn't enough to illuminate it. Instead, the dim light cast shadows on all the trees and bushes, giving them a sinister look.

Sophie stripped off her gloves and touched her hot cheeks with her hands. Breathing in and out. She hadn't felt this out of control in years. Mrs. Ellis had successfully beat most emotion out of her.

"Please tell me what Rebecca said to upset you before dinner," Ethan asked tentatively from behind her. "I'm sure this is only a misunderstanding that I can explain."

She stood silent for a few moments, trying to put her words in order like she would put together the gears of a clock. "Rebecca was not unkind."

"Something has upset you," he said, touching her shoulder.

Sophie stepped forward, breaking their contact. If he touched her, her tenuous resolve would be lost. "They all seem to assume that everything is settled between us."

"Is that such a bad thing?"

"Yes!" Sophie exclaimed, finally turning to look him in the eye. "You know how I feel about courtships. You know my past. This . . . this is all much, much too soon for me."

Ethan reached his hand out to her. "I know the Trentons abandoned you, but that doesn't mean that I will."

"How could you possibly understand?" Sophie cried, wringing her hands. "Someone like you with your beautiful house and your beautiful family . . . You will *never* understand what it's like to be thrown away! To be treated like you're even less than a servant, to not know if you'll have a roof over your head the next day. To watch your sister be starved and belittled and know there is nothing you can do to help her, *nothing* you can do to make her life better. You could never understand."

"I'm trying to . . ."

Someone must have opened a window at that moment; the sounds of happy chatter floated out into the garden.

"I can't do this anymore. I can't be here," Sophie said, feeling nauseous again.

"Please stay. I'm sure we can resolve this together—"

"There's nothing to resolve. I don't belong here . . . with you. Please call me a carriage. Every moment here pains me."

Ethan nodded slowly. "Of course . . . if you wish it."

"Thank you."

He left the garden and Sophie was finally alone. For the second time in a week, tears threatened to spill from her eyes. This was all her fault. She should have kept Ethan at a proper distance from herself, from her heart. She knew better. Reaching into her pocket, she felt for her pocket watch and ran her fingers over the engraving on the front until she felt calm again.

The door to the house opened; Ethan stood holding it for her. Sophie sniffed and walked through it.

"The carriage is ready, and I've brought you another bowl—just in case," he said with a ghost of a smile.

He was trying to cheer her up, but Sophie could not return the smile. Her chin quivered as he led her to the front door on the opposite side of the house.

"May I accompany you home?"

"No, thank you," she said.

He winced. "I don't need your thanks."

"I have nothing else to give."

"This is goodbye for a little while then," he said, his voice choked with emotion. "I'm leaving tomorrow for Birmingham and I'll be there for several weeks. I've put off this business too long. Perhaps I can call on you when I return?"

Sophie looked down at the bowl in her hands. She didn't know what to say. She had no idea where she would be living in a few weeks.

Ethan opened the carriage door for her and then offered his hand to assist her in, but she didn't take it, electing to clamber in on her own. She knew she ought to say something, but no words would come. He stood waiting for her response for several moments before he closed the door to the carriage and said to the coachman, "Drive on."

As the carriage jerked forward, Sophie ran her fingers through her hair and felt the forget-me-not flowers. She plucked them from her tresses and watched them wilt in her hands.

At last, the carriage arrived at Hyde Street. Mr. Taylor let Sophie in, his expression more curious than condescending. She brushed past him without a word and went straight upstairs to her room.

"Sophie?" Mariah said in surprise, sitting up against

the pillows. When she saw the look on her twin's face, she dropped the book she'd been reading and scrambled out of bed.

Sophie fell into the arms of her sister, the only person she trusted, and cried and cried.

SEVENTEEN

SOPHIE OPENED THE FRONT OF Mrs. Spooner's clock, which had fallen five minutes behind, and wound the minute hand forward carefully, as winding it backward could break it. She cranked the thirty-hour weight until it was at the top and then closed the front, grateful to have something to focus her mind on besides Ethan.

"I don't understand why Mrs. Trenton refused to be my friend," Mariah said as she placed her teacup on its saucer. She picked up a cucumber sandwich and took a bite.

Sophie returned to her chair and picked up her cold cup of tea. "It doesn't surprise me at all. She's a horrible woman."

"She's not horrible."

"She *is*."

"Now, now, dears," Mrs. Spooner said. "I'm sure she

does want to see you, Mariah, but seeing you reminds her of wronging you."

"But I forgave her," Mariah protested.

Mrs. Spooner shook her head slightly. "But has she forgiven herself?"

Sir Thomas walked in with a harrumph.

"Still gossiping, I see, like a bunch of lasses," he said. "With no thoughts of my profession or that my painting should have been completed nearly a fortnight ago."

Mrs. Spooner stood up. "You're right, dear, we weren't thinking about you at all—it was a refreshing change. Come, ladies. Let's go finish Joan of Arc."

Mariah and Mrs. Spooner helped Sophie back into her armor while Sir Thomas cursed their slowness from the stairs. When Mrs. Spooner announced that Sophie was decent, he growled, "About bloody time."

Sophie tried to conceal her smile. She liked Sir Thomas, despite his being egotistical, domineering, and short-tempered. She could hardly believe the painting was almost done. She wouldn't miss dressing up in enough metal to build a steamboat, but she would miss Sir Thomas and his wife.

"Hold still, dreadful girl!" Sir Thomas shouted.

Sophie stuck her tongue out at him and then resumed her position, holding as still as she was able for over an hour. Periodically she would glance at her sister, who was painting with a pursed look on her face. Sophie hated Mrs. Trenton even more in that moment for troubling Mariah so.

Exhaling slowly, Sophie reminded herself that she'd already determined to not let that woman take any more of her time or emotions. She had to make good to herself on that promise. But the thought that replaced it was equally traitorous: Her mind kept picturing Ethan in the park with the sunshine in his hair, and the hope and happiness she'd felt in his presence.

"Prudie!" Sir Thomas barked. "Make her stop! She's making a mooning face."

Mrs. Spooner stood up from the chair where she'd dozed off and walked over to Sir Thomas's easel. She examined the canvas carefully from the very top to the very bottom. It was as if the studio itself was holding its breath, waiting for her pronouncement.

"It is complete, Sir Thomas," Mrs. Spooner said finally. "Not another brushstroke."

"Not another brushstroke?" Sir Thomas repeated.

Mrs. Spooner placed a hand on her husband's thick arm. "Not a one. Now, go away, dear. Get yourself some brandy and celebrate. I'll take care of the framing and arrange with the gallery to come collect it for the presentation."

"Are you sure?" he asked, a note of uncertainty in his voice.

"Sir Thomas, this is why you married me," Mrs. Spooner replied. "I always know when a painting is complete. Now go, before you traumatize the young ladies any further."

Sir Thomas left the studio with something strangely

close to a smile on his face. Mrs. Spooner helped Sophie out of the suit of armor and back into her dress. Sophie looked at the pile of metal pieces on the floor. "If it weren't metal, I would suggest we burn it to celebrate."

Mrs. Spooner reached a hand into her voluminous apron pocket and pulled out a five-pound note, handing it to Sophie. "My dear, I think this is a much better way to celebrate."

Taking the note, Sophie smiled. "Yes, it is."

Mrs. Spooner walked over to Mariah, who was still steadily painting. She examined her small two-foot-by-two-foot canvas as Mariah put down her paintbrush and started to clean up.

"You are making great steps forward, Mariah," Mrs. Spooner said. "You shouldn't stop yet. You're finding your rhythm."

"Our aunt will want us," Mariah explained. "She should be waking up from her afternoon rest very soon."

"She only needs one of us," Sophie said. "I'll go."

"But I need a model to paint."

Mrs. Spooner smiled. "I'll have a footman bring up a mirror, and you can paint until you can no longer hold up that brush."

Mrs. Spooner gave them both a benign smile before leaving the room. Sophie looked intently at Mariah, who had picked her brush back up and continued to steadily stroke the red paint into flame-like curls around Sophie's face.

"Are you all right?" Sophie asked. "Should I stay?"

Mariah shook her head. "I wanted some time to myself, and I think now is as good a time as ever."

Sophie nodded, then opened the attic door and climbed over the short brick wall to Aunt Bentley's house.

EIGHTEEN

SOPHIE HAD NOT SAT DOWN on the bed for more than five minutes when Adell knocked on the door and said that Aunt Bentley wished to see her. Sophie picked up a hairbrush and gave the red curls around her face a few quick swipes. She pinched her cheeks and straightened the lace on her dress before following Adell downstairs to the sitting room.

"Ah, Sophie," Aunt Bentley said, a piece of paper in her hand. "I was hoping that you would help me write and address these additional invitations to Charles's party."

"As you wish."

Sophie sat down next to her aunt and began to copy the words of the invitation in her best penmanship, for Mariah's handwriting was much cleaner and more elegant than Sophie's. She carefully wrote and addressed more than fifty invitations to people she'd never even heard of. *At least Adaline will be at the party,* Sophie thought. Her family's invitation had already been sent out with the first batch of letters.

"I see that you're smiling," Aunt Bentley said.

"I'm fond of Miss Penderton-Simpson—Adaline," Sophie explained. "She's a delightful companion and a good friend."

"If only Charles would realize as much," Aunt Bentley said with her usual scowl. "I cannot see why he is holding back when she has everything a young man could wish for—and such excellent family and business connections."

Sophie nodded absentmindedly, then put down her pen carefully so as not to spill the ink.

"Adaline certainly has all those things, and more. She has a vivacious charm and a lovely personality. But if there is no spark between them, it is not Charles's fault."

"'Spark?'"

"Attraction," Sophie said simply. "If he doesn't feel warmly toward her, he shouldn't ask her to marry him."

Aunt Bentley scoffed. "You're showing your naivety again, Sophie. Love is imaginary, like fairies and monsters. People who delude themselves into believing in love make foolish matches like my sister."

"Did you not love the late Lord Bentley?"

"He didn't want my love, he wanted a wife," Aunt Bentley replied flatly. "And I flatter myself that I upheld that position with honor and purpose."

"I'm sure you did."

Aunt Bentley smiled at this and then laughed derisively. "*Spark*, indeed. Nonsense!"

Sophie turned her head to hide her own smile. She felt more than a spark of feeling for Ethan. It was more like a bonfire—wild and out of control.

For the first time ever, Sophie felt pity for her aunt. No one loved her. Sophie certainly didn't. Mariah was trying to, but she was continually rebuffed. Charles seemed indifferent in her presence, and her husband apparently hadn't loved her. The only people who loved Aunt Bentley were dead: her father; her mother; and her sister, who'd died alone and in the direst poverty.

How lonely it must be not to be loved.

It certainly was Aunt Bentley's own fault. She'd refused to take care of her sister's children, and even now she was only willing to accept one of them. Aunt Bentley was more worried about her position and fortune than she was about personal relationships. And soon she would be all alone. Sophie's visit would end, and Charles would return to New York.

If I keep pushing people away, I'll end up all alone, too.

It seemed so simple. Yet, to Sophie, it was as earth-shattering a thought as a thousand-ton hydraulic press. She didn't want to be like her aunt. She wanted to be able to love others and open herself to love. To trust others to not fail her. To trust herself to not fail them. She had to start letting people into her heart and into her affections.

She only hoped that she wasn't too late.

Mariah woke up on the floor of Sir Thomas's studio. She stretched out her arms and legs, and the blanket that was covering her fell off. Her neck felt stiff and her whole body felt as if she were the one wearing metal armor. Gingerly she got to her feet.

Mrs. Spooner walked through the door. "Awake at last, are we?"

"I'm so sorry, I didn't mean to—"

Mrs. Spooner smiled. "Genius cannot wait. Let's see your portrait, then."

Mariah felt her temperature rise as Mrs. Spooner came near the canvas and began inspecting it with the same circumspection with which she'd examined Sir Thomas's *Joan of Arc*.

Sophie's portrait looked forward defiantly, her curly red hair streaming over her bare shoulders, onto the black dress and out of the painting. Mariah's soft face turned away from Sophie, her curls pulled back, her dress white with a high collar.

"You're not at all the same," Mrs. Spooner said finally. "What do you mean to do with your painting?"

Mariah flushed. "I don't have any plans."

"All the better," Mrs. Spooner said practically. "Mr. Poulton will be arriving today to frame *Joan of Arc*. With your permission, I'll have him frame your painting as well."

Mariah tugged at her sleeve. "How much does that cost?"

"Consider it a gift," Mrs. Spooner said. "I have a knack for discovering fine artists, and I mean to add you to my list of discoveries."

"Me?"

"You," Mrs. Spooner said with a wide grin. "I'll even venture to have your painting displayed publicly, if you'll trust me with it."

"Of course, I can't thank you enough!" Mariah cried, her eyes beginning to water. "You've done so much for me and my sister. There's no way to repay you . . ."

"Friendship requires no payment," Mrs. Spooner said. "Now, go home and see what mischief your sister's been up to, and leave everything to me."

NINETEEN

MARIAH COULD HARDLY BELIEVE HOW quickly the next seven days passed. Her aunt required so much help with the party arrangements that she barely had time to dress before dinner or switch places with Sophie. Not that how Mariah looked mattered; Charles had spent the last week visiting his country estates without even bothering to say goodbye.

The night of the party, Mariah sat still as Sophie pinned each curl into place. "Are you sure you don't want to go?"

Sophie laughed. "Ethan's in Birmingham, and I'm afraid Charles is no inducement for me."

They heard a knock at the door and Mariah's eyes opened wide. Sophie placed her finger to her lips and tiptoed toward the bed.

"Who is it?" Mariah asked.

"Aunt Bentley."

Mariah heard Sophie curse softly as she hit her head on the side of the bed frame. Mariah waited for Sophie to finish shimmying underneath before she walked to the door and opened it.

"Do you need something?" Mariah asked, acutely aware of the second pair of boots on the floor beside the bed.

Aunt Bentley didn't speak immediately as she entered. She seemed to take up half the room with her enormous dress of dove-gray silk. Mariah stood dumbly holding the doorknob, unsure of what she was supposed to do. Their aunt had never visited their room before.

Aunt Bentley looked around the room, taking in every detail. Mariah hoped she wouldn't notice Sophie's hair poking out from underneath the bed.

"I received a visit from a lawyer today," Aunt Bentley said finally.

"Yes?"

"Captain Trenton died three days ago," she said. "His lawyer came to inform me that you and your sister have each inherited two thousand pounds. I'm glad you were prudent enough to visit him. Your attention has received its reward."

"I . . . I-I can't believe he's dead," Mariah said, tears springing to her eyes.

"Don't become maudlin, Sophie," Aunt Bentley snapped. "You only saw the man once in several years and excessive displays of emotion went out of fashion when the Prince Regent died."

Mariah wiped at her tears. "I'm sorry. It's such a surprise, is all."

"I meant it to be a happy surprise," Aunt Bentley said, stiffening. "Two thousand pounds will make a great deal of difference in your future as well as for Mariah. You will not be rich, but you will never have to be dependent again."

Mariah sniffed and flushed at her own duplicity. "Thank you, Aunt Bentley. You've been very good to me."

"You'd better finish getting ready," she said brusquely. "My guests will soon arrive."

Without another word, she left the room. Mariah rushed to the bed as Sophie stuck her head out.

"Poor Papa," Mariah said, crying again.

To her surprise, Sophie's eyes were full of unshed tears.

"You know what this means, Mariah?"

"What?"

"That he truly loved us," Sophie said. "And he didn't forget us, and that means more to me than the money."

Sophie walked to the table and picked up the handkerchief to hand to Mariah, but instead brought it closer to her own eyes, examining the embroidery. "Is this the Bentley crest, Mariah?"

Mariah took the handkerchief from her sister and put it to good use on her eyes first, and then her nose. She could feel Sophie's scrutiny as she said lightly, "Charles lent it to me once. I should have returned it already. I will tomorrow."

"You'd better return it before he leaves," Sophie said. "Aunt Bentley mentioned that he would only stay here tonight, and then he plans to stay the night in Dover before he sails."

Mariah turned from her sister, unable to meet her eyes.

"We can talk about this tomorrow," Sophie said. "Let me powder your face a little, to cover up that you've been crying. We can grieve tomorrow."

Mariah felt numb as her sister powdered her face. Sophie pinned four more curls before pronouncing Mariah perfect. Standing up, Mariah looked in the mirror: the white silk dress made her appear paler than usual.

Sophie pinched Mariah's cheeks. "For color." Then she helped Mariah pull on her long white gloves and dancing slippers.

"What are you going to do while I'm gone?"

Sophie gave her a sad smile. "I think the best way for me to honor Papa is by using his telescope. I mean to sit on the roof and search for him in the stars."

Mariah nodded, overcome with emotion.

Sophie hugged her. "Don't forget to smile!"

Mariah gave her a wan smile and then left the room. Aunt Bentley and Charles stood waiting at the bottom of the stairs in the grand foyer.

"There you are, Sophie," Aunt Bentley said. "I was just telling Charles about your good fortune."

Mariah didn't trust herself to speak, so she looked down and merely nodded. She heard the knocker and glanced first at the door and then to Charles. Their eyes met for a moment before he looked away.

"Come stand by my side, Sophie," Aunt Bentley said. "We must welcome my guests."

Charles stood on the other side of Aunt Bentley. He might have been in another room for the lack of notice he gave Mariah. The first guests to arrive were the Penderton-Simpsons. The parents barely acknowledged Mariah, but Adaline gave her a brilliant smile. "My dear Sophie, it's been too long since I've seen you—or Lord Bentley."

She looked archly from Mariah to Charles. He cleared his throat. "I'm afraid that I've had business with my estates to settle before I go out of the country again, Miss Penderton-Simpson."

"That's a very good excuse," Adaline admitted gaily. "Still, you must make it up to me tonight."

"With pleasure," Charles said. "May I have the first two dances?"

Adaline blithely accepted, and Mariah tried very hard to smile. More guests arrived, and Charles's attention went to them. Mariah didn't recognize most of the guests, but she had a shrewd suspicion that Sophie would have. A beautiful blond young woman named Lady Gordon positively winked at her!

At last, Aunt Bentley proclaimed that they could leave their post and join the party. Charles went at once to claim his dances with Adaline, who beamed in his arms. Mariah didn't have to watch them long before she was asked to dance by a Mr. Heath. His face was pocked like ground beef, and he tread on her toes twice.

Mariah was relieved when he led her off the dance floor. She stood there, uncertain for a moment, and Mr. Heath circled the room and came back to her.

But before he reached her, another gentleman stepped in front of him and asked, "Might I have this next dance, Miss Carter?"

He must have arrived late, because Mariah hadn't seen him before. He was tall with blond hair, bluish-green eyes, a straight nose, and a strong chin. Mariah shyly held out her hand. The unknown gentleman pulled her into his arms and whisked her away to the dance floor.

"I've come to beg for forgiveness, dear friend."

Mariah's breath hitched, and she stumbled through the dance step. Who was he and why was he asking for Sophie's forgiveness? How was Mariah to know if she could give it or not?

"I, uh . . . well . . . that is—" Mariah stumbled through her words as well as her steps.

"I should have listened to you. I shouldn't have rushed you. Please say that we may still be friends."

"Um . . . I, uh, I don't know . . . I shall, um . . . have to think about it."

He then did an intricate dance turn that required all her dancing skill to follow. She deftly turned and spun reversely in his arms. It was a difficult dance move and she executed it perfectly. She looked up at his face and the man's pleasant countenance had changed to a serious frown.

"You're not the Miss Carter I know."

Mariah panicked and lost her step. "Wh- . . . I . . . Then who c-could I be?"

"Her identical twin sister," he said simply. "I should've known that Sophie wouldn't have left you behind."

Again, Mariah lost her step and the man led her back to the correct dance figure.

"Where might I find, Sophie, if that's her name?" he said, looking at her intently. "Or is it yours?"

Mariah blinked. "Wh-who are you?"

"Ethan Miller at your service, Miss Carter."

Mariah laughed in relief, pulling her hand from his to cover her mouth. They stood there in the middle of the dance floor for a moment before Mariah noticed several eyes on her. She placed her hand back into Mr. Miller's and they continued to dance.

"I'm Mariah. Mariah Carter," she said softly. "You know the real Sophie Carter."

"I'm glad of that."

"Aunt Bentley only invited one of us to stay," she explained breathlessly. "Sophie wouldn't come without me. So we've taken turns being 'Sophie.' If we knew *you* were coming tonight, she would've been here."

Ethan laughed; it was a deep, melodious sound. Mariah liked him for it.

"Let me guess," he said quietly. "The whole charade was Sophie's idea?"

"Yes," Mariah admitted. "But I also agreed."

"And not one person has guessed there are two of you?"

"You're the first."

Ethan spun Mariah around as they continued through the set. "May I ask again, where might I find Sophie?"

"Usually the spare sister stays in our bedroom," Mariah said. "But tonight, she's on the roof stargazing."

Ethan grinned and Mariah found herself returning his smile. He led her to the side of the room and bowed over her hand.

"Miss Carter," he said formally.

Mariah watched Ethan walk away as Charles escorted Adaline to her side. He bowed over Adaline's hand.

"Thank you for the pleasure of those two dances," he said.

Adaline tittered. "I have permission to dance a third with you, should you ask me."

"I wouldn't wish to be so cruel as to monopolize you from the rest of the party," Charles said. "Sophie, may I have this dance?"

Mariah offered her hand, and Charles clasped it in his. Once on the dance floor, he lightly took hold of her waist with the other. He didn't speak, and Mariah foolishly enjoyed being in his arms. She closed her eyes and moved with the music, the slight pressure of his fingers directing her every step.

"I suppose I wouldn't be behind in offering you my congratulations, Sophie," Charles said in a hard voice.

Mariah blinked and opened her eyes.

"Miss Penderton-Simpson says that everything is all but settled between you and my cousin."

Mariah found herself blushing.

"Your face says it all."

She bit her lip. "Charles, I was wondering if I could speak to you privately for a moment. Perhaps in the library? There's something I would like to say."

"I'm not sure it's anything I would like to hear," he said stiffly.

"Please. I need to say it."

"As you wish."

When the music ended, he took her hand and led her out of the room. He didn't speak again until they arrived at the library and he closed the door behind them.

"Nothing is settled between myself and Mr. Miller," Mariah said.

"What?" Charles said. He took an involuntary step toward her before checking himself.

"I've wronged my aunt twice, and I'll leave it to your discretion how much to tell her," Mariah said. "The first is that I was not invited to stay. My sister, Sophie, was. We've always been together, and so we both came to London—one sister staying hidden and the other taking turns being 'Sophie.'"

"That . . . is too incredible to believe."

"My sister and I are identical in appearance," she explained. "But we're not at all the same in personality. Did you not notice the differences between us? Wasn't our behavior, our expressions, varied enough to give you pause?"

Charles ran his fingers through his dark hair. "I never supposed."

Mariah grasped the table for support. "And the other wrong was that my aunt specifically asked me not to try to engage your interest. And I did try. But I realize now that it was both wrong and foolish."

"Foolish?"

She shook her head. "You were never interested in me, *Mariah*. You were only interested in 'Sophie' because your cousin was. Another area in which you could compete with him."

"That's not true—"

"I'd hoped it wasn't," Mariah said. "But Ethan realized I wasn't Sophie within seconds of meeting me tonight."

"Did you expect me to guess?"

"Of course not," she said. "I'm only disappointed that

you never knew me well enough to tell the difference between us."

"Do you know *me* well enough to make such an assertion?" Charles demanded.

"I know you well enough, Charles, to tell you that you'll never beat your cousin," Mariah said, shaking her head. "And it's not because he's better, older, richer, or wiser. It's because he's not competing with you. Every success you have, he will celebrate it with you. Every mistake you make, he will commiserate with you. He doesn't need to prove himself to anyone. He's like my sister, Sophie: whole and complete."

"Miss Mariah Carter." He said her name slowly, as if it was new to him. "Can you say that you are whole and complete?

"No," she said, pressing her hand to the center of her chest. "My life has been an empty canvas, and I thought I had to wait to find someone to paint my life into a masterpiece. But I was wrong. *I* am the painter and *I* am the only person who can make my life into a masterpiece. And I'm the only person who can make me whole and complete."

"And how are you going to do that?"

Mariah attempted a smile and let go of the table. "I'm going to learn how to live on my own. Trust myself. Make mistakes. Learn from them. And then hopefully, someday, find someone whom I can love wholly, because I'll finally be whole."

"I understand," Charles said slowly.

Mariah took a deep breath and let it go. "We'd better return to the party. My aunt will be wondering where we are."

"You go first," he said. "It will be better if we don't enter at the same time."

Charles opened the door to the library, and Mariah gave him a small curtsy before leaving the room.

TWENTY

SOPHIE WALKED OUT ONTO THE roof and felt the slight chill of evening. She pulled her shawl closer around her shoulders before setting the telescope case down and opening it. Bringing the telescope to her eye, she adjusted it until her view was clear. Captain Trenton had told her that the North Star eventually calls all sailors home. As a child, Sophie had not realized that he had meant death. She scanned the skies for a few moments before locating the Little Dipper constellation, then the brightest star in its handle. The North Star.

The North Star guided sailors in the night. It allowed them to know which direction they were sailing. Sophie lifted her other hand and saluted the North Star, as she used to salute Captain Trenton.

"May the wind always be in your sails."

Sophie needed to decide which direction she wanted to sail. And now, with the income left to her from Captain Trenton, she could choose. She and Mariah could afford a small country cottage or rented rooms in a city. She could invent and Mariah could paint.

But would she be happy?

The last seven days had felt like an eternity without Ethan. He had become her North Star. His light eclipsed everything and everyone around her. Just being near him made her happy. Without him, she felt lonelier than she'd ever felt before, even with Mariah at her side.

Sophie lowered the telescope.

Something had changed between them. Sophie would always love her sister, but she could sense that Mariah was keeping things from her. They were growing apart; or rather, growing up. They were becoming their own people, and although Sophie felt a pang of remorse, she didn't regret it. It was time for Sophie to be Sophie and Mariah to be Mariah. Their destinies were no longer inseparably intertwined.

She heard the door to the roof open and was so startled that she nearly dropped her telescope. Sophie quickly stashed it back in its box before turning around.

Ethan walked outside carrying a gas lantern, light seeming to emanate from him. She longed to throw herself into his arms, but her feet would not move.

He placed the lantern on the brick parapet. "Did you miss me, Sophie?"

"More than you'll ever know," she whispered.

"I'm so sorry—"

Sophie forced her feet to step forward. "No. *I'm* sorry for the terrible words I said."

"The truth is always terrible," he said. "And you're right. I'll never truly understand what you and your sister have been through."

She gasped in surprise. "Oh dear! Poor Mariah. You must have discovered her."

Ethan seemed to be struggling not to smile. "She is a *much* better dancer than you."

Sophie stepped close enough to give a playful shove to his shoulder. "I know. But that's still unkind of you to say."

He caught her hand and held it in his. "I'm sorry that I rushed you. That I was indiscreet in my attentions and allowed my sisters to assume things were more definite between us."

"I do care for you, but trusting other people is difficult for me."

Ethan kissed the back of her hand and Sophie felt strangely weightless.

"We have all the time in the world, just like your clocks," he said. "There's no need to rush into anything."

"I'm still going to be an inventor," Sophie said. "Captain Trenton left me a small legacy and I mean to pursue my dream."

"I believe you," Ethan said, twirling her around as if they were dancing. "You'll turn the world on its axis, and I only hope to be by your side when you do it."

"I would like that very much," she said breathlessly.

Ethan gently pulled her close to him and with his hand smoothed back the curls from her face. Sophie couldn't breathe.

"From the first moment I met you, I've been entranced," he whispered.

"Then you'd better kiss me."

Ethan lifted her off her feet and pressed his lips to hers. It was as if they were two parts of the same clock, in perfect motion together. One giving, the other receiving as they turned in small, perfect circles.

At last, Sophie pressed her hand to Ethan's chest and he instantly pulled away from her. "I must catch my breath."

"You should invent a device that makes breathing optional," he offered.

"The very thing," Sophie said. "But perhaps until I do invent such a marvelous device, we should breathe and talk about our plans. Mariah and I can no longer masquerade as the same person. And even if we could, my aunt only invited us for this one season."

"I have a plan. You and Mariah can come stay with my mother," Ethan said. "She could help both of you find the perfect positions . . . And now I think about it further, you ought to run away with me this very moment, and we'll come back tomorrow for Mariah. There's currently too many Sophies in this house."

"Now?" Sophie said. "It's pitch-black and nearly midnight."

"The perfect time to run away."

"I suppose it is more difficult to slip away undetected in the daylight," Sophie admitted, and then clapped her hands together. "I've got it. I'll run away tonight with you, and when we come back tomorrow, I can pretend to be Mariah."

"It's a good plan," Ethan said. He held out his hand to her. "Shall we?"

Sophie went back to pick up her telescope, tucking the case underneath her arm before taking Ethan's hand.

"You're running away with a telescope?"

"It never hurts to be prepared," she said. "Oh, and I need to leave a note for Mariah. You can't run away without a note. It simply isn't done."

"Even if you're technically dancing downstairs?"

"Especially if your doppelgänger is dancing downstairs."

Ethan picked up the lantern by the handle and opened the door to the house for Sophie. She led him down the servants' staircase and to her room. He didn't enter but respectfully stood waiting in the doorway.

Placing the telescope on the table, Sophie picked up a pen and dipped it in the ink to write:

M.,

As you know, E. has discovered our masquerade. He has invited us both to come stay with his mother until we find suitable positions and a more permanent home. So you will no longer have to pretend to be me. In fact, I'm going to pretend to be you! Tomorrow, E. and I will come pick you up and he'll introduce me to Aunt B. as Mariah. Once we leave, we can switch back and then we'll never have to pretend to be each other again. I'll be an inventor and you'll be the most celebrated artist in all of England. I must go.

Love, S.

Sophie placed the letter on the table, then took a bonnet from the wardrobe and tied it on. She then covered her shoulders with a shawl and pronounced herself ready.

"I've never run away before," Sophie confided in a whisper. "Shouldn't I be climbing out a window or something equally hazardous?"

"I thought the front door."

"That isn't very dashing of you and we'd get caught. There's a party downstairs."

Ethan's lips twitched. "Alas, I forgot my stepladder in my other coat."

"Luckily, I have a rope in the wardrobe. I'll climb down

the side of the house into the garden. Then we can escape through the alley."

Ethan nodded. "I'll meet you in the garden. Please don't climb down until I get there. I want to make sure you don't fall."

He closed the door behind him, and she opened the wardrobe, locating the rope at the bottom. She tied the rope in a knot on the bed frame and opened the window. Peering through it, she saw a man standing in the garden.

Ethan must have practically flown down the stairs!

Sophie threw her rope out of the window and then, holding tightly, swung one leg out and then the other. She lowered herself slowly down the exterior of the house, grateful for the protection of her gloves from the friction of the rope. Swinging to the side a few feet, she carefully missed her former adversary—the prickly bush. When she reached the bottom, she exhaled in relief.

"What in the blazes are you doing?"

She let go of the rope and turned. The man brooding in the garden was not Ethan, but Charles. "Why are you not at the party?"

Light spilled into the garden and Ethan stood in the doorway. Charles looked from Sophie to Ethan and back to Sophie with a scrutiny that made her feel uncomfortable.

"Are you eloping?"

"Of course not," Sophie said defiantly. "I'm running away."

"Charles," Ethan said, closing the door behind him and walking toward his cousin. "I have something to say of a rather awkward nature."

"I know about Mariah Carter," Charles said sharply.

Sophie was rarely ever surprised, but she was downright shocked for the second time that evening. She tripped over the rope on the ground and stumbled a few steps before grabbing Ethan's arm to balance herself. "You do?"

"Excellent," Ethan said, steadying her. "Sophie is going to stay with my mother tonight, and we'll all come back tomorrow for Mariah. Please keep the secret for a little longer. We don't want to give the gossips anything to talk about."

"Like a young woman running away in the night with a single gentleman?" Charles said in the same disapproving tone.

"Blame that on your guardian," Sophie snapped. "If she'd had the decency to invite both Mariah and me to stay with her, we wouldn't have been forced to pretend to be the same person. And I wouldn't need to be leaving in the middle of the night."

"We'd best be off before we meet anyone else," Ethan said.

Charles nodded, and Ethan briefly touched his arm as they walked past him and out of the garden. Sophie led him down the alleyway to his carriage on the street. Ethan handed her into the dark vehicle.

"Home, Winkler."

Ethan climbed into the carriage and sat beside her. Sophie could only see the outline of his face from the gas lanterns on the side of the carriage. The carriage lurched forward, and Sophie fell into Ethan's arms.

"I missed you so much, Sophie," Ethan whispered.

She pressed her lips to his.

TWENTY-ONE

IT TOOK ALL MARIAH'S SELF-CONTROL not to weep at the party. Charles didn't return to the ballroom for nearly a half hour after she did, and he didn't look at her again until they stood by the door to bid the guests farewell. When he finally acknowledged her presence, she couldn't tell if his expression held anger or contempt. Possibly both.

What a mess I've made of things, Mariah thought as she walked slowly back to her room. She schooled her face into a smile. She couldn't let Sophie know that she'd betrayed their secret . . . twice. She opened the door and saw no sign of her sister. The bed was made, but a rope was tied to the corner post, and their window left open. Mariah saw a scrap of paper on top of the desk. She hurried over and read it.

She gasped. Sophie was gone. Mrs. Miller seemed like a

kind woman, but Mariah could not help but feel a pang of regret at leaving. She would miss this house and all the books inside it. She would even miss Aunt Bentley and the opportunity to learn more about her mother. But most of all, if she was being honest with herself, she would miss Charles. Their talks about books. Their walks. And their adventures together.

She didn't bother to undress. She climbed into the bed face-first and buried her head into the pillow, finally releasing the tears that had been threatening to come out all evening.

Mariah woke up when Adell entered her room with her breakfast.

"Miss Sophie, you ought to have gotten undressed last night," Adell scolded, placing the tray on the table beside the bed. "Your dress is all wrinkled. Although, how you manage to get in and out without my help is a mystery."

Mariah wanted to put the pillow over her head and hide from the daylight, but she couldn't hide from her feelings for Charles.

"Would you help me dress today, Adell?"

"Of course, miss," she said. "I'm always willing to help. It's my job."

Adell helped Mariah out of her beautiful—but very wrinkled—gown and into a morning dress of light green with a large white collar. After Mariah dismissed Adell, she sat down at the table to sip her hot chocolate and reread Sophie's letter about leaving their aunt's house. *Aunt Bentley*; Mariah cringed when she thought about how Aunt Bentley would take the news of their charade. Mariah knew she would be livid, but would she reject her as Mrs. Trenton had? Or could Aunt Bentley forgive them as she hadn't been able to forgive their mother?

Mariah felt tears well up in her eyes, but she forced herself not to cry. If Charles was leaving today, then she needed to give Aunt Bentley the miniature for him. Mariah collected all her painting supplies and the art lesson letters from Mr. Ruskin and put them in the old carpetbag she'd brought from the Ellises'. She opened the table drawer and pulled out the small oval picture of her aunt. It was nearly done; she just needed to finish a few details. She dipped her paintbrush in the water basin that Adell had brought for Mariah to wash her face with. Then she carefully opened the black paint, dipped the brush in, and meticulously added the lace circles to the collar on her aunt's dress.

When she was finished, Mariah washed her paintbrush and restored it to its place among her supplies. She stood up, resolutely breathing in and out. It was time to find out if her aunt knew the truth, and it was time to tell her that she was leaving today.

Mariah found her aunt in the yellow sitting room reading the morning newspaper.

"Sophie," Aunt Bentley said in surprise, putting down her newspaper. "I didn't expect to see you until the afternoon. You seemed quite done in after the party."

"There is something that I need to tell you," Mariah said.

Aunt Bentley shook her head. "There is no need. Charles has already explained about your invitation."

Mariah pressed her palm over her racing heart, relieved that he'd kept her confidence.

"Do sit down, Sophie. What are you holding?"

Mariah sat by her aunt on the settee and with trembling hands held out the miniature. "It might be a little wet still," she said. "Be careful that you only handle the sides for the next hour."

Aunt Bentley delicately accepted the little painting. "It looks exactly like me!"

"I hope so," Mariah said quietly.

Aunt Bentley brought it closer to her face and peered at every detail. She then placed the miniature on the side table.

"Thank you, Sophie," she said. "I see that you've inherited your mother's talent for art. She drew a sketch of me when we were girls, and Mama thought it was rather good."

"I didn't know that about my mother."

"The less said about her the better," Aunt Bentley said with an icy shift of tone. "She was a disappointment."

Mariah didn't know what to say in response and was relieved when the door opened.

"Charles!" Aunt Bentley called. "Don't stand in the

doorway. Come see the miniature Sophie painted of me for you."

Charles looked from Aunt Bentley to Mariah as he skulked into the room. Aunt Bentley handed the painting to him. Mariah felt light-headed as he sat down between them. He was close enough to touch and how she longed to place her hand on his arm. To express her gratitude for his every kindness to her.

"Very fine," he said after a few moments of quiet.

Mariah watched his face eagerly, but his eyes never looked in her direction.

Aunt Bentley seemed unaware of their constraint. "I was about to talk to Sophie about her plans to stay with the Millers."

"I hope I haven't offended you by accepting Mrs. Miller's invitation without consulting you first."

"Not at all," Aunt Bentley said with a rare smile of approval. "It's a prudent move on your part to secure a good match."

"Mrs. Miller was also kind enough to invite my sister, Mariah, to stay with her," Mariah said, trying to ignore her reddening cheeks.

"Your filial feelings do you credit, Sophie," Aunt Bentley replied. "It was thoughtful of you to ask Mrs. Miller to include your sister in her invitation."

Mariah looked down at her shaking hands and clenched them into fists. "Mr. Miller has already gone to Lyme Regis and escorted my sister here to their home in London. I believe she'll be coming with Mrs. Miller today to fetch me . . . I'm sorry if our haste causes you any inconvenience, Aunt Bentley. You've been so generous to me, inviting me to stay and purchasing my clothes. I can't thank you enough."

Charles stood up, walking over to stare out the window. As if he could not bear to even look at Mariah.

Aunt Bentley wrinkled her nose and sniffed. "The Millers are fond of having their own way—which their fortune, of course, allows them to. I'll have Adell pack your clothes. Did Mrs. Miller tell you a time, or are we to sit around all day at their convenience?"

"I-I'm sorry . . . I don't know what time," she admitted. "But before I leave, I was hoping to pay a short visit to Sir Thomas Watergate and Mrs. Spooner next door."

"I wasn't aware you were at all acquainted with *those* people."

"We met quite by chance," Mariah explained. "Sir Thomas is a great artist and has been so kind as to give me some advice on technique. I wouldn't wish to slight them."

"I suppose a short call would be adequate," Aunt Bentley said. "Would you like me to accompany you?"

"No!" Mariah said, almost too quickly. "I mean, I really don't think that it is necessary. I won't be there longer than a quarter of an hour, and I'm sure you wish to speak to Charles privately before he leaves for New York."

"Yes," she agreed. "There is much to go over about the estate."

"I'll miss you, Aunt Bentley," Mariah said, and was surprised to realize how true those words were.

Aunt Bentley sniffed and blinked several times. It was the most emotion Mariah had ever seen from her aunt; perhaps she was actually fond of Mariah in her own way. "Let us not get maudlin," she said bracingly. "Pierce, the second footman, will accompany you on your call."

"Thank you, Aunt," Mariah said, a *farewell* hidden in her words. She took a step toward Charles but lost her nerve. "Goodbye, Charles."

He nodded but didn't say a word.

Mariah walked down the steps of her aunt's house, twenty feet to the next house, and back up the steps, Pierce faithfully trailing behind her.

The Watergates' butler answered their door and ushered Mariah into the sitting room. She was about to sit on the couch when Mrs. Spooner burst in.

"My dear, which one are you?"

Mariah laughed, something she wouldn't have thought herself capable of an hour ago. "Mariah Carter, ma'am."

Mrs. Spooner took both of Mariah's hands and squeezed them. "Sit down, dear girl, I see that you're making a formal call. With a footman, too! How fancy of you."

Mariah sat next to Mrs. Spooner and smiled. "I'm afraid that it's not so much a formal call as a formal farewell.

Mrs. Miller has kindly invited both Sophie and me to stay with her."

"I'll miss my attic guests," Mrs. Spooner said with a sigh. "I daresay the only ones I'll find now will be mice."

"I'll miss you, too. Both of you," Mariah said. "I've learned so much from your husband about painting, and so much from you about kindness."

"Are you going to be staying with Mrs. Miller indefinitely?"

"For a little while; Sophie is looking for an apprenticeship with an inventor and I'm hoping to continue pursuing my art education and find my own employment. I have a small legacy that will keep me."

"I'm glad that you're not abandoning your art. Ah!" Mrs. Spooner said, tapping a finger against the side of her nose. "I have some news for you. The Royal Academy of Arts will debut Sir Thomas's *Joan of Arc,* and they've agreed to display your painting in their gallery as well."

"*My* painting?!"

"I entitled it *Sisters,*" Mrs. Spooner said. "I hope you don't mind. I've a knack for naming things, you know."

"Mind?" Mariah cried, wiping happy tears from her eyes. "I'm now doubly indebted to you."

"Off with you," Mrs. Spooner said with a warm smile. "Say farewell to your uppity aunt and go stay with the Millers. I'll see that Sir Thomas sends you an invitation to the debut."

Mariah gave Mrs. Spooner one last hug, then returned

to her aunt's house. She took off her hat and quickly climbed the stairs. When she opened the door to her room, she saw the housekeeper, Mrs. Kimball, and Adell standing by a trunk. Mrs. Kimball gave her a curt nod and Adell bobbed a curtsy.

"We're all done packing your things, Miss Carter," Mrs. Kimball said. "Come, Adell."

With another nod, Mrs. Kimball left the room, Adell trailing behind her. Mariah lay down on the bed. She could feel fresh tears rising but willed them not to fall.

It was time to go.

This house was not her home—it never had been. Charles didn't love her, and she didn't need to be loved by him. She had herself, she had her sister, and she didn't need anyone else. Mariah fell into a fitful sleep and was awakened by a smart rap on her door.

"Come in."

Adell gently pushed open the door. "Lady Bentley would like you in the front sitting room, miss."

"Thank you, Adell," Mariah said. "I'll come immediately."

She straightened her red curls, tucking one strand of hair behind her ear. Then she sighed and walked the familiar path down the hall to the grand staircase and onward to the sitting room. She could hear the squeak of the front door opening—Sophie was here.

Her aunt was sitting on a sofa with a book in her hand—which she was not reading. Charles was still standing by the window, his face shadowed by the light. His complexion almost looked gray, the same color it had been when he was sick.

"Sit, Sophie, and look employed," Aunt Bentley said brusquely. "We don't want the Millers to assume we waited all day for their arrival."

Which, of course, they had. Mariah sat down in a chair, just as the butler opened the door to the sitting room.

"Mr. Miller and Mrs. Miller," Mr. Taylor said, "and Miss Carter."

Mariah sighed in relief, but still felt her color mounting. She stood and shook hands with Mrs. Miller, who smiled at her, then looked over her shoulder to see Sophie and Mr. Miller. Ethan stepped toward her and bowed over her hand. Sophie threw her arms around Mariah and squeezed her tightly. Mariah pulled back and saw that Sophie was glowing with happiness in a borrowed gown.

"Miss Mariah Carter, allow me to introduce you to your aunt, Lady Bentley," Mrs. Miller said with a knowing smile.

Sophie smiled and curtsied to Aunt Bentley, whose eyes were as large as coins.

"My goodness, child," she said. "I had no idea you were so exactly the same."

"We may look alike, Aunt Bentley, but we are not at all the same," Sophie said with a wink at Mariah.

"Miss Carter," Ethan said, taking Sophie by the elbow and turning her toward Charles, "may I introduce you to my cousin, Lord Bentley."

Sophie curtsied. "Lord Bentley."

"Miss Carter," Charles said blankly. He took her hand and briefly bent over it.

Mrs. Miller kept the conversation going for a quarter of an hour, before Aunt Bentley called for the butler and instructed him to have "Miss Sophie's" things brought down and put into the carriage. Mrs. Miller thanked Lady Bentley for a lovely visit and went to wait for the rest of the party by the door. Sophie and Ethan followed behind her.

"I hope to see you soon, Aunt Bentley," Mariah said, surprising Aunt Bentley by embracing her. The older woman stood stiffly for a moment before softening and patting Mariah on the back.

Mariah turned to Charles and held out her hand. After a moment of hesitation, he took hers; his hand shook a little.

"I said some words last night that I'm sorry for this morning," she said softly so that only Charles could hear. "I hope you prove everything you've set out to prove, especially to yourself. But most of all I hope you find happiness."

Charles didn't say anything. He bent over her hand before letting it go.

Mariah walked to Sophie and gratefully allowed her sister to put her arm around her waist. They left the house and entered the carriage, Ethan and Mrs. Miller seated on one side and Sophie and Mariah seated on the other.

"What a relief that's over," Mrs. Miller said, as they

pulled away from the Bentleys' house. She smiled kindly at the sisters. "Now, Sophie, introduce me properly to your sister."

"Mrs. Miller, this is my sister, Mariah," Sophie said with another of her dazzling smiles. "She's a very talented painter and has all the sensibility I lack."

Mariah blushed as Sophie and the Millers laughed.

"Mariah, I'm delighted to formally meet you," Mrs. Miller said. "And I'm thrilled to have you stay with me for as long as you wish. All of my daughters are married, and I find myself quite without any female company. You're doing me a great favor."

"Thank you, Mrs. Miller," Mariah said with a sniff. "I hope I won't be a burden for too long."

"You couldn't be!" Mrs. Miller insisted with a wave of her hand. "I am delighted to have you for a companion while you pursue your art."

Mariah looked into the woman's face and saw only sincerity and caring. Her own eyes began to water; for so long she'd craved the love and attention of a mother figure. Sophie quickly supplied a handkerchief for her sister and gave her a one-armed hug.

"I would like very much to be your companion," Mariah said wetly.

Mrs. Miller beamed. "There's just one thing. I insist that my companions have only the most stylish of clothes, so I'll have to take you both shopping for your own wardrobes. And

I daresay each of you will like to select clothing that reflects your own unique personality."

"Are you sure?" Mariah gently teased. "Sophie will want to purchase trousers."

Everyone in the carriage laughed.

TWENTY-TWO

"I'M AFRAID THAT MISS CARTER is simply too old to be accepted for an apprenticeship," said Mr. Moore, owner of Moore's Curios Shop. "I never accept apprentices over the age of fourteen."

"Thank you for your time, Mr. Moore," Ethan said politely.

Sophie could hardly manage a curtsy to Mr. Moore, because the only time his beady eyes had looked at her during the interview, they'd been focused on her chest rather than her face. She sighed as she put her hand on Ethan's arm.

He patted her hand lightly. "Don't lose heart. I have two more interviews lined up."

Ethan helped her back into the carriage and they drove for several blocks to a large building with a garish sign that read LONG'S EMPORIUM. They walked inside and Sophie was surprised to see a tidy showroom with every item for sale displayed perfectly, not a speck of dust to be seen. There was a young man standing on a stool dusting the higher shelves. His shirtsleeves were rolled up, and Sophie could see bruises on his arms. When he noticed them walk in, the young man quickly unrolled his sleeves and clambered down from the stool to bow to Ethan and Sophie. She instantly felt sympathy for him.

"We have an appointment with Mr. Long," Ethan said, handing the young man his card.

"This way, sir."

They followed him up a narrow staircase to a spotless parlor with two sofas and three chairs. He picked up a bell on the table and rang it. Mr. Long, presumably, came into the room. He had a narrow face lined with black sideburns that reached down to his jaw. Behind him, a woman in a white cap came rushing into the room with one hand on her cap to keep it on her head. Sophie thought she must be the housekeeper.

"Mr. Miller, allow me to introduce my wife, Mrs. Long."

Mr. Long cleared his throat and Mrs. Long bobbed an awkward curtsy before looking at her husband for direction. Mr. Long raised his eyebrows at her, and she shrank a little from him before saying, "Do please sit down."

"You have a lovely home," Sophie said, sitting on a sofa next to Ethan.

"We do indeed," Mr. Long agreed. "And it's a good

thing, too, because I require all of my apprentices to live with us, and Mrs. Long treats them like they're her own children, don't you, Mrs. Long?"

"I-I do," Mrs. Long said, her eyes wide and fearful. "M-my very best."

Sophie knew that fear and pitied the woman.

"I'm sure you do," Ethan said encouragingly.

"There's no need to beat around the bush," Mr. Long said as he looked at Ethan. "I'd be prepared to take Miss Carter on for my usual premium."

Sophie cleared her throat. "What is your usual fee?"

Mr. Long glanced her way, but his eyes returned to Ethan's. "Five hundred pounds."

"Five hundred pounds!" she exclaimed. A quarter of her legacy from Captain Trenton!

"It's not a bad premium for a seven-year apprenticeship, when you consider housing and board are included," Mr. Long explained.

"Do your apprentices receive wages?" Sophie asked.

"They receive a small yearly stipend for clothing and other necessities."

I've already worked eight years without wages, I'm not about to work any longer for free, Sophie thought furiously.

"Thank you, Mr. Long. I'll consider your offer," she said, standing. "Mrs. Long, goodbye."

"Don't consider too long, Mr. Miller," Mr. Long said. "I only have the one opening and it won't be vacant long."

"We will let you know shortly," Ethan said, and again touched his hat before squiring Sophie down the stairs and out of the establishment. She was relieved to leave the heat of the shop and the oppressive atmosphere. Even the close air of the carriage was preferable.

"If you're worried about the money—" Ethan began, but Sophie placed a finger on his lips.

"Don't. I know you're only being kind, but I cannot and will not accept any money from you. Mariah and I already live in your home and your mother purchases our clothing. You know that I wish to be an independent woman."

Ethan kissed her finger and gently held her hand. "I respect your independence, Miss Carter."

"Thank you very much, Mr. Miller," Sophie said. "And I would not apprentice to Mr. Long even if he offered to teach me for nothing."

"Why not?"

"Did you not see the bruises on his apprentice?"

Ethan shook his head.

"And how his wife startled in fright every time he spoke?"

"I'm sorry. I'm afraid it escaped my notice."

Of course Ethan hadn't noticed. He'd never known fear or its twin sister, hunger. Sophie subconsciously shook herself. It wasn't his fault that he didn't recognize the signs. "Where are we going next?"

"Mr. Elias Cooper, horologist."

"A clockmaker?"

"I thought that your previous experience with clocks would be to your advantage," he said with an apologetic smile.

"I hope so."

Mr. Elias Cooper's horologist shop was tucked in the back of an alley with only a small sign above the door. Ethan opened the door and a bell hanging from the doorknob chimed. The shop was tiny and very untidy. The walls and shelves were lined with all sorts of fancy clocks that Sophie had never even seen before—a cuckoo clock, a triple-decker clock, a mahogany beehive shelf clock, a steeple clock with reverse fusee movement, and wall clocks with painted pictures beneath the clock's face. Other clocks had glass windows that showed their pendulum swinging back and forth.

Through a back door came a slight, older gentleman with round spectacles and an impressive gray beard that reached past his waist. He looked at Sophie through his spectacles as if appraising her.

"Mr. Cooper, may I introduce you to Miss Carter?" Ethan said formally.

Sophie stuck out her hand, but Mr. Cooper turned away from her. Self-consciously she let it fall to her side. When he turned back to them, he was holding a large shelf clock in his hands.

"I prefer demonstrations to words, Miss Carter," he said as he set the shelf clock on the table. "I would like you to first tell me what is wrong with this clock and then, if you can, fix it."

A smile formed on Sophie's face as she pulled off her

gloves. She lovingly touched the wooden casing of the shelf clock—it was mahogany—then opened the back and saw that it was a thirty-hour clock, time and strike, and weight driven. She turned the crank to raise the weight, which should have started the clock ticking, but it didn't.

Carefully she checked the wheels, the rack, the snail, the ratchet, the hour hand, and the minute hand—they all looked to be in working order. She looked closer at the verge, the movement part that touches the pendulum and causes it to go back and forth, and noticed that it was crooked.

"The verge is bent," Sophie said, then carefully bent the part back into position. She instantly heard a beautiful telltale *ticktock*: The clock was working again. Sophie closed the back and, out of habit, dusted it off before turning back to Mr. Cooper.

"Very good, Miss Carter," he said. "Can you also repair a spring-driven clock?"

"Yes."

"Your skills have not been exaggerated."

"I'm eighteen years old," Sophie said, her eyes darting to Ethan. "Some of the other masters thought I was too old to be apprenticed."

"You're not too old, per se," Mr. Cooper said, stroking his long gray beard. "I accept apprentices up to the age of twenty-one."

"Excellent," Ethan said with a hopeful smile.

Mr. Cooper stroked his long beard again. "Where did you learn how to repair clocks?"

"From Mr. Nathaniel Ellis," Sophie said. "He is a retired navy sailor who serviced ships' chronometers. I helped him in his clock shop for the last eight years."

He clucked his tongue. "He taught you well."

"Mr. Cooper, may I ask what you would teach me if I were to be your apprentice?"

"Since you already seem to understand basic clock maintenance, I would probably first start with oscillation and regulators."

"I'm already familiar with both."

"The different levers?"

"I know how to repair and set the top lever, maintenance, count, warning, J, and hammer levers."

He rubbed his beard again. "I see. Are you at all familiar with German cuckoo clocks?"

"I confess, I'm not."

"Fascinating little creatures," he said. "I could teach you all about them."

"Then you would be willing to take me on?"

Mr. Cooper laughed, a low raspy sound. "I would be a fool not to. You're clearly a very talented young lady."

"Thank you," Sophie said, exhaling. "I'll think about it, if I may?"

"You can have as much time as you'd like—we have an abundance of time in this shop," Mr. Cooper said with another raspy laugh at his own jest.

Sophie smiled. "You do indeed. Thank you, sir."

"Best of luck, Miss Carter," Mr. Cooper said, and he did not wait to watch them leave but turned his back to them and started fiddling with a cuckoo clock.

Ethan closed the door behind them. "Why didn't you accept his offer on the spot?"

Sophie lifted her chin. "Because he couldn't teach me anything that I wanted to know."

He nodded. "I see. Shall we keep looking?"

"No. Standing in his shop, I realized that I didn't need to apprentice myself to anyone: clockmaker, tinker, or inventor," she said, feeling a sense of calm in her soul. "I'm going to open my own shop and create my own inventions."

"Excuse me, Miss Sophie," the butler said with a bow, handing her a card. "A Mrs. Spooner to see you."

"Thank you, Mr. Jenkins," she replied. "I'll come at once."

Sophie stood and followed Jenkins to the sitting room, where Mrs. Spooner looked uncomfortable and out of place, sitting on the edge of the sofa.

"Mr. Jenkins, would you please be so good as to order tea for us?"

"Of course, Miss Carter."

Sophie held out her hands to the lady. "Mrs. Spooner, it's a delight to see you."

Mrs. Spooner took Sophie's thin hands into her plump

ones and gave them a squeeze. "The delight is all mine, Miss Carter."

"We're friends, you must still call me Sophie!"

Mrs. Spooner laughed. "I will then, Sophie. And I should, as a friend, give you leave to use my given name, but I would much rather you didn't. It's Prudence. Even shortened to Prudie, it's insufferable. What were my parents thinking?"

Sophie laughed with her and gestured for her to sit. "I still believe I should call you Lady Watergate."

"Me, a lady?" Mrs. Spooner said, shaking her head. "I haven't the manners to be called a lady, nor the birth, as I'm sure you're well aware."

"Your manners are much better than your husband's," Sophie persisted. "And he's called Sir Thomas."

"He was born into a higher class."

"But it's *your* money that makes him the artist he is."

Mrs. Spooner shrugged. "Money can't buy birth. I know you mean well, Sophie, but I wouldn't wish to embarrass him or myself."

Sophie took her hand and gave it another small squeeze. "You wouldn't embarrass Sir Thomas. I don't think anyone could."

Mrs. Spooner gave a loud chuckle. "I trust you've received Sir Thomas's invitation to the premier of *Joan of Arc* at the Royal Academy of Arts?"

"Yes, indeed!" Sophie replied. "And I'd be delighted to see Lady Watergate there as well."

"Who is she?"

"*You* are," she said. "And London society will know it, and they'll adore you just as you are."

"I suppose I could come," Mrs. Spooner said reluctantly. "I wouldn't have to speak to nobody."

"Except for Ethan and myself," Sophie said. "He's been eager to see the painting ever since I first told him about posing for it. He can hardly wait—I daresay we'll be there so early that the doors will still be locked."

Mr. Jenkins entered the room with a tea tray. He set it on the sofa table and bowed deeply to the ladies. Sophie nodded regally. He stood up straight and walked out of the room.

"His manners would put a duke to shame," Mrs. Spooner remarked, putting a hand to her bosom.

Sophie laughed so hard, she spilled the tea she was pouring. "I know! It quite disconcerts me. But he's so very efficient and really quite kind. Unlike my Aunt Bentley's odious butler, Mr. Taylor."

Sophie handed a teacup to Mrs. Spooner.

"Your sister's painting will be displayed that night as well," she said.

"Yes, I'm equally eager to see it."

Mrs. Spooner lifted her cup to her lips, but she didn't drink. Instead she placed it back on the saucer. "Is Mariah still pining for Lord Bentley?"

"Charles?" Sophie asked incredulously. "How could she fancy *him*?"

Mrs. Spooner laughed. "Different tastes, my dear, different tastes. She seemed quite despondent when I saw her in Oxsham's Bookshop yesterday, despite her fancy new clothes."

"Oh," Sophie said, looking down at her cream lace gloves that were so delicate a spider could have spun them. She felt dreadful. She'd been so wrapped up in Ethan and finding an apprenticeship that she hadn't noticed Mariah's melancholia.

"Speaking of wardrobes," Mrs. Spooner said. "I've a notion that I believe will cheer her up and make Mariah's painting unforgettable. But I need your help."

"Please, tell me," Sophie said, leaning forward.

TWENTY-THREE

"WE'LL BE DREADFULLY LATE!" Mariah cried, stamping her foot impatiently. "Ethan already left with his mother and grandfather!"

"I won't be more than a minute now," Sophie called. "Miss Barker is finishing my hair."

Mariah looked down at her white silk dress. The sleeves went all the way to her wrists, and the collar was high on her neck. The waist was pointed with a bell-shaped skirt and two ruffles. Mariah's lady's maid, Miss Hansen, had parted her hair down the middle and braided each side into a bun at the back of her head. It looked rather plain, but Miss Hansen assured her that it was very fashionable and how Queen Victoria wore her own dark locks.

At last, Sophie opened the door, and Mariah's mouth

dropped open in surprise. Around Sophie's face were countless red ringlets. Her black dress combined velvet and silk, complete with pointed bodice, scooped neck, and lace-trimmed skirt and sleeves. It was as ornate as Mariah's was simple. They were foils of each other, just like in Mariah's painting.

"Good gracious!" Mariah exclaimed. "But you haven't seen my painting yet . . . How—?"

Sophie spun in a circle so that Mariah could see the full effect of her gown. "It was Lady Watergate's idea, and I thought it was an excellent one."

"I had no idea!"

Sophie linked arms with her sister. "What an entrance we'll make."

"A late one," Mariah grumbled.

"Lady Watergate suggested we be late," Sophie explained. "Although, I didn't mean to be quite *this* late."

When they arrived in Trafalgar Square, Mariah saw the familiar National Gallery building with its domed roof and Roman pillars. She thought instantly of the last time she'd been there—with Charles. She felt a pain, as real as any physical injury, somewhere between her chest and her heart. She had not seen him in over a month, but the separation did nothing to ease the bitterness of their parting. Aunt Bentley had called on Mrs. Miller once to tell her that Charles had not sailed to America. He'd taken ill and traveled to his estate in the country to recover.

She hoped he was well and wanted to see him again—and yet dreaded it.

The Royal Academy of Arts occupied the east wing of the National Gallery. The footman assisted the sisters from the carriage. Sophie linked arms with Mariah, and they proceeded up the stone steps and into the building. When they entered the main gallery, there was a sudden hush, and it seemed to Mariah that every eye in the large room was upon them.

The quiet didn't seem to daunt Sophie, because she immediately began to walk through the room, pulling Mariah alongside her. She nodded to several acquaintances as the crowd seemed to part for them. Sophie led them first to *Joan of Arc*—framed, it looked majestic, and Mariah would have followed the woman in that painting into any battle.

"It turned out rather nice," Sophie remarked.

Mariah touched her heart. "It's a masterpiece! I daresay people will still be coming to see it in one hundred years."

"I'm sure Sir Thomas thinks so," she said with a mischievous smile. "Let's go over and talk to him and Lady Watergate."

Mariah was surprised to see Mrs. Spooner looking plumper and prettier than ever in an elaborate velvet dress, a shade somewhere between maroon and crimson, with large bell-like sleeves. Sir Thomas looked decidedly less elegant in a black suit with a rumpled cravat. They stood alone, several feet away from his painting.

"*Lady Watergate*, always a pleasure," Sophie said in a loud voice with a wink. "And Sir Thomas, I believe your *Joan* is quite the hit."

Mariah managed to add, "Lovely to see you, Lady Watergate and Sir Thomas."

Sir Thomas only grunted in response. Ethan came up to them, and Sophie released her hold on Mariah's arm to take his arm instead.

"Sir Thomas, your painting is exquisite," he said.

"It is indeed," said another voice from behind them.

The group turned to see who had spoken. He was a young man with brown curly hair, soulful eyes, a mustache, and a goatee. On his arm was a tall young woman with abundant coppery-gold hair, a small mouth, a distinct chin, and a long neck. Mariah thought her entirely paintable.

"Gabriel," Sir Thomas said. "I'm glad you could make it."

Lady Watergate cleared her throat. "Allow me to introduce Mr. Dante Gabriel Rossetti, one of the founders of the Pre-Raphaelite Brotherhood, and Miss Elizabeth Siddal. Like you, Sophie, um—Miss Carter, she has been a model for paintings."

Mr. Rossetti gave a curt bow, and Miss Siddal curtsied. "Watergate, you are a man of real genius," Mr. Rossetti stated. "Your painting has the marvels of finish and imaginative detail, unequalled by anything except perhaps Albrecht Dürer's finest works."

Mariah looked at Sir Thomas and was shocked to see him

blushing. He tried to speak, but she couldn't understand his sputtering in Gaelic.

"Come, Miss Carter," Lady Watergate said, pulling the focus off Sir Thomas. "Allow me to show you where your painting is. I hope you like the frame I selected."

Mariah allowed herself to be led to the corner of the room. The frame Lady Watergate had chosen was gold with ornate carvings of grapevines and six-inches thick. It made the painting appear larger and more significant. Mr. Eustace Miller, Mrs. Miller, and Aunt Bentley stood observing her painting.

And so did Charles.

Her heart pounded most uncomfortably at the sight of him. But Mrs. Miller held out her hands to Mariah and embraced her, and the thudding in Mariah's chest calmed a little.

"A triumph, my dear Mariah, a triumph," Mrs. Miller said loudly.

Mariah felt the tears rise. Mrs. Miller, upon whom she had no claim whatsoever, had welcomed her into her home and treated her like family. She turned to Mr. Eustace Miller, who gave her arm a squeeze. "We'll have to be buying you more painting supplies, girl. You've got talent and I'm not too blind yet to see it."

"Thank you, Mr. Miller," Mariah said, wiping a tear from her eye with a gloved hand. "You've been so kind."

"Here, please take my handkerchief," Charles said

quietly. He held out a familiar white cloth with the Bentley family crest embroidered in the corner.

Mariah's hand brushed his as she accepted the handkerchief, bringing it to her eyes and dabbing at the tears on each side.

"Very creditable," Aunt Bentley said. "You and Sophie both seem to be blessed with artistic talents."

Mariah was already blushing, but at this comment, she felt her face go positively fiery. She heard Sophie's laugh. She and Ethan had come to join them in front of her painting.

"But I am sure you'll agree with me, Aunt Bentley, that Mariah is greatly my superior in talent," Sophie said. "Her work has so much life in it. I may be *slightly* biased, but I've never seen a better painting."

"The colors and contrasts are incredible," Ethan added.

"Sophronia," Mrs. Miller said, "I see Mrs. Heathcote over by Sir Thomas Watergate's painting. Shall we go speak to her?"

Mrs. Miller didn't wait for Aunt Bentley's assent, but took her arm and steered Aunt Bentley away. Over her shoulder, she added, "Come, Father, Ethan, Sophie."

Sophie laughed again and winked at Mariah before obediently following Mrs. Miller.

Mariah and Charles stood alone before the painting. The hammering in her chest was so wild she wondered if Charles could hear it.

"I'm so glad that you are recovered . . . again," Mariah

murmured, but she couldn't quite bring herself to meet his eyes. "I was so worried."

"You needn't worry anymore," he replied, and Mariah could feel his gaze on her.

She folded the handkerchief and held it out to him. He closed his hands over hers and said in a low voice, "Keep it."

Mariah finally found the courage to look at him. "I'm afraid that I'm obtaining quite a collection of your handkerchiefs."

"There is no person to whom I would rather give them," he said, letting go of her hand.

Then why have you not called on me? But Mariah wasn't bold enough to ask. She tucked his handkerchief into her pocket. "Will you be at Mrs. Miller's party the day after tomorrow?"

"Yes, I'll be there."

"I was only wondering . . . supposing . . . perhaps that you might have plans to return to New York. Now that you're well."

"No," Charles said, shaking his head slightly. "I have no immediate plans to return to America."

"Oh. Well. If it's not too impertinent for me to ask," Mariah said in a breathy voice, "what *are* your plans?"

Charles rubbed his neck tiredly. "While I was recovering at my estate, I had plenty of time to contemplate my life. Who I was. What I wanted. And not what others wanted for me."

"And . . . ?"

Charles let his hand drop and he gave her a smile that warmed her whole body.

"I discovered that I liked living in the country," he said. "I liked the view of the English Channel from my south fields. I liked the trees. I even liked the dirt. I liked the business of the estate and the duties of a landlord. And I loved the quiet—the seclusion of a country life."

"Do you mean to give up your place in your grandfather's business?"

"Yes," Charles said simply. "I inherited many business shares from my mother, and I intend to keep up with the business world and invest in it but give my days to something that I care about. Something that makes me happy. And I have you to thank for it."

"Me?" Mariah echoed in surprise. "What did I do?"

"You made me think about my life and about why I was on the path that I was on. I wasn't happy. The family business wasn't making me happy—competing with my cousin wasn't making me happy. I thought long and hard about what brought me joy, and that's when I realized that it wasn't London but rather my estate, my books, and everything that I'd taken for granted in my pursuit of accomplishments. You went out into the world to find yourself; I had to go home to find myself."

"I'm delighted for you," Mariah said, unable to contain her smile. "Have you told your family? Your grandfather?"

"Yes," he said. "I'm in disgrace. They think it's a result of my fever, that my brain must have been addled."

Mariah laughed and then covered her mouth with her gloved hand.

Charles grinned. "But I keep telling myself, if Miss Mariah Carter can be a painter, why can't I be a farmer?"

"Do you mean to farm the land yourself?"

"The home farm at the very least, Mar— Miss Carter," Charles said. "Possibly more of my land as I improve at it."

"Please, call me Mariah."

"Mariah." He said her name slowly, caressing every syllable. "I've wanted to speak to you—"

"Charles," Aunt Bentley's voice sounded from fifteen feet away. "Come and meet Mr. Rossetti. A most interesting young man."

Charles sighed and then took Mariah's gloved hand and lightly kissed it. "Au revoir."

As he walked away, Mariah clutched her own hand as if she were afraid it would fall off.

Charles kissed my hand!

The fluttering in her chest expanded to her whole body, and it seemed a medical miracle that she was able to remain standing at all. She turned away from Charles and Aunt Bentley, to find Mrs. Miller at her elbow.

"Trust Sophronia to interrupt a promising conversation," the older woman said with a sigh. She took Mariah by the arm and began to walk with her, nodding to several acquaintances and introducing Mariah to countless more.

Mariah managed to smile and mutter polite nothings, but her mind was on Charles. What had he been going to say when Aunt Bentley had interrupted him? Could he possibly still care for her after she had deceived him? After her harsh words the night of the party?

TWENTY-FOUR

MARIAH PICKED UP HER CHARCOAL pencil and slowly practiced outlining leaves depicted in *Baxter's British Flowering Plants*. Mr. Ruskin's letter said the next step was to lay the tracing paper over the book and see how accurate she'd managed to be. She was carefully lining up her sketch with the printed one beneath it when Mr. Jenkins came into the room.

"Lady Bentley to see you, Miss Carter," he announced.

Mariah instantly stood and curtsied as her aunt swept in behind Mr. Jenkins.

"Miss Car— Mariah," Aunt Bentley said with a curt nod. "I'm actually here to speak to Mr. Eustace Miller about Charles. Do you know when he will be home?"

Mariah shook her head. "I'm sorry, Aunt Bentley.

He went out visiting with Mrs. Miller, and I'm not sure when they'll be back. Is there anything I can assist you with?"

Aunt Bentley's hat was slightly crooked, and her shawl barely clung to one arm. Mariah had never seen her aunt look anything but polished and felt alarmed by her disarray. She led Aunt Bentley to a sofa.

"Shall I call for tea?" Mariah asked.

"No tea," Aunt Bentley said. "Tea will not make one drop of difference."

"What are you hoping to talk to Mr. Miller about?"

"Charles," Aunt Bentley said, taking her handkerchief out and sniffing into it.

"Has his sickness returned?" Mariah asked anxiously.

"No, no," Aunt Bentley said with a wave of her hand. "*Worse!* He has proved to be just as headstrong and foolish as my sister, with no thought about his adopted family and the sacrifices we've made for him. Only about what *he* wants."

Mariah stiffened at the mention of her mother but attempted to soothe her upset aunt. "What *does* he want?"

"To be a gentleman farmer, of all things," Aunt Bentley said reproachfully. "After all my efforts to ensure his place in his grandfather's company and in the highest society, he plans to forsake it all."

"Sometimes we have to love people for who they are and not for who we want them to be."

"He was *my* ward. He inherited *my* husband's estate. And all my plans for his future will come to naught," Aunt Bentley continued, as if she had not heard Mariah at all.

"Do you wish for his happiness?"

Aunt Bentley scoffed. "His *happiness*? He refuses to offer for Miss Penderton-Simpson. He says he has no regard for her. What more could he possibly desire? She has birth, beauty, breeding, and is an heiress to add to the bargain."

"Miss Penderton-Simpson is very lovely," Mariah agreed, "but we can't always help our feelings. And if he has no regard for her, you would not, I'm sure, wish for him to marry without *some* affection."

"He has no affection for me, it seems."

Mariah moved closer to her aunt on the sofa and cautiously put an arm around the older woman's shoulders.

"I'm sure Charles has great affection for you," she said carefully. "You were more than just his guardian: You're the only mother he's ever known."

Aunt Bentley shook her head vigorously. "Just as selfish as my sister. Just as foolish."

Mariah removed her arm from around her aunt and clenched her hands tightly in her lap.

"Your sister—*my* mother—is dead. You lost the opportunity to spend the last year of her life with her because you didn't agree with her choices. If you don't wish to lose Charles, too, I suggest that you support him and stop worrying what society may or may not think about it."

"You know nothing of society," Aunt Bentley admonished. "You're little more than a child."

"Charles is no longer your ward. He's a grown man now and is capable of making his own decisions. If you want his love, respect him," Mariah said, standing up. "I'll let Mr. and Mrs. Miller know that you called. Is there any other message you would like to leave? I would be happy to relay it for you."

Aunt Bentley stood, a look of disbelief on her face. She, Lady Bentley, a baroness, was being dismissed by her niece, the daughter of a wayward sister and a navy nobody.

"No message."

Mariah picked up the other side of her aunt's shawl that was askew and placed it gently back over her shoulder. Aunt Bentley gave a stiff nod and left the room.

She sat back at the table and looked at her leaf sketch, but her mind was on Charles. Absentmindedly she closed the book. She picked up one of her letters from Mr. Ruskin and turned over the last page, finding her sketch of Charles. She traced the lines of his face with her finger, lingering on the curve of his lips.

"You look very serious this morning, Mariah," Sophie remarked as she slouched down on the settee.

"I'm writing a letter to Mr. Ellis," Mariah said with a little sniff. "I told him that we were well and where we're staying. I thought perhaps we might include small gifts for the children. I can do it myself, if you'd rather not."

"Of course, I would be happy to purchase gifts for them," Sophie said. She looked at her beautiful yellow dress and delicate kid boots, remembering when she had arrived in London with her worn gray dress and one dilapidated pair of boots. "New material for clothes, too. And something nice for Mrs. Ellis . . . maybe some cloth for a new dress."

"That is kind of you," Mariah said, not even attempting to hide her knowing smile. "I thought you were finished with Mrs. Ellis."

Sophie smiled ruefully in return. "I suppose we're never truly finished with our pasts—they follow us wherever we go, like phantoms. Whoever we become is because of who we once were. I can't love Mrs. Ellis, but I can be grateful to her for taking us in when no one else did. Her life hasn't been an easy one, and perhaps if the world showed her a little more kindness, she would be more kind. She certainly couldn't be any meaner."

"*Sophie!*" Mariah scolded with a laugh. "Shall we go?"

Sophie and Mariah left the sitting room to find Jenkins standing at attention in the hall.

"Mr. Jenkins, always where I need you," Sophie said. "Would you please call a carriage for us?"

"Yes, Miss Sophie." He bowed deferentially and went about his task.

She and Mariah put on their hats and black lace mantilla shawls. Mr. Jenkins returned to escort them out the front door and open the door to the carriage—a privilege he never allowed a mere footman. Even if the footman would be accompanying them and he would not.

Mr. Pool, the third footman, trailed behind them like a puppy as the sisters ran their errands. He sat on the outside of the carriage and carried all their packages from the shops. Sophie selected six different pairs of children's boots at a bazaar. Mariah chose several bolts of sturdy cloth at a shop next to it and material with blue flowers for Mrs. Ellis.

They were on their way back to the Millers' house when Mariah touched Sophie's arm. "Oh, look! There's a toy shop. Could we stop here as well?"

"Yes, please," Sophie said. She leaned her head out the carriage window and asked the driver, Mr. Winkler, to please stop at the toy shop. Winkler expertly maneuvered the carriage through the busy London street, and Mr. Pool opened the door for them. Sophie was about to follow Mariah into the toy shop when she spotted a well-dressed man placing a sign on an empty shop next door: FOR LETTING, SEE MR. HICKMAN, REGENT'S STREET 115.

Sophie walked up to the older gentleman, and he tipped his hat to her.

"Are you looking for a new tenant, sir?" she asked him.

"I am indeed," he replied, tucking his thumbs into his striped waistcoat. "Mr. Edward Hickman's the name."

"How much?"

"For what?"

"To rent the shop for a year?" Sophie said, pointing to the sign on the door.

"One hundred pounds per annum," the gentleman said.

"May I see the inside?" Sophie asked eagerly.

The gentleman raised his eyebrows. "Do you know someone who would be interested in letting it?"

"You're looking at her."

"*You*," he said, his surprise obvious.

"Me."

"Oh," he said, eyeing her curiously. "Well, you are certainly dressed very stylishly, if I do say so myself. Are you a milliner or a haberdasher, miss?"

"Clockmaker and inventor," Sophie replied with a smirk. "Shall we go inside?"

He nodded, pulling out the brass key and unlocking the door for her. Sophie walked into the poorly lit room, the only light coming from the single front window. The space was narrow, probably only ten feet wide, but at least twice that distance long. It was completely devoid of furniture, but she didn't need to see tables or chairs to know what it could look like. She could use the money from Captain Trenton and build a row of shelves all along the east wall to display an assortment of clocks for sale. Then she could put a few worktables in the back area, a few serviceable chairs up front for customers, and her shop would be ready for business.

"I'll take it," Sophie said, holding out her hand. "One hundred pounds per year."

The gentleman reached out his hand and shook hers firmly. "I'll bring you the contract on Monday. What's your name and address, miss?"

"Sophie Carter," she said proudly, handing him her card with her name and address engraved on it. "And I'll have a bank draft ready for you then, Mr. Hickman."

"It's a pleasure doing business with you, Miss Sophie Carter."

"Might I lock it?" Sophie asked as she followed him outside the shop. He reached into his coat pocket and handed the brass key to her.

Sophie placed the key into the lock and turned it, laughing aloud. She was locking her very own shop!

"Thank you," she said, and held out the key to Mr. Hickman.

He shook his head. "You can keep it. It's your shop now, after all."

She could have embraced him, but she restricted herself to shaking his hand warmly with both of hers.

"Sophie, there you are!" Mariah cried, hurrying over from where the carriage stood by the curb. "I was worried."

Mr. Hickman bowed yet again to Sophie and sauntered down the street, whistling.

"Who was that man?"

"My landlord," Sophie said impishly, hooking her arm through Mariah's. "You're looking at the new proprietor of this shop."

Mariah let out a sound that was halfway between a shriek and a laugh. "I am so happy for you," she said, and squeezed Sophie tighter than a corset.

"If you don't strangle me before I can open it."

Mariah released Sophie but took her hands, and the sisters jumped up and down together, squealing and laughing. Mr. Pool waited patiently by the carriage until their celebrating was over to open the door for them.

"What are you going to name your shop?"

Sophie shrugged and climbed into the carriage after her sister. "I don't know. I'm sure I'll think of something spectacular."

"And I'll paint the name on the front window," Mariah promised.

They spent the rest of the ride back to the Millers' trying to come up with the perfect name for the shop.

As Mr. Pool helped them out of the carriage in front of the house, Ethan walked up to them with his hat in hand, his own carriage right behind theirs. "Out starting a revolution?" he asked.

"Only a bit of shopping," Sophie replied. "And I found myself the perfect shop."

Mariah and then Mr. Pool passed by them, the footman's arms full of brown paper packages.

"For shopping?" Ethan asked.

"No, no!" she said excitedly, pulling the brass key from her pocket and waving it in the air. "I saw a small shop for rent just a few streets away from here. I talked to the owner, and it's mine for the next year!"

"Sophie, you're a genius," Ethan said, grabbing her waist and spinning her around.

Her stomach flipped in delight. Even when her feet touched the pavement again, she still felt like she was flying.

"You're brilliant," Ethan said. "Now you can take on your own apprentices in your very own office."

"Shop," Sophie corrected.

"Office-shop," he said, grinning. "Oh, Sophie, I'm so delighted for you. When I said that I'll always support you and your dreams, I meant it. My only request is that you allow me to manufacture your notification clock when it's ready for production."

Sophie felt surely her heart would burst. "If we weren't on a public street, I would kiss you."

"I daresay we can remedy that problem."

Sophie laid her head against his shoulder. "I really should be getting dressed for the party."

"Must you dress this very moment?" Ethan asked as they walked through the front door of the house, hand in arm. "I wanted to give you a gift before the party."

"A gift?" Sophie repeated in surprise.

"I believe it's customary for a gentleman to present a token of affection to the lady he loves—" Ethan's face suddenly flared a brilliant shade of crimson. "I mean . . . rather, um . . . to the lady with whom he is, um . . . acquainted in a f-friendly manner."

The lady he loves.

Since Sophie had told him to slow down, Ethan had carefully avoided any words of affection. But he had just said that he loved her. *Loved her.* And she didn't feel sick or scared. She felt *wonderful*. All warm inside as if she'd drank a whole cup of hot chocolate in one swallow.

"All right then," Sophie said, trying not to smile. "If I ever go into battle again as Joan of Arc, I suppose I'll need a token of your affection. But I do hope it doesn't clash with my armor."

"It won't," Ethan assured her with a smile and a shake of his head.

He led her to the back of the house and outside into the small rose garden. The air was thick and sweet. The red blooms were as large as her fist, and the trees gently swayed in the summer breeze.

"Close your eyes," Ethan said.

Sophie dutifully shut them—mostly.

"You're peeking."

She closed her eyelids all the way.

"Now open your eyes."

When Sophie looked, Ethan was holding a velvet box. He flipped it open with his thumb; inside was an oval locket with a cluster of diamonds on the front that seemed to capture all the light in the garden in little rainbows. He opened the locket and on one side was a painted miniature of Mariah and on the other, Sophie.

She subconsciously touched her bare neck, struck speechless. The necklace was more spectacular and beautiful than anything she'd ever imagined, but it was the paintings that meant the world to her. In the locket, she and her sister would always be together.

"You said that you had no heirlooms from your mother, so I hired your sister to paint these miniatures. Hopefully, something that you can pass on someday," Ethan said, sounding nervous and unsure. "And I noticed that you touch your neck sometimes at parties and I thought perhaps you were wishing for a necklace . . . If you don't like it, I can always get you a nice set of diamond-studded clockworking tools instead."

Sophie took the velvet box from his hands and examined the little paintings, before closing the locket and seeing the sparkling white jewels. "I was disappointed in the Koh-i-noor diamond because it was so drab, and you assured me that well-cut diamonds do sparkle."

"I hope these diamonds are sparkly enough for you."

"They're perfectly sparkly . . . and I love what is inside of them even more. Thank you," Sophie whispered, before closing the velvet box and throwing her arms around him. She covered Ethan's face in kisses—his chin, his cheek, his eyes, his ears. He laughed, and Sophie pulled his head down and pressed her lips hard against his. Ethan put his hands through Sophie's hair and then slowly down her back, pressing her closer to him—for Sophie, they could never be close enough. She locked her fingers around his neck and kissed him again.

"I love you," she whispered.

Ethan gently brushed a curl from her face. "And I love you."

TWENTY-FIVE

SOPHIE PATTED THE DIAMOND LOCKET around her neck subconsciously as she looked down at her cream silk dress with a scooped neck and lace-trimmed skirt and sleeves. Her dressmaker had boasted that Queen Victoria wore a similar dress of Spitalfields silk to the grand opening of the Great Exhibition.

The Great Exhibition—the whole reason why she had written to her Aunt Bentley; why she had come to London; how she had met Ethan in the park and he took her to see the hydraulic press, the Koh-i-noor diamond, and the watches from Switzerland. From her apprenticeship interviews to her idea for a notification clock. So much had come from that one event, her one wish to catch even a glimpse of a bigger world.

"Ready, my love?" Ethan asked.

Sophie glanced up with a guilty grin. "I was admiring my finery."

He looked her up and down. "I don't blame you; there is plenty to admire. I could stare at you for a fortnight . . . possibly longer."

Sophie laughed. "Come, we don't want to be late for a party in your own house."

Ethan leaned in to kiss her, and she playfully pivoted away from him. "You'll muss up my hair."

"I won't disturb one curl."

"Liar," Sophie said, and leaned toward him for a soft kiss.

Ethan gently kissed her lips and then held out his arm. "Shall we, Miss Carter?"

Sophie linked her arm in his. "Yes, indeed, Mr. Miller."

He led her down the stairs to a large ballroom already full of people. Sophie released Ethan's arm and walked farther into the room until she saw Mariah, but her sister didn't notice her, deep in conversation with Charles. Sophie rolled her eyes.

"You cannot roll your eyes already," Adaline said, suddenly at her side. "The dancing has yet to begin."

"Adaline! I haven't seen you in an age."

Sophie embraced her friend, who was wearing an exquisite dress of scarlet velvet trimmed with black ribbons and worn with black lace undersleeves.

"Your sister seems to have quite captivated Lord Bentley,"

Adaline said bluntly. She nodded toward Mariah and Charles, who were talking as if they were the only people in the room.

"He does seem taken with her," Sophie said thoughtfully.

"If he'd been half as attentive to *me*," Adaline teased, "I would have sent for my dressmaker and started fittings for my wedding dress."

"I'm sorry—" Sophie started, but didn't know how to finish.

"That he preferred your sister to me?" Adaline said. "Don't be. I daresay there are other aristocrats to be caught. Although, probably not so young or so handsome."

"To be married just to be married, I think would be miserable," Sophie admitted. "Even with a title."

"Your relationship with Mr. Miller hasn't made *you* miserable."

Sophie couldn't contain her smile. "Being with him does make me happy. But I also think that I'm happy because I have interests all my own."

"Do tell," Adaline said, raising her eyebrows.

"I've told you before," she said. "I'm an inventor."

"A lady inventor?"

"Yes, and I have my very own clock shop," Sophie said proudly. "I haven't invented anything new yet, but I'm learning more and more about mechanisms. I keep experimenting and trying, and someday I know my invention is going to work."

"And I will be the first one to purchase it," Adaline stated. "Whatever it is."

"Thank you. You are a true friend."

"The truest," Adaline said with a wink.

Sophie bit back a smile. "You are! And I should hate to see someone I care about who is smart and compassionate and entirely delightful trapped in a loveless marriage for the sake of position."

"You want me to become a professional spinster?"

Sophie laughed. "No, but I believe you need to find something that brings you joy, whatever it may be. And then when your aristocrat comes along, with his many titles and large estate, you will only be the happier."

"I see your point, my dear Sophie," Adaline said. "But the only talent I seem to have is for society gossip."

Sophie wrinkled her nose in thought and then said, rather more loudly than she meant to, "You could be an authoress."

"An authoress?"

"Mariah has been reading all sorts of novels written by ladies."

"I'm sure my parents would not approve."

Sophie raised her eyebrows in response. "Even better."

"You're right," Adaline said in a conspiratorial whisper. "Their disapproval only makes the prospect more inviting to me."

"You could publish your works anonymously, and everyone who's anyone will be all agog to discover who the writer is of your fascinating stories."

Adaline grinned and fanned herself with her ivory-handle

fan. "Sophie, that does sound quite scintillating—perhaps I'll put my pen to paper and see what comes of it."

"And if you don't like writing, you must find some other interest."

"Yes, yes, enough serious talk," Adaline said, steering them around a group of older ladies chatting. "Did you hear that Lady Simford is about to become a double duchess?"

"A double duchess?"

"Yes, she is the dowager Duchess of Simford, and the rumor around the city is that she has accepted an offer of marriage from the elderly Duke of Essex, who was her suitor forty years ago. But because of some disagreement they parted, and she married the Duke of Simford."

"That is exactly the sort of story that would be a great novel."

Adaline laughed and squeezed her arm. "No more seriousness, Sophie. I'm here to dance."

They strolled together onto the dance floor, where Adaline was instantly asked to dance by a handsome young man. Sophie had only walked a step farther when Ethan appeared and offered his hand. Once she was in his arms, the familiar comfort and feeling of rightness settled in her chest. Over his shoulder, she saw Lady Watergate leading a very reluctant Sir Thomas to the dance floor. Sophie grinned and leaned in a little closer to Ethan, who tightened his hold on her waist. Together they turned around and around—dancing in perfect synchronization, like the wheels of a clock.

TWENTY-SIX

MARIAH FELT SELF-CONSCIOUS STANDING by Mrs. Miller and Mr. Eustace Miller, welcoming the guests to the party, but Mrs. Miller had been adamant that she be there. Mariah was now her dearest companion and should take her rightful place greeting the guests.

Despite the self-consciousness, the warm feeling of belonging surged again inside her heart. In a few short weeks, Mrs. Miller had somehow become the mother that Mariah had always wished for. She had also selected Mariah's gown of celestial blue silk with its wide-collared neck that showed off her shoulders and throat. Mrs. Miller introduced her to guest after guest as her "very dear companion, Miss Mariah Carter." Mariah mechanically held out her hand and smiled, until she saw his profile. Charles was here.

She breathed in too quickly and began to cough.

"Grandfather, Aunt Miller, Miss Carter, how do you do?" Charles asked.

"Fine," Mariah managed to say between coughs.

"Charles, why don't you take Mariah to get a drink?" Mrs. Miller suggested with a smile, and then turned back to speak to Aunt Bentley.

He took Mariah's elbow and guided her into the room. He picked up a glass off a footman's tray and handed it to Mariah. She sipped the wine slowly, then hiccupped.

"Oh dear," she said, covering her mouth with her hand. She hiccupped several more times.

"I am so—*hic*—embarrassed," Mariah groaned.

"Why?"

"I was so—*hic*—nervous and—*hic*—now I can't stop—*hic*—hiccupping."

"Why are you nervous?"

Mariah felt her color rise, but managed to squeak, "You."

Charles pointed to himself, clearly trying to suppress a smile. "*I* make you nervous."

"Yes—*hic*—yes—*hic*—"

Mariah could see people around her staring at them. Sophie and Adaline Penderton-Simpson were both watching her.

"I must—*hic*—go."

Without sparing another look at Charles, she walked quickly around the groups and out of the room. She passed through the hall, to the kitchen where she set down her wine-glass, and outside to the small garden behind the house. She took off her gloves and used her hands to fan her hot cheeks.

How mortifying!

She heard footsteps and turned to see Charles at the door, illuminated by the gas lamps of the kitchen. Mariah turned away from the light. She bit her lip, hoping to stop the tears of embarrassment from falling down her cheeks and ruining her silk dress.

"Allow me," Charles said quietly. He pulled out a handkerchief from his pocket, but instead of handing it to her, he dabbed at each tear on her cheeks. He then placed the handkerchief in her hands, covering her hands with his.

"I am so—*hic*—sorry I seem to always—*hic*—take your handkerchiefs."

Charles smiled and leaned in conspiratorially. "I only carry them for you."

Mariah didn't know what to say, so she blurted out, "I cannot—*hic*—seem to—*hic*—stop hiccupping—*hic*."

Charles gently touched her neck. "May I offer you a solution?"

She nodded.

He cradled her face with his left hand, then leaned forward and gently placed his lips on hers. Mariah forgot her self-consciousness, her embarrassment, even her hiccups. Nothing existed but Charles and herself and the magic of a first kiss. He lifted his head and looked down at her, smiling, his hand still warm against the side of her face.

"Did I cure you of the hiccups?"

"Most effectively."

"Mariah, I . . . I began to say something at the Royal Academy, and I wish to finish it."

"All right." She could barely breathe as he stood so close to her.

"Only that I love you, Mariah."

She couldn't speak. She was too overcome with emotion. Tears formed in her eyes.

"Oh, I . . . Please, don't cry again," Charles said, and stepped back, his hand falling from her face. "I didn't mean to upset you."

"These are tears of happiness," Mariah said with a watery chuckle.

He cocked his head at her. "You cry when you're happy?"

"I seem to cry over everything," she confessed, wiping the tears from her cheeks with his handkerchief. "I must tell you that I have loved you for so long and so very, very much."

Charles took her into his arms. His second kiss was nothing like the first—it was hard, passionate, and absolutely marvelous. When he lifted his head, Mariah caressed the planes of his face with her fingers just as she had done to the sketch of him. The curve of his upper lip. The line of his jaw. The arch of his eyebrow. Charles closed his eyes and exhaled slowly.

They heard footsteps approaching and awkwardly broke apart. One of the kitchen maids dumped some liquid on the grass before looking up and suddenly seeing Mariah and

Charles. "Oh!" she exclaimed. "I didn't see you there, Miss Carter. I am most sorry."

"We were just going in," Mariah said.

Charles followed Mariah through the kitchen, past the stares of all the servants, and to the hall. Mariah turned to look at him. "Am I presentable?"

He gently tucked a curl behind her ear. "You are perfection."

Mariah felt the delightful fluttering of her stomach again . . . and then hiccupped. "Oh no—*hic*—not again!"

"I believe we know how to solve this particular problem," he said.

Mariah smiled and raised her face to be kissed.

EPILOGUE

"I CAN'T BELIEVE I FINALLY DID IT," Sophie said, her hands clenched into fists in the air. "I'm an inventor—a *real* inventor. I created a clock that notifies people at whatever time they select. I always hoped, but I began to doubt I would be a success."

Sophie gently stroked the Notification Clock prototype on the worktable of her very own shop. Ethan came up behind her and put his arms around her. He gently moved her hair and kissed her neck. "I never doubted for even a moment that you were going to be a great inventor."

She turned around in his arms to face him.

"It's a very good thing you have your own shop," Ethan said. "I fear if we shared an office, we would be terribly inefficient . . . at least at working."

"Very well, then," Sophie said, twisting out of his arms. "Mr. Miller, I would like to know when my product will be available on the market."

"Typically, it will take close to a year to complete production."

"That is acceptable."

"As your principal investor and manufacturer, I've been thinking about the name of your invention," he said.

"The Notification Clock."

"I thought perhaps we could call it 'the Alarm Clock.'"

"Why would anyone want to be alarmed?"

"All right, how about 'the Timer'?"

Sophie paused to consider it. "'The Timer' is much too vague," she said. "Any clock tells time."

The prototype began to ding loudly on the desk and Ethan turned off the alarm.

"What was that notification set for, Sophie?"

"To remind me to kiss you," she said. She put her arms around his neck and kissed him very thoroughly.

Mariah held the sailboat rope tightly, humming her mother's favorite song, "I've Been Roaming." The wind was blowing so hard, she had to hold her bonnet down with her other hand. Charles finished letting down the sail and tied his end of the rope to the opposite side of the sloop. Mariah released her hold on her hat—she needed both hands to tie a stopper knot. Taking the loose end of the rope, she tied it around one hand, twice, then tucked the rope under the two loops and let it slip off her hand.

A gust of wind blew her bonnet off her head and out into the waves of the English Channel.

"I never liked that hat anyway," Charles said, as he came to stand by her side.

Mariah laughed and reached her arm around his waist. He put his arm around her shoulders and dropped a kiss in her hair. They watched the view of the south fields of the Bentley estate become more and more distant as the wind caught the white sail and propelled them forward.

Tomorrow, she would come back and paint this scene.

"Where shall we go today?" Charles asked.

"On an adventure, of course."

"Every day is an adventure with you, Mariah," he said, and kissed her.

AUTHOR'S NOTE

THE GREAT EXHIBITION OF 1851 was a seminal point in British history and industrial predominance. There were exhibits from all over the world, and only a few were highlighted in this book. From the Koh-i-noor diamond to the enormous hydraulic press to Sèvres china to the first public toilets, the Great Exhibition was an unforgettable event. The Crystal Palace was a real building, but it moved from its original location in Hyde Park to Penge Common and unfortunately burned down in 1936.

Sophie Carter is fictional and therefore didn't invent the alarm clock (or notification clock). That honor belongs to the French inventor Antoine Redier, who was the first to patent an adjustable mechanical alarm clock, in 1847.

Mariah Carter is also fictional, but the Royal Academy of Arts was real, and many Victorian painters debuted their works there. The National Gallery in Trafalgar Square opened in 1838, and you can still visit it today. The Regent's Zoo, or the London Zoo, was opened to the public in 1847.

Lady Bentley sings the English folk song "I've Been Roaming," lyrics by George Darley.

Sir Thomas Watergate is a fictional character, but the reform movement in art called the Pre-Raphaelite Brotherhood did exist. Dante Gabriel Rossetti, a famous painter, was a founder of the Pre-Raphaelite movement. His muse, model, and (later) wife, Elizabeth Eleanor Siddal, was a milliner in Cranbourne Alley, London, before being noticed by the painter Walter Deverell. He asked her to be his model and introduced her to the art world. "Lizzie" did more than model; she was also a poet and an artist, producing many sketches and a few paintings. John Ruskin was her patron and paid her a yearly income to support her art.

John Ruskin was a prolific art critic, writer, and lecturer. He taught several ladies drawing by correspondence and eventually published a book in 1857 entitled *The Elements of Drawing*. I borrowed lines from that book to serve as John Ruskin's words and his epistolary advice to Mariah. Effie Gray was his wife at the time this novel takes place, but their marriage was later dissolved.

ACKNOWLEDGMENTS

SINCE THIS IS A SISTERS' BOOK, I want to first thank my amazing sisters, Michelle and Stacy. You taught me how to curl my hair, flirt, wash laundry, and pick myself up after a fall. Thank you for reading countless pages of my writing. You are both strong, smart, and capable women and I look up to your examples (even if you're both shorter than I am).

I often tell people that I married Mr. Bingley because my husband is the nicest, most patient man alive. Jon, I am so grateful for your love and endless support. I couldn't write without my family; all my love to Andrew, Alivia, Isaac, and Violet. To Mom and Dad, thank you for buying my books by the case and giving them away to everyone you know. You're the best!

To my longtime besties, Dannielle and Katie: friends can be like sisters and our shared memories make us family.

A huge shout-out to my beta readers: Maren, Erin, Lisa,

Nichole, and Susannah. Thank you for being willing to read early drafts and for giving me thoughtful feedback.

I am so grateful for book bloggers, YouTubers, Instagrammers, reviewers, teachers, and librarians around the world who have supported my book. Especially Krysti and Sarah from YA & Wine: You two are amazing, and I'm so grateful for your friendship as well as your bookish support.

The writing community in Utah is incredible, and I'm so thankful for the encouragement I've received from other authors. A special thanks to Tricia Levenseller, Kathryn Purdie, Emily R. King, Sara B. Larson, and Caitlin Sangster.

I was blessed to debut with so many talented authors whom I now call friends: Tiana Smith, Addie Thorley, Crystal Smith, Sofiya Pasternack, Erin Stewart, RuthAnne Snow, and Jennieke Cohen. I couldn't have picked better partners for my publishing journey.

To my agents, Jen Nadol and Jennifer Unter, I can't thank you enough for your support on this book and I look forward to making more stories with you.

To Sheldon and Tyler, you give the best medical consultations for fictional characters; any mistakes are my own.

I am so grateful for the Swoon Squad (other Swoon Reads authors). Your wit, wisdom, and wonderful books have enriched my life.

I'll be forever indebted to Jean Feiwel and the Swoon Reads imprint for publishing my stories. A huge thank-you to the rest of the Swoon team: Lauren Scobell, Holly West,

Kat Brzozowski, and Emily Settle. Emily, you are a delight to work with and the best editor around.

Katie Klimowicz, thank you for my incredible cover and interior book design. Cheers to my copyeditor, Juliann Barbato, for helping me polish my book until it shined. I appreciate the wonderful work of my production editor, Ilana Worrell. And I'm so grateful for my publicist, Madison Furr, for her enthusiasm and support.

Dear Reader, thank you for joining me on this adventure. May you always have a fresh cup of tea, a new book to read, and enough bravery to sail toward your dreams.